MW01532382

CAMPANELLI:
SIEGE OF THE NIGHTHUNTER

Frederick H. Crook

ALL RIGHTS RESERVED

No part of this book may be reproduced or transmitted in any form or by any means, electronic or mechanical, including photocopying, recording, or by any information storage and retrieval system, without permission in writing from the author, except in the case of brief quotations embodied in reviews.

Cover Art:
Arvin Candelaria & Velvet Lyght

Stories by CL

http://www.storiesbycl.com/

Publisher's Note:

This is a work of fiction. All names, characters, places, and events are the work of the author's imagination.

Any resemblance to real persons, places, or events is coincidental.

Solstice Publishing - www.solsticepublishing.com

Copyright 2016 Frederick H. Crook

Campanelli: Siege of the Nighthunter

by

Frederick H. Crook

Dedication

Much love and appreciation to my wife, Rae. She's my biggest fan, and without her I could not be who and what I am today. This is also for my family and friends, who have been very supportive and understanding over the years.

For Michael Shockey.

Part One

*F*or a weekend evening, the hospital was quiet. Even with the waves of influenza raging through the streets of Chicago, the full facility seemed at peace. The staff was more lighthearted than on the weekdays when Detective Frank Campanelli visited. The nurses even smiled as they briskly fulfilled their duties, wandering from room to room and administering whatever care they were called upon to perform. As he walked by them, he saw the sides of their white anti-bacterial masks lift upward with the movement of their cheeks as their eyes brightened.

The Sentinel Squad's second-in-command was not sure, but he thought he recognized one of them from a couple of days before. She was petite, blonde, if her eyebrows were any indication, and had apparently grown fond of Marcus Williams, Frank's partner and the man he was visiting this Sunday evening. If he was correct, she had been in his partner's room the previous Thursday, and though Williams was encapsulated within a germ-free tent and hard to hear, the young lady was being entertained. Frank walked in to the sounds of laughter, which died almost immediately upon his arrival.

The young woman unsealed the outer door to William's room and cleared Campanelli to enter.

"Thank you, Miss..." Frank bid her, fishing for her to complete the sentence.

"Linda," she provided as the anti-bacterial mask widened at the cheeks. Unlike Thursday, she brightly welcomed him and cheerily sealed the airlock afterward. Frank adjusted his anti-bacterial suit's visor and swung the inner door out of his way.

"Hey, Frank," Marcus called from his bed. The tent was gone.

"Hey, yourself," the honorary captain greeted and stepped to the chair next to the patient. He sat and gestured to the world beyond the hospital room door. "This is not a complaint, you understand, but why is everyone so cheery around here?"

Marcus gave a short, weak chuckle. "Damned if I know." He laughed a little harder as he looked over his friend and partner's appearance. "Nice hat."

"You like it?" Frank adjusted the black fedora set awkwardly over the medical tunic's hood and looked at his partner's face from the corner of his left eye.

Marcus laughed again, causing a slight cough. "Where the hell did you get that?"

"Well, an old friend strongly suggested it," Frank answered in a mild voice as he removed it. He turned it over and over in his hands and inspected it like it was new. "I've actually had it a long time. I'm surprised you haven't seen it."

"I haven't, but it suits you."

"You think so?"

"It goes with the briefcase," Williams joked. The black briefcase was something that Frank had been given by the chief of the Chicago Police Department's Organized Crime Division, Earl Sebastian just days prior. It was crammed with documents and crime records that Sebastian had regarded as too sensitive to commit to the department's computer network, which had become less than reliable of late. "Where is it?" he thought to ask.

"I left it in the car," Campanelli admitted in a whisper.

"Frank," Marcus blurted in mild, perhaps feigned, shock, "the Chief is not going to like that."

"Well, keep your mouth shut and he won't find out." Frank adjusted the fedora and looked to the sealed portal. "I'm heading straight home after this."

"Good. You just got that commendation for taking down DeSilva and Ignatola. I'd hate to see you fired."

Campanelli's retort was a sharp, grunted chuckle. "Said the guy that took a bullet meant for Mayor Jameson."

The two men shared wise grins, clearly pleased with the other's feats. Neither felt like a hero, but they did not mind complimenting each other.

"Doctor says I'll be out in a few days," said Marcus.

"Bullshit," Frank spat. He knew the handgun round that struck his partner near the collarbone and chipped the bone had been of a rather large caliber. It had missed the vest completely, though by millimeters.

"I'm serious, Frank," Marcus stared at him plainly for a moment. "This is the third time I can thank military science for saving my life. If it weren't for these genetic alterations, I'd never heal this fast."

Campanelli smiled. "Go Navy."

"I should be able to return to duty a week from Monday."

"That's amazing," the Captain of Detectives granted. He considered the state of technology in this post-Great Exodus world where the best minds had left for the colony planet of Alethea. Williams was still a young man, though long retired from the U.S. Navy, and during their short partnership, Campanelli had become very fond of the giant ex-SEAL. Frank had lost much in his life, including his wife and son back in his home town of New York and did not want to lose anyone else. He had hated to leave Williams lying on that stage in front of the Daley Center, but it had paid off in bringing in the shooter's employer.

"You okay, Frank?" Marcus asked. Frank's eyes had glossed over in thought.

"Yeah, pal," Campanelli spoke up, "I just can't wait for you to come back to work."

"Me neither. It's not in my nature to lie still for so long."

"I know."

A handful of quiet seconds passed.

"So, since the Ignatola ring's been broken up, have you noticed a drop in the human trafficking?" Marcus asked.

Campanelli smiled. "You asked me that last week. The answer's still yes."

"Did I? Wow. Sorry," the big man said with knitted brows. It was clear that he was searching his memory for the conversation.

"Forget it," he said, then laughed at his unintended pun. "You were pretty stoned on pain meds, bein' fresh outta surgery and all."

"True."

"So, do you remember the mayor and Superintendent Dehner presenting the DSA to you?" the honorary captain fished.

"That, I do." Marcus Williams smiled brightly. "I'm putting the ribbon right next to my Blue Shield Award, which they also gave me that afternoon."

"I knew it! Faker," Campanelli chided and laughed. Frank had earned the Distinguished Service Award from the CPD already and had no wish to earn the Blue Shield, which was the result of being shot while protecting the mayor. Not wanting to augment the size of his decorated partner's cranium, he kept the fact that he was also to be presented with the Richard J. Daley Police Medal of Honor when he returned to duty. This would have been given to him during the annual awards ceremony the previous week, but Williams was recuperating. It was announced during the ceremony, where Campanelli had accepted it on his partner's behalf.

The medal was in the black briefcase.

"What's funny, Frank?" Marcus inquired, having caught the strange smirk on his older partner's face.

"Oh, nothing." He adopted a somewhat convincing expression of innocence.

"Frank," the impatient patient pressed.

"It's nothing at all."

"Uh-huh."

The two colleagues spent the rest of the visit speaking of the disappearance of Chief of Detectives Dmitri Vanek and his family, the internal power struggle over his vacated position, and other meaningless but entertaining banter. Frank kept to himself, and would most likely always have to, the fact that he had apprehended the Vanek family at O'Hare Airport and, out of pity for their child, had let them board the helicopter belonging to Maximilian DeSilva. The fact that Vanek and family had not been heard from since helped Campanelli sleep at night, as it meant they most likely were able to escape the planet and board a starship bound for Alethea. Confessing to anyone that he had let the family escape would have ended his career and earned him a jail term, which, considering the poor, disease-ridden conditions of the area prisons, was a sure death sentence.

When it was time for Frank to leave, he signaled for the nurse via his bio-electronic implant. In moments, she arrived to unseal the door. He bid his healing partner a good evening and was led to the locker room, where he was able to shed the anti-bacterial suit.

Sunday, June the first, was a cool day in Chicago. Frank did not mind, for between his trademark black overcoat and fedora, he was comfortable. He walked to his car, got in and commanded it to drive him home, where Tamara would be waiting for him. It was nearly five o'clock and surely, a nice dinner awaited him.

***

Hours later, in the dead of night, a creature emerged from the Chicago River. It had no clear idea where it was, as it had become lost. It had not left that body of water for weeks, other than to feed in its most brutal method, but had traveled unplanned and untracked distances every day.

With only the top of its head having broken the water's surface, its eyes peered through the darkness for many minutes before it slowly made its way to shore. The amphibious hominid had chosen to emerge from the protection of deep water for two reasons. The river had split into two directions. One went south while the other continued northeast. Secondly, it was desperately hungry.

The tall biped slipped out of the water, closed and retracted its gills. Water slipped out of its freshly opened nostrils and its skin felt the faint light from the stars and the sliver of the moon. The pigment darkened from pale pink to a deep charcoal upon a thought command. Its feet stepped onto the soil of the embankment and it was then that the entity discovered a bridge spanning the river. It climbed to the surface of a raised road, where it gracefully and silently hurled itself over a metal fence. It stared at its feet for a time, taking in the sensation of cool, rough concrete. The biped shifted its weight back and forth for a few moments, for it had swum so long that standing felt strange.

Making a fist of its right hand, the creature rapped it upon the fence it had climbed over. The metal rang in the quiet night. It knew that metals had become a sort of rarity sometime after its activation date, so when it turned its attention upon the iron structure of the bridge, it could not help but quickly run to it.

Carelessly, it traversed the short distance without stealth in mind. Its big feet slapped the poorly maintained street. It palmed the middle spine of the structure, causing a flesh on metal sound to reverberate. It was cold, gritty with rust and magnificent in its uniqueness. According to the computer in the creature's mind, this bridge's appearance corresponded to that of the Ashland Avenue Sanitary and Ship Canal Bridge of Chicago, Illinois. Reading more information, it was discovered that the bridge broke in the middle, allowing each end to rise into the air.

Amazing! I wonder if it still works.

The male hominid turned to look at the brick bridgetender building just across the street, but as he took a step toward it, a sound came to its sensitive ears and it froze in a crouch. He listened hard, raising the gain on his hearing devices. It was a car.

Automatically, the military grade implant processed the sound and displayed its findings. It listed the drive type, manufacturer, and production years of the model. The shapes of the headlights confirmed the information, matching up perfectly with the diagram he saw projected upon his lenses.

It was then that he remembered his hunger. As the electric light danced upon his body, he commanded it to change pigment. The feet he turned as black as the one true piece of clothing that he wore upon his body, his utility belt. His upper torso turned bleach white up to the wrists and neck, simulating a long-sleeved shirt. Everything below his belt was set to brown, as his hands, neck and face went to his natural state, quite close to his Caucasian origins. His hair, naturally black, remained so, but he swept it straight back with his hands.

Almost as an afterthought, his optics changed colors. His irises went from pale yellow to brown for the sake of appearances and his sclera switched from a dull, non-reflective orange to a convincing off-white.

As his training had taught him decades prior, he reached out to the oncoming vehicle's onboard computer and began to hack it with his implant's software tools. In seconds, he had access to the vehicle's functions.

The car approached, but slowed as the driver found the pedestrian in his headlights. Immediately, the human occupant knew something was wrong. The engine quieted and the brakes applied more intensely than he had demanded with his foot.

"What the...hell?" the driver mumbled. His heart began pounding intensely. There was something odd about the man in his lights. There was a strange intensity in his eyes and something about his appearance was wrong.

The rebellious automobile stopped dead, placed its transmission in park and opened the driver's side window.

Deeply frightened, the man could form no sound in his throat, and irrationally, he reached out with both hands and grabbed at the disappearing glass partition.

"Shit! Sh...shit!" he shouted. His panic had brought about an asthma attack. The man's chest tightened and, for a fleeting second, he debated over what to do next. There were two items in his glove compartment: a handgun and his inhaler.

The glistening wet stranger began to stride toward the disabled vehicle. Seeing this made the driver's decision for him. He stretched his torso to reach the glove compartment as his chest heaved and his breathing wheezed from deep within it. In a heartbeat, the pistol was in his grip.

Then, the locking mechanism clicked. The driver righted himself just in time to see the driver's door swing open and a blur of something long and black reach for him. Asthma or not, the man screamed.

With barely a tearing sound, the seatbelt was sliced away and before he could bring his weapon to bear, two long arms reached in and scooped him from the seat. With well-practiced efficiency, the predator had thrust his long sharp nails into his victim's body, skewering it like a dinner fork would a cantaloupe, giving the assailant the grip to launch the lighter man into the air. Seeing the weapon at the last second, he tore it from the other's grip quickly and cleanly, though he had felt the weak bones under his grip snap and break.

The man's body was sent tumbling high into the air, disorienting him immediately. He landed on the sidewalk opposite his car with a crunch.

The attacker inspected the weapon, identified it as something antique and only somewhat effective. He dropped it and moved to the crumpled human mess on the sidewalk in three long strides. He looked into his prey's face. Barely conscious as the human had landed on its head, it made things all the easier.

There was no trace of guilt in what the predator was about to do. That emotion had long left him along with so many other sensations and sensibilities that he had been trained and otherwise conditioned to accept. The powerful hominid had been out of its element and without guidance for far too long.

He drew his triangular blade from its sheath once again and slit the victim's throat long and deep. In moments, the predator sank its teeth into the steamily warm flesh and feasted for many long minutes after prying the chest cavity apart with its powerful grip. There, the steaming heart and liver were focused upon. In between bites, the monster listened and looked about for signs of discovery. The unseasonably cold night was deadly silent beyond the grotesque sounds of frantic feeding.

After the predator had his fill, he transmitted the commands to his dinner's car to restart the motor, close the window, and set the interior heat to seventy-two degrees. The chill that had seeped into his flesh was months old and he craved for it to be gone.

To rid his body of his victim's blood, he dashed to the bridge and dove into the frigid river. Emerging from the same place as before, the well-fed predator leapt over the iron fence, ran to the waiting car and closed the door after him. The warmth of the cabin covered his naked flesh like a warm blanket.

Oh! Yes! Heat!

The tall killer shed cold water into the warming seats and carpeted floor as he pressed himself into the cushions for comfort. The coloring of his disguise was allowed to melt away to his natural pale pigment of skin and eyes. He regarded the world beyond the windshield for a time while he hugged himself to retain the warmth. His eyes were attracted by the mass of lights that turned the black sky to a glowing silvery blue over downtown Chicago, and though he normally avoided a larger populace, he decided at that very moment that it was time to stop wandering. It would be nice to have a rich hunting ground for a while.

Though his body had been genetically designed and conditioned to be omnivorous with a strong tendency toward a diet of vegetation for efficiency, this predator had exposed himself to the pleasures of poultry, fish and meat for so long it had developed a preference.

This preference over plants and vegetables had not been simply for the taste, but he had also developed a thrill for the hunt. He had grown to love the challenge and he thrived on it.

He accessed his implant, fed his approximate location into it, and plotted a route into the depths of Chicago. He felt out the brake and accelerator pedals with his large bare feet and placed the transmission into drive.

With tires screeching into the night, the stolen sedan stormed across the aged Ashland Avenue Bridge at a reckless, frame-rattling speed.

***

The mechanical ringer of the wired antique telephone ripped Frank from a deep sleep marred by a fleeting, none-too-pleasant dreamscape. As he opened his eyelids, blackness gave way to nothing but more blackness. He was not surprised by this, however, as his implant had deactivated when he had gone to sleep, shutting down his full service ocular lenses. His ears told him that he had forgotten to bring the old phone into the bedroom for the night yet again.

"I'll get it," Tamara mumbled. She was no more awake than he, but she could see in the night with her natural vision.

Campanelli sat up, put his bare feet to the cold wooden floor, and thought the command for his *CAPS-Link* device to initiate.

"Time," he called as he stood.

"*Four-oh-three, A.M.*," the voice-clock answered.

"Shit." A phone call at this time was never anything good and always work-related. However, since being moved from the Violent Crimes Division's Homicide Squad and into Sentinel, these calls had become rare. Of course, it had only been less than a month.

Frank's optics came online just as he felt his way out of the bedroom. It remained dark, but not for long. His lenses adjusted.

"He's right here," Tam said into the receiver and covered the microphone. "Detective McLain, Frank."

"McLain? He's homicide," he grumbled. He took the phone from her and patted her shoulder. It was not her fault his old underling had called the wrong number.

"Campanelli," Frank said into the phone. He placed his right fist on his hip and waited for what he assumed would be a short, "beg your pardon", out of the mouth of Kirby McLain.

"Frank? Kirby here."

"Yeeesss?"

"Pardon the early call, Cap'n," McLain started. He was one of the few that called Campanelli by his honorary rank, a leftover from Frank's NYPD days. "We've got somethin' I think you really need to see."

"What is it, Kirby?" Frank dropped his annoyance. From the background noise, he could tell that McLain was outside and from his manner of speech, whatever it was had ventured way out of the ordinary. A big man like Kirby McLain, a career police detective, should have seen everything by now.

"Frank...we have a body. Sort of," McLain explained in his deep, gravelly voice.

"Go on," Campanelli said with patience. At six-foot-four and three years his senior, Frank cut the man some slack. He remembered while listening to Kirby's frequent pauses, that he had lost a good part of a lung to cancer the previous year. As a result, his speech was partitioned by pauses every few words.

"It's been torn apart and, apparently, somethin' got to the body and ate it. Parts of 'im, anyway."

Frank grunted in disgust. "Okay, Kirby, who is he? Why are you calling me?"

"We've checked his ID and he's...not even supposed to be here."

"He's on Sentinel's list?"

"Yessir."

"Okay, where?"

Kirby McLain told him.

"Got it," Frank replied. "Give me a half hour. No one touches anything."

"I've already ordered that done," Kirby confirmed.

"Good. On the way." He hung up the telephone and strode into the bathroom. He ran the water and prepared for a speedy shower.

Tam had gone back to bed and he did not blame her. In months prior, she would have simply stayed up, as she would get ready for work and leave around five. Since her diner had been burned to the ground by DeSilva's thugs during her kidnapping, there was no reason for such an early rise. Besides that, she was still recuperating from her facial injuries. The bruising around her left eye was yellow and fading fast. Soon, she would be fully recovered.

With his shower completed, he dressed. In his haste, he deferred on the tie, leaving the top button of his shirt free. He donned his fedora, shoulder holster and overcoat. Quickly, he stepped into the bedroom, gave the sleeping Tamara a kiss on the temple, and grabbed his folded RadarCane from his nightstand.

Frank flew down the stairs and out of the apartment building, reaching his waiting car. Its engine was already running and so was the heater. As he approached, it opened the door or him and closed it once he was inside.

Campanelli had fed the cruiser's computer with its destination via his implant, so it wasted no time buckling him in and backing out of the parking spot. At four-forty in the morning, even if it was a Monday, traffic would be nearly non-existent. Even so, as it turned onto Eighteenth Avenue and headed west, the detective set the car to Condition Two, bathing the night in blue and white flashing lights. The siren squawked and chirped only when the car detected other vehicles and intersections. The crime scene was little more than two miles from his place.

In less than five minutes, Campanelli arrived at the northern end of the Ashland Avenue Bridge. His police lights alone were enough for the uniformed officers there to wave him through. Frank took manual control of the automobile as it rolled onto the bridge from the pavement. The tires sang along the odd pavement and thudded on every iron grate.

He parked behind a marked CPD cruiser and shut the car down. He stepped out into the cool early morning air and cinched his overcoat tightly against the breeze. Frank looked about the old bridge, already searching for anything unusual as he strode to the crime scene ahead of him, lit by multiple headlights of marked and unmarked cruisers and their spotlights. Blue strobes gave the scene that familiar haunting eeriness.

What Campanelli saw lying near the curb was so horrifying, he took a misstep on a risen bit of the bridge's surface. He stepped to Kirby McLain's side and could form no words.

"Good morning, Frank," McLain offered in a hushed voice. The look on his face mirrored the Sentinel Squad's second-in-command, although due to the size of the man, it was augmented. His lips were drawn downward at the edges, his eyebrows were pinned halfway up his generous forehead, and the lines that ensued there were deep and wide. Considering that Frank could barely comprehend the level of horror he was witnessing, he sympathized.

"Good morning, Kirby. You said that you had ID'd him," he said, almost as a question.

"Yeah," McLain uttered reverently out of the side of his mouth. "Name's Werner. Herman Werner."

Frank searched McLain's chiseled features for a few seconds, mostly to give himself something else to look at. Kirby's head was tilted downward as his naturally colored blue eyes studied the body with what appeared to be heartfelt grief. Campanelli knew this to be genuine of the man. McLain had suffered many personal losses in the choice to remain on Earth instead of heading off to Alethea. He had lost a wife and son, just like Frank had, only McLain's losses were stretched out over months of cancer treatments. In the end, none of the care had mattered. Both wife and son passed in the same year. Then, adding insult to injury in the form of further injury, the cancer in his lungs was found. Despite it all, Kirby McLain persevered, fought the cancer through the available old medical technology and returned to the job. He even got his hair back, though it was a bit thinner and more of it gray.

As much as Frank wanted a cigarette at that moment, he refrained out of respect for the man.

In moments, the CPD computer's information was relayed back to Campanelli, who read it from his projected display.

"File says he's been missing for over a year. Suspected of leaving the planet with his wife. He was wanted for armed robbery and grand theft auto," Frank read off.

"Yeah." McLain nodded. "I bet he wished they had taken that ship."

Campanelli sidestepped around the towering McLain and moved closer to see the deceased's face. It bore little resemblance to the photo in the computer. "How did you ID him, Kirby?"

"Expired driver's license in his wallet." He hesitated to take a breath. "It was soaked in blood. Dennis fished it out," he finished with a gesture to the coroner, Dennis Gherling, who was taking some close looks of the remains, and certainly committing some stills to his implant's memory.

"Dennis," Frank greeted as he stepped closer.

"Hi, Detective Campanelli," the younger man replied as he leaned even closer to the body's gaping opening at the throat.

"What can you tell me?"

"Well, it's perplexing, really. The medical scanner shows a nasty skull fracture at the back, his right shoulder and collar bone are shattered. Ribs are, obviously, torn open and pried out of the way until they broke." The coroner rose and joined Frank on his right side. "Heart and liver were cut out and are missing. It was done in a hurry, too. There's plenty of scoring to the bones and esophagus. I can't tell, but the same blade that slit his throat may have been what was used to remove the organs."

"So, the breaks tell me he was assaulted with something heavy first," Frank surmised.

"No, I don't think so," Gherling replied and showed Campanelli the recording on his medical scanner's screen. "If it were a pipe or solid piece of metal used for a club, there would be multiple strikes to the body. These breaks are consistent with a single impact."

"I see. So, Dennis, what impacted him?" Frank asked as he adjusted his fedora and leaned closer to the small screen.

"I found concrete dust deeply embedded in his scalp, neck and shoulders."

"The ground came up and hit him, Dennis?" Campanelli laid on him sarcastically.

Gherling gave a mild and brief smile. "Oh, no. Take a look at these punctures and tears in his arms, buttocks and legs." He bent down to the body and pointed them out with gloved fingers. "These are from claws or talons or something. The attacker...well...grabbed him and launched Werner into the air, where he came down on his upper body on the curb here."

"Get outta here," Frank scoffed.

"No, I mean it," the coroner insisted. "Look, the punctures line up with a pretty large hand. The attacker grabbed Werner here and here." Gherling demonstrated by assuming a crouched posture with both his arms stretched out in front of him. He bent his knees and made as if he were dragging something. "It grabbed his right wrist and left leg and pulled, manhandled him, dug these claws into the flesh, turned him and with one...*incredible* move, took Werner by the ass and *threw* him skyward."

"*Gherling*," Frank mused and gave him a crooked grin of doubt.

"And it could not have been an animal, Detective Campanelli, because of the presence of thumbs. The fifth digit's claw enters the flesh at different angles from the other fingers, like a thumb would, sir." He demonstrated with his own hands, curling the fingers and thumb menacingly.

Frank glanced to McLain who returned it expressionlessly.

Gherling pushed on. "There are tire tracks in that lane there," he pointed and walked briskly to the two black streaks in the light gray pavement. "The killer tore out of here in a real hurry."

Campanelli stared at the tracks for a time and nodded in thought. McLain joined him. "I don't know. This is all very hinky."

"I know how crazy it sounds, Detective Campanelli," Gherling conceded.

"'Crazy' is not the word for it, Mr. Gherling!" Frank spouted. He turned back to the victim and waved over the body with his right arm. "What you are describing is far from plausible. This man weighed, from the looks of what's left, about two hundred pounds. Now, what has claws and is powerful enough to throw such a man high or hard enough to bust him up like that?"

"Frank," McLain tried to interject.

"And then, after that, slices the man up and steals a couple organs?" Frank continued.

"Frank," Kirby tried again.

"What is it, Detective?" Frank said and took a breath.

"There are also bite marks on the body," Kirby explained. "Chunks of his left shoulder and neck were bitten into."

"That's right, sir," Gherling affirmed.

"Oh, now I've heard everything." Frank threw his arms into the air and let them drop to slap his thighs.

"There was also a gun," McLain said, halting Frank's further objections. "It was found a few feet from the tire tracks. An antique revolver in thirty-eight caliber."

"Now we're talkin'. Was it fired?" Frank asked, turning his back on the young coroner.

"No. Scratch marks in the frame and chips in the wooden grip indicate that it was dropped," Kirby finished.

"Do you buy this scenario, Kirby?" the Captain of Detectives nearly whispered.

"I don't know, Frank," McLain admitted as he looked down on his shorter colleague. "I've never seen anything like this. If it weren't for the presence of concrete embedded in the skin, I'd have thought a truck hit 'im."

Frank nodded. "Well, things may become clearer when the sun comes up. Was there an owner found on the revolver?"

"Stolen from an owner in Georgia more than thirty years ago," Kirby said.

"All right. Forward that and the body in for autopsy. I'm going to call Rothgery in on this."

Dennis Gherling remained silent, though the expression on his face was one of protest.

"No offense to you, Dennis," Frank supplied quickly, "but I think you've been up too late for too many nights in a row watching horror vids."

"I understand the level of crazy involved in this, Detective Campanelli," Dennis replied flatly. "I'm not offended. I simply have to follow what the clues tell me."

Kirby McLain received a relayed message across his implant as Gherling spoke. Frank noticed the expression of interest upon his colleague's face and waited.

"Frank, check the blotter…madman in a car," McLain explained and let Campanelli search for himself.

Frank linked with the CPD server and found the report labeled, "Madman in a Car" on the list of calls. A sedan of unknown manufacture had been seen driving northeast at high speed across the park of Benito Juarez High School, just north of their crime scene, narrowly missing an early morning jogger. The car had continued accelerating upon exiting the park's widened path and onto Blue Island Avenue, a street which began at that location and maintained a northeasterly direction. The caller was convinced that the vehicle had reached a speed of perhaps eighty miles per hour and was showing no signs of slowing down.

Blue Island Avenue terminated at Roosevelt Road one mile further.

"Forty-three minutes ago," Campanelli noted with a frown.

"There's one after that, Frank," McLain added. "Vehicle crash at Desplaines and Harrison."

"Not much there," Campanelli said as he read the newer report. "The driver dumped the car in a foundation on the corner."

McLain glanced at the two long black streaks on the pavement where they stood. "Our guy?"

"It's a possibility." Frank nodded. "Why don't you have the area cordoned off and we'll have a closer look at the car."

"Right," Kirby agreed. He composed the order and submitted it to the CPD server. The police on scene would be alerted to the update and touch nothing.

"I'll meet you over there," Frank said and turned to Dennis Gherling. "Get everything over to Rothgery's lab."

"Sure thing," Gherling replied.

Once he was back in his cruiser, Frank made a tight U-turn and headed north on Ashland. Soon, he passed the abandoned Benito Juarez High School. It was here that the car left Ashland and drove onto the park's walkway. Frank continued on to Roosevelt Road before hanging a right. Setting the car on Condition One, his lights flashed, but the siren was kept quiet. He arrived on the scene of the crash in a few minutes. He had seen Kirby's cruiser in the rearview mirror the entire ride.

As ordered, the two responding units had taped off the area and the four uniformed officers milled about, waiting. Frank parked near them, got out of the car and approached the gathering. The oldest of them, a Sergeant Mueller, stepped forward and met him.

"Morning, sir," Mueller said.

"It is for some," Campanelli replied, not unkindly. "Morning Sergeant," he amended, then turned to the other three. "Gents." They returned his greeting.

"What's the Sentinel Squad doin' answering to a car wreck, Detective?" Mueller asked with a smile. His breath steamed up in the cool early morning air as he adjusted his cap.

"We'll see if there's a reason for me to be here," Frank answered honestly. "I'd rather be at home in bed."

In a moment, McLain joined Frank and the sergeant, who led them to the edge of the concrete crater left behind from the deconstruction of a building.

"The car was movin' at quite a clip when it blew a tire," the sergeant explained and pointed behind them. "The wheel cut a nice path, here. It went to the right, up the curb," he spoke as he gestured to the markings on the pavement, "and still had enough momentum to carry it down there." He pointed with a flashlight to the wreckage some dozen feet below them. It would be a while before the sun would shine upon it.

"Has anyone been down there?" McLain asked.

"I have," Mueller admitted. "Got a rope ladder attached over there. Car's empty. The driver left some blood. I honestly can't believe it, but it seems he walked off. He was hurt, that's for sure."

Campanelli adjusted his vision for night and looked about the deep, wide concrete canyon. There were hundreds of such remnants throughout the city. Over the two decades prior to the outlawing of the migration to Alethea in 2109, the largest, oldest structures of every major city became targets for reclamation of steel and other metals. As a result, nothing taller than forty floors could be found anywhere in Chicago. Many railroad tracks and iron bridges had been consumed as well, making the Ashland Avenue Bridge a true rarity.

The foundation in front of Campanelli, McLain, and Mueller was a rather unremarkable square hole in the ground. The floor was covered with dirt, debris, and miscellaneous trash caught up between the forces of wind and gravity. It appeared no different than any other scar in the landscape of Chicago, and Frank knew for certain that it was not the only one with a car in it.

"Well, I'm going down to take a look," Campanelli announced.

"Right behind ya'," McLain uttered.

The rope ladder was well-anchored to a light pole and was hung over the southwest corner of the foundation. Frank dropped to his hands and knees and, entirely without dignity, sent his left foot down to feel for the first rung. Mueller came over and lent a hand to the Captain of Detectives. As his foot grabbed hold, the ladder twisted and knocked Frank's fedora to the depths below.

"Shit," he muttered.

"You all right, Detective?" a concerned Mueller asked.

"Yeah, no problem," Frank answered tersely.

He slowly descended and after what felt like minutes, his feet found the floor. His eyes, still set for night, found the hat. The air was strangely still at the bottom of the square pit. He picked up his fallen fedora, slapped it against his overcoat to rid it of the dirt and placed it back on his head.

"Come on down, Kirby," Frank shouted up. "I'll hold the ladder still."

Mueller assisted the much larger McLain in finding the first rung and down the big man came, no faster than Frank had, however. Neither man trusted the rope very far.

Together, both detectives stepped to the mangled automobile. The gloom of the pit and the eerie silence prompted McLain to pull his pistol from his shoulder rig. Frank said not a word in protest, as he had thought of doing the same.

The sky above them had begun to lighten to a shade brighter than midnight blue. It would not be long until sunrise and Frank was grateful.

The detectives approached the driver's side of the ruined automobile. Frank shrunk back from a sudden blazing light and blocked it with his hand. His implant compensated quickly.

"Excuse me," McLain offered. He had lit the area with a large flashlight. "I find a good light reveals a little more than implanted lenses.

"It's okay. Forget it." Frank blinked hard while trying to remove the blue and red streak that the large light had caused. His full service prosthetics were far more accurate and sensitive than the standard commercial grade models that everyone else used. It was a fact not appreciated by those with normal sight.

In truth, Frank knew that Kirby was correct. There was simply no substitute for light, even though it threw shadows. With his eyes fully adjusted, he looked where Kirby shined.

Naturally, the car was heavier in the front than the rear, so it had struck the concrete nose first, shoving the engine compartment upward and back. The dashboard was destroyed as a result, bent from left to right. Gauges, in-dash fans, and speakers were exposed and were hanging by their wires.

The anti-collision devices had all worked. The steering yoke was flush with the ruined control panel, having retreated upon threat of impact. The seat had moved the opposite way by angling back and the air cushioning devices had deployed and deflated once the danger had passed. Still, the impact had been great. The entire frame was twisted and not one panel of glass remained intact. The driver's door, right rear passenger and trunk lid had been thrown open and bent forward.

Campanelli looked into the open trunk. Two spare tires, a case with clothing in it, and some miscellaneous handyman tools lay about.

"There's blood all over the seat," McLain announced.

"I'm sending a message to Gherling. I want him to go over this whole car."

"I thought you didn't like the boy," Kirby said and gave a crooked smile.

"Did I give that impression?"

"You were leanin' on 'im pretty hard," the taller man confirmed as he studied his co-worker's face.

"Well, to hear that nutty tale at four-thirty in the morning was a bit much," Frank explained.

"That it was." Kirby nodded and went about the car with the light. Finding nothing but more wrecked car, he turned his light on the ground near the driver's side. "More blood here."

"Yup." Frank moved closer to inspect the seatbelts. With both hands, he gave them a tug. "The driver had to cut himself loose. Strange, the hardware's not bent."

"Maybe it was cut before," McLain opined from over his shoulder. "To remove Werner earlier."

"Good point."

"Must have been some knife," Kirby said as he bathed the area in light. "Look at the material."

"Whatever it is, it's surgically sharp," Campanelli affirmed. The ends of the seatbelt straps were sliced clean, without fraying of any kind. It could very well have been the same knife used to remove the victim's organs.

Both veteran police detectives had witnessed plenty of hard crimes in their lifetimes, and both had seen things they could not explain and further, did not wish to try. Thoughtful silence washed over them both like a cold wet blanket.

Kirby washed his flashlight's beam over the area many times, convinced that the driver was hurt and had to be nearby. But the longer he took to inspect the destroyed vehicle, the more convinced he became that the person driving should have been killed.

Similar thoughts were running through Frank Campanelli's mind. In his experience, fatalities had occurred from much less serious accidents. The car had been traveling at a high rate of speed, blown a tire and had enough momentum to carry it some forty feet into this concrete pit.

"Where the hell is the driver?" Campanelli whispered. He had avoided asking the question, for every bit of reason within him agreed with McLain's unspoken assessment.

"Yeah." McLain murmured as he swept the light over the expanse once again. "And how the hell did he get outta here? Sewer access?"

"Possibly."

"I guess we'll get those answers when the sun comes up."

"Agreed," Frank answered.

***

From across eight lanes of highway and atop a vacant office building, the two detectives were being carefully watched. The killer felt his broken nose, found the separation and placed it within the vice-grip of his fore and index fingers. With a click that made his eyes tear for a moment, he squeezed the bones into place.

The ring and pinky fingers on his left hand would be a different matter. Both were broken at the proximal phalanx and would need to be set and placed into a splint, at the very least.

The impact had also taken a toll on his feet and legs, but there was nothing beyond some deep lacerations. The area over his ribs and other parts of his body that he had not yet discovered had been injured would soon bruise badly.

He watched the two detectives climb out of the foundation. His magnified view had brought them up close and personal with him, so he recorded their faces for future reference, if needed.

The naked and battered hominid pulled himself up to his feet and limped to the access door on the roof. He had a building to explore and injuries to heal.

***

That evening, nearing five o'clock, Frank packed up his briefcase and prepared to drive home to the apartment building across Eighteenth Street and the District One Station. The events of the day weighed heavily on his mind. He had attended to regular Sentinel business later that morning, and had driven to the station to take care of the paperwork that had backed up on his desk over the last month. Meanwhile, he stared at the phone, waiting for Lincoln's phone call. It never came, and when Frank walked past the forensic genius's labs, they had been closed and locked.

At first, the closed department angered Campanelli, but then as he stormed through District One's rear exit, he noted Rothgery's white and rusted van. It was his personal as well as professional ride, unmarked for privacy, and very utilitarian. His assistant, Teri Wilkins, was apparently still on the job as well, for her tiny electric econobox lay waiting in the large van's shadow. Among the visitor's vehicles, Frank discovered the coroner's black wagon. Gherling was also on the premises.

As much as Frank wanted to go back inside and burst through the lab doors, he knew better. H. Lincoln Rothgery's work ethic was untouchable. When those doors were locked while he was in, whatever was happening beyond them had become top priority.

Once home, Frank parked the cruiser next to Tamara's convertible and walked steadily, but tiredly, up the steps. The apartment complex was sparsely populated and, as always, quiet. The other four families in residence were on the other side of the building. He transmitted his identification to the residence's computer with his *CPD-Link* and the door unlocked for him.

"Hi, Frank!" Billingsley called before he had even placed his hand on the knob.

"Hello," he returned as he pushed the door out of his way. The home was filled with the aroma of a nice supper on the stove.

"Oh, ick!"

"Ick? What ick?"

"Ick, as in you sound terrible," she said as she came to where he stood.

"Oh, that ick," he said as he tossed his hat and briefcase into the closet.

She swung her arms around his neck and held him still for a kiss. "Better?"

"Yeah." He smiled. His blue eyes shared it, but only briefly.

"What is it?" she asked as she stepped back.

"That call this morning," he uttered as he removed his overcoat and draped it over the hanger. "Bad."

"Oh?" Tam watched him carefully, fearing the worst. She had expected the Ignatola crime family to retaliate against the police department for the Sentinel Squad bringing down their boss, but she hoped that she was wrong.

"Yeah," he said and turned back to her, unsure of what to say as he tried to read her face. He swiped his palm over his short gray hair and looked to the floor for a brief second. "It just wasn't pretty, is all. What's cookin'?"

"Some Italian beef with some mostaccioli in red sauce on the side," she said in an upbeat tone that did nothing to alleviate her concerned expression. She followed him into the kitchen and watched him closely. Frank was tired and she could tell. He had forgotten his RadarCane in his coat pocket. She would retrieve it later for him when he was not looking. His forgetfulness irritated him.

"That smells wonderful!" he exuded with his nose over the pot of red meat sauce.

"Yeah, I've been waiting to find all the ingredients at the stores for a long time," she explained as she watched him retrieve his bottle of bourbon. *Damn it.* "I found the pasta just today."

"Smells almost ready." Frank poured, took a sip then leaned back against the counter and raised his hand to his neck. Had he the time to put on his tie that morning, it would be about now that he would loosen it.

"Frank," Tamara ventured as she stirred the sauce. She watched his face for a reaction.

"Yeah." He locked his eyes on hers.

"Was it...them?" she dug while her eyes squinted in emphasis.

"Them? Who? *Ignatola?*"

"Yes, Frank. Them...or maybe one of DeSilva's thugs?" Her voice raised as her mind went through the possibilities faster than her mouth could convey them.

"Tamara, *no,*" he assured her as he removed his suit jacket. His eyes never left hers. *I kind of wish it was, after what I saw.*

"Are you *sure,* Frank?" she pressed while her eyes teared.

"Yes." His response was immediate and certain.

Tam believed him right away. "Oh, thank God," she let out in a rush of breath and took a seat at the table. She rested her forehead on one hand and fought tears of relief.

Frank stepped to her and placed his hand on her shoulder. "This is what's been bugging you for the past week? Well, longer than that, I think."

"Yes, Frank," she responded weakly.

"Listen to me," he began as he crouched next to her. "Those poor dumb bastards are in jail, awaiting trial. Some are already in Joliet and some are in county. A couple of those jokers had Federal raps already pending and were shipped outta state."

Tam moved her hand from her face and found his face with wet eyes. "DeSilva's men."

"Dead. Well, except for his driver. I'm trying to pull some strings to get him a light sentence in minimum security. The kid don't deserve to die for crashin' a few squad cars."

Tam smiled as she remembered the young African-American limousine driver. Frank was right, he was just a kid and did not need to be exposed to the rampant disease and influenza of the prison system.

"What do you say, kiddo? Can we eat?" He smiled and kissed the top of her head as he stood up.

With the weight lifted from her heart, Tamara smiled and bounced up from the kitchen chair like a woman half her age. The pair set the table and settled down to eat.

Campanelli could not keep himself from thinking of the murder and the wrecked car, however. He wished he had taken the time to visit Marcus, but he had chained himself to his desk with the expectation of Rothgery's call. He promised himself he would drop by the hospital tomorrow.

"I think I found a new place to open," Tamara said in between bites of her Italian beef.

"Oh? Where?"

"It's on Michigan. Next to that mart where you buy your cigarettes."

"Oh, yeah. I know that place. They're selling?"

Tam nodded and grunted in the affirmative. "They're moving west," she supplied once her mouth was no longer full.

"Do you know where?" he asked, more as the second in command of the Sentinel Squad.

"Now, Frank," she admonished with a wagging finger, "these people are pushing seventy-five years old."

"That's still a good age to take your chances and try to migrate."

"Honestly?" She regarded him with disbelieving eyes and tilted her head. It was a pose that suggested utter doubt. He was quite familiar with it as Tamara Billingsley was naïve about a great many things.

"I've seen older." He shrugged and took a sip of bourbon.

"Well, forget it this time, copper," she teased. "They're a married couple trying to get out of the city."

"We've got too much of that, too."

"I know," she answered. She did not want to start that discussion again. Though the holovision news channels speculated that the population of Chicago would stabilize with the end of the Ignatola/DeSilva human trafficking ring, Frank had insisted that it would only slow down. People were still leaving the city for what they hoped would be safer towns or rural areas.

With dinner finished, Frank and Tamara quickly cleaned their plates. Tam sent Frank to the living room to rest. It was clear that he was exhausted, especially after being wakened so early in the morning.

Frank retrieved his lighter and a cigarette from the pack in his suit jacket. He placed the tobacco between his lips and stepped into the living room. He dropped into the couch cushions, lit the cigarette, and thought the command to activate the holovision set. A re-run of an old comedy show appeared above the projector. Campanelli recognized the show immediately and smiled. He wanted to stop thinking about the morning's grisly puzzle, but he knew better. The half-hour program rolled into the next one, and as both were familiar, they did little to distract him from shifting the facts around in his head.

More than once, he was tempted to link with the CPD computer to check his messages, peruse the case file with Gherling's pictures, or reach out to Rothgery for an update. A moment later, it mattered not. The six o'clock news broadcast began.

"Chicago police have a shocking murder case on their hands as of this morning," the lovely female anchor announced with a hint of distaste. *"A body of a wanted man was found on the south side of the Ashland Avenue Bridge. No name has been released to the public, but according to a source within the department, the middle-aged male victim was on the Sentinel Squad's wanted list. It was also stated that the body had been badly mutilated and bitten by his assailant."*

"Jesus, Frank," Tamara said as she joined him on the couch.

"There were no signs of an animal attack and a handgun was found on the scene, unfired. There have been no suspects as yet, but it is being given a high priority by homicide and Sentinel detectives," the anchorwoman finished and changed the subject.

"That was the call this morning?" Billingsley inquired. She crossed her arms and her expression was that of horror.

"Yeah."

"Who was he?"

"Just what the girl said, Tam," Frank explained, wishing to keep it vague. "Just some guy that we thought had bought his way on one of the human trafficking networks. That's all."

"Yes, but to mutilate the body and bite into it...*blech*!" Her body shivered as she said it. She curled her legs underneath herself and looked at the newswoman with the same horrified expression. Her blond curls took a moment to settle upon the shoulders of her tan blouse.

Normally, Captain Campanelli would be annoyed by the leaking of the news item, but his mind was too occupied with Gherling's account on how Werner was murdered and how the perpetrator had escaped a car crash that should have been fatal. He decided to contact McLain in the morning and see what his detectives had found.

The rest of the newscast and a couple of holovision shows passed quickly, and Frank, exhausted, turned in early. Tamara remained awake for a time, as she had since before she left the hospital. She had become accustomed to reading old books and staying up late to do so. With her diner gone, there was no reason for an early rise.

Frank shut his implant down none too soon. Its network of power cells was mostly depleted, and if he had attempted to stay awake, he would have been doing so blindly within minutes. It would take much of the night for the implants to glean enough electrical energy from his brain and nervous system to recharge them.

Though drained physically, Campanelli could not relax his mind. Gherling's reenactment of the Werner murder was ludicrously hideous and unbelievable. It took a special kind of maniac to tear a body apart like that, remove organs, and leave bite marks. Further, without a formal registration on the vehicle, it could not be determined that the car was driven by the victim, the murderer, or even a witness until Rothgery and his team swept the wreck for DNA. There was plenty of that, given the amount of blood in the car, but waiting to find out was tortuous.

Frank wanted sleep, but the visions of Herman Werner's gutted body and that of the twisted wreck of a car that should have yielded no survivors persisted, and had he any excess energy whatsoever, it would have been enough to keep him awake, attempting to solve the puzzle.

With the cool night air slipping in through the windows, Frank drifted into a tumultuous sleep.

***

Tamara awoke the next morning to the bed moving. Frank was awake and had risen for the day. She listened to the water in the shower running and the gurgling of the coffee maker while she drifted in and out. When the holovision had been turned on and the apartment was permeated with the inviting aroma of coffee, she dragged herself out of bed and put on her robe.

"Good morning," Frank called from the couch where he sat watching the news.

"Mornin'," she mumbled as she shuffled to the coffee maker. She had been up very late, curled up on the couch, reading one of Frank's many books from his impressive library. Sir Arthur Conan Doyle's Sherlock Holmes was quite entertaining. She had blazed through *The Adventures of Sherlock Holmes* and *The Hound of the Baskervilles* in less than a week and she had begun an earlier work, *The Sign of the Four*, the previous night.

"How late were you up?" Frank asked when he joined him on the couch.

"Not sure. Three, I think."

"I take it you're enjoying the books." He looked over at her and smiled.

"A little too much, maybe," she said and sipped her coffee.

"Nah," Frank answered with a dismissive wave of his hand. "I think you're enjoying those books just the right amount. I wish I could read more."

Tamara placed a hand on his knee. "You know, I never thought about that."

"Hmm? Oh, not having enough juice left over to stay up and read?" He tapped his temple, indicating his implant.

"Yeah."

"Well, yesterday was an exceptional day. I get some time for a book now and then, but I wish it was more."

"I guess I take my vision for granted," Tam said and yawned.

"Everyone takes their senses for granted," Frank said and sipped some coffee. "No one expects them to be lost in some accident or illness."

Tam decided to change the subject. "Any updates on the biter?"

"No. Just a repeat of the same thing," Frank answered and stood up with his cup in his hand. "I should get going. I need to find out what Rothgery's found. He's been too quiet for too long."

Frank kissed her on the forehead and, after a few more minutes of preparation, he donned his hat and coat and bid her a good day before closing the door behind him.

The morning was cool and sunny. Campanelli decided to walk to the forensics lab, which was on the far side of the building. However, he figured that today was a fact finding day. This murder, though not directly his case, was still a priority, and to bring it to a quick close would be beneficial to the city.

Frank picked a cigarette out of the pack in his overcoat's inner pocket and lit it before entering his code to open the gate, something his cruiser would normally do automatically. Overhead, the seven o'clock train passed along the elevated tracks. With less than seven hundred thousand people in the city, with few of them having daily business out of town, there were only four trains running in the morning, and four in the evening.

Campanelli puffed on his cigarette and looked both ways before stepping into the street. Traffic, as always, was light. He found an opportunity and took it, stepping leisurely across the roadway.

Frank accessed the CPD server and checked his messages. To his relief, there was one from H. Lincoln Rothgery, asking for Campanelli and McLain's presence in his lab at their earliest convenience. McLain had replied and indicated that he would be there at eight a.m., not quite an hour from then.

Frank spent much of that hour in his office, dealing with more reports and paperwork until it became close to the appointed time, when he stepped out front of the station and smoked another cigarette. After a time of reflection, he stomped it out and re-entered. He wound his way through the hallways until he reached the forensics lab. When he approached the door, he found it partially open. He pushed it out of his way and went in.

Rothgery's lab was one cavernous room featuring a garage door that opened onto a short driveway on one end. The wrecked sedan from the previous day had been deposited within the lab. Under the light, the gaping and twisted front end of the vehicle beheld indelible ugliness, like a gargoyle statue from a haunted mansion. Workbenches, storage cabinets, and loaded shelving units lined the garage area and were sporadically placed throughout the rest of the lab. Not one shelf went unused. The cabinets were bulging with tools, artifacts and equipment. The room was as versatile and multifaceted as Rothgery's skillset and job responsibilities. The unused portions of the room were as yet unlit that morning as Lincoln sat at his main desks in the center of the rectangular room, near the door.

"Campanelli," the forensic genius called from his seat. "Come on in." He remained seated, staring at a brightly lit monitor a bit closely. Not equipped with bio-electronics by choice, Rothgery's glasses should have been enough to see whatever it was on the screen, but appeared not to be adequate considering his hardened expression and concentration.

"*Good morning*, Lincoln," Frank said with emphasis. H. Lincoln only gave such greetings when he was not busy or was in a good mood, which was almost never.

"Yeah, well, we'll see about that," Rothgery answered. "You'd better have a look."

Frank removed his fedora and stepped around the connected network of desks to get behind his friend and co-worker. As he did, Kirby McLain entered.

"Gentlemen," McLain greeted.

"Close the door," H. Lincoln directed. His eyes never left the center monitor.

"Yes, *sir*," Kirby replied and did so as he smiled crookedly at Campanelli, who shrugged it off.

"Okay, so I've gone over the body with Gherling's help and we've found some interesting things."

Frank scowled when he found the picture on Lincoln's monitor. It was a close up of Werner's sliced throat. McLain moved next to the Sentinel detective and stared upon the unpleasantness over the forensic scientist's left shoulder. He raised his eyebrows as he studied the screen, causing the deeply carved forehead ripples to appear again.

Rothgery looked around to verify that he had their attention and continued. "The killer cut this man's throat deep, scraping the blade against the esophagus. This left microscopic traces of the blade behind. It's carbon fiber, very long and most likely military grade. The fibers are high quality and very durable."

"Did you find any pieces large enough for a serial number?" asked McLain.

"Strangely, no. Considering the strips we were able to extract from the body, they should have yielded at least one string. But we've found nothing."

"What does that mean, Lincoln?" Frank inquired next. He knew that commercially made knives had been mandated to include a multitude of serial numbers woven into the blades on a microscopic level. No matter what it was made of, when a blade was used, there was a good chance that pieces would be left behind. That would render the weapon traceable to its owner, who was obligated to register the weapon. Manufacturers of carbon fiber, carbon nanotube, and metal blades turned to including their brand stamps and batch numbers at such a scale.

"It might mean a few things, Frank," Lincoln said as he turned to look into his face. "The quality indicates that it's a newer more refined carbon fiber, let's say under forty years old, but the lack of any stamping tells me it's older, before serial numbers were mandated by law. Kind of a conundrum, unless it's something made for the special forces. Those serial numbers aren't found in the blade material."

"Most likely, it's a stolen weapon, anyway," Kirby commented.

"That's a good bet," Rothgery agreed. "The throat was sliced open in one long stroke. I'd say the blade is eight to ten inches. Also, if you look at how wide the flesh was spread apart, we're looking at a triangular blade."

"What do you mean? Like a bayonet?" Frank asked.

"Exactly."

"A carbon fiber military-style bayonet without serial numbers," McLain restated. If he was surprised, he hid it well.

"Everything I see is pointing to that, yes," H. Lincoln affirmed.

"Okay, well, what about Gherling's idea that Werner was thrown through the air?" Campanelli pushed on.

"I agree with him."

"You're kidding," McLain inserted. The smile was long gone. Even though he could not figure out another alternative, he had expected it to be disproved by something he had not considered.

"Not at all," Lincoln said as he turned his chair to face them both. "The way his bones are broken, he was either thrown through the air and left to fall onto the curb, or someone smacked him over the head and shoulders with a solid piece of concrete. What's more likely?"

"Amazing." Frank ran his hand over his short gray hair and over his face. The strength of whoever killed Herman Werner was staggering. A dedicated weightlifter with nothing to do but train be easy to find, however. As he gazed upon the gargoyle parked inside the room, he rethought. There was no way, in his judgment, that a bodybuilder capable of throwing a man into the air would have escaped the collapsed vehicle. *Unless there's a third party involved.*

Lincoln caught Frank's gaze. "We found two different types of blood, two sets of DNA in the car."

"Go on," McLain prompted.

"Herman Werner's and the killer's. No ID's been matched to his," Rothgery stated and stood from his chair. He stepped between the two detectives and moved casually toward the sedan. "The killer's DNA has been engineered, as has the blood, but there's no identification to be found in the cells. *He* is a he and appears to be of military origin, but it goes beyond anything I've ever seen."

"So, you're telling me that the killer is a soldier. American?" Frank asked as he stopped next to Lincoln and stared at the driver's seat of the ruined car.

"I can't even determine *that* without a serial number in the DNA sequence, Frank."

"Soldier or not, Mr. Rothgery...how the hell did he get outta that?" McLain asked from Lincoln's other side. The big man waved his hand over the wreckage as he spoke. "That should've been fatal...engineered genes or not."

"I agree." Rothgery slid his glasses from his Roman nose and rubbed his eyes with his free hand. "Gherling is still researching the DNA and the blood while Teri is carrying out more tests."

"You said Werner's blood was in the car," Frank stated.

"Yeah," Lincoln said, then nodded. "Not much of it, though. A lot of the DNA we found in it was from hairs in the carpets and seats. My opinion is that he had used the car for some time. Months, perhaps close to a year."

"So, Werner was cut out of the seatbelt...then thrown through the air." Kirby stepped up to the side of the car and studied the sliced seatbelt. In the bright light, the precision cut was much more impressive.

"Definitely," H. Lincoln affirmed as he replaced his eyeglasses. "And...before I forget...there are teeth marks on the body."

"We saw those," Frank said. He leaned back on the workbench behind him and crossed his arms. "The bites on the shoulders."

"I'm not talking about those, Frank."

This took Kirby's attention from the wreck to the forensic genius. "What are you trying to say, Mr. Rothgery?"

"I'm saying he had a little nibble on some muscle tissue while he cut out the heart and liver. It's also confirmed that the heart and liver were eaten." Lincoln met McLain's eyes then looked to Campanelli.

"God," Kirby uttered and stepped away from the sedan as if it exuded heat.

"How do you come to that, Lincoln?" Frank asked.

"Pieces of both organs were left behind in the car. Nothing more than shreds, really. Seems he had to pick them out of his teeth as he drove."

Frank lifted his right hand to his chin and rested it, keeping the left arm tucked. "You're telling me that we have a soldier of unknown origin turned cannibal, running around the streets of Chicago."

"From everything we've gathered so far, Frank, that's about the size of it."

"Have you tried plugging the DNA into the modeler?" Kirby asked.

"I was just about to address that, Detective McLain." Rothgery stepped away from the workbench and faced both veteran policemen. "We've verified the sequence a couple dozen times or so. Taken from samples of the blood in the car and from saliva found from Werner's chest cavity..."

"Christ," Kirby groaned.

"...the modeler can't read it and spits out a general synopsis instead."

A DNA modeler was a holographic generator that could read an entire strand of DNA and display it in a three dimensional image. It resembled a holovision, but was connected to a specialized computer. Rothgery's was almost a half-century old, but kept in great condition by the scientist himself.

"Malfunction?" Frank asked.

"Not really," H. Lincoln answered. "It would have trouble with any military encoding of DNA. We would have a hard time analyzing your partner's strand, since he was a Navy SEAL, but we'd still end up with a partial image as least as good as a pencil sketch."

Campanelli grunted in understanding. He had not known that about the machine, but the fact did not surprise him. The unit was, after all, old technology. There had been plenty of time for the military to work out ways to defeat such a device.

"The reports from the modeler also vary after each run, so it's ever the more perplexing after every attempt," Lincoln provided. "That's not unheard of, if we made it run with only a partial strand it's prone to speculate. I had Teri run what we had through the FBI's database and came up with nothing."

The three of them stood for several long moments, regarding the wrecked car in utter, contemplative silence.

"Gentleman," H. Lincoln Rothgery finally said, "I believe there's a monster loose in Chicago."

"Maybe he was just passin' through," Kirby McLain said as he looked over to Campanelli for his opinion.

"All we can do now is wait," the Captain of Detectives croaked through a dry mouth. Staring into the twisted mouth that was the entrance to the driver's seat of the antique automobile, it seemed to mock him. Bent and broken as it was, the machine had seen something that they could not. The murderous monster that had victimized Werner so disgustingly efficiently, sat in that seat, touched that steering yoke, caused *that* damage, and had survived it, all without fear of being identified.

"We can't just sit back and do nothing, Frank," McLain stated flatly.

"What are you going to put in the bulletin, Kirby?" Frank asked without much life in his voice. He understood the frustrations that McLain was feeling and sympathized, but the horrifying nature of the case subdued the fire in his demeanor. Campanelli felt that he was in some sort of fog, kept at bay and helpless in the face of the killer's will.

McLain stewed quietly for a moment. He stepped from the counter he had been leaning on and stared hotly into Frank's face, then looked to Rothgery's. The expressions of both men were not challenging. In fact, the Sentinel detective and the forensic scientist were plainly baffled. Kirby McLain knew that Frank was right, for the most part.

"Aw, hell," Kirby exuded and turned to face the ruined automobile once again. "All I can do is…spread the word to the patrol units and my detectives. I'll have 'em look for anyone unusually large, probably wounded. We may get lucky."

Frank nodded with his arms still folded across his chest. Lincoln simply regarded the homicide detective with kind, regretful eyes peering over his glasses.

With that, McLain bid them both a "Good morning," and left. As his footfalls faded down the hallway, Frank ran his hand over his short gray hairs. While his eyes could not seem to leave the old sedan, his scalp itched.

A question from Lincoln snapped him out of his trance. "What are you thinking, Frank?"

"I'm thinking it's time for me to go visit my partner," he answered as he moved to leave.

"I meant about the case, Frank."

"I did, too," Campanelli answered as he scooped up his fedora. He gave Rothgery a two-fingered salute and left, closing the lab's door behind him.

***

Frank walked back home for his car and went to Cook County Hospital. From the driver's seat, he stared unfocused through the windshield with all the facts Rothgery had fed him bouncing around in his mind. Despite his natural and trained logic, he did not want to believe that some military-grade monster was loose in the city. In all his years in the NYPD and CPD, he had never heard of such a thing, and had always assumed veterans like his partner, Marcus Williams, represented the avant-garde of the military. Like most citizens who wished their child to be considered for the elite forces, Marcus's parents had him tested while still in utero. From that moment on, a candidate fetus would receive genetic modification and allowed to have a natural birth. As the baby grew, he or she would be tested and adjusted physically and behaviorally every two years until adulthood, where the subject would be inducted into whatever branch of service they preferred, if available. Psychosis of this magnitude should not have been possible.

Marcus Williams had been among the last to have the distinction and proud honor of being a Navy SEAL, a section that no longer existed. Outside of some Green Beret units and paratroopers of the army, the only other force that could be considered elite were the Marines, and they had been scaled way back in numbers.

The cruiser turned from Harrison Street onto Damen and then into the parking lot of the hospital, where it stopped to let off its driver and rolled away into the parking lot. Frank walked through the front entrance and into the elevator, trying to think of a way to present the detail of this case to his mending partner.

To Campanelli's surprise, Marcus had been allowed to leave the constraints of his anti-bacterial hospital room. Frank found him on the same floor, walking the hallway, escorted by not one, but two young nurses. Neither of them were the nice blonde from the previous visit.

"At ease, Lieutenant," Frank chided from behind them.

Marcus stopped his shuffling walk as his spine stiffened. Warily, he turned around to see the speaker. "Jesus, Frank," he exuded and chuckled with relief.

The two nurses smiled, but Campanelli could tell they would rather have been left to their duty. "Good morning, Marcus. Ladies," he greeted them with a tilt of his hat. He introduced himself and asked them for a moment of the patient's time. Cheerily, but reluctantly, they granted it and wandered off.

"Gee. Thanks, Frank." Williams shifted his weight from one leg to the other, holding tightly to his wheeled I.V. tree.

"Sorry to piss all over your road to recuperation, my friend," Frank said lowly enough not to be overheard. He smiled crookedly. "You are looking surprisingly well. Now I understand why." He glanced over his shoulder as the nurses disappeared around a corner.

"I'll catch up to them later," Marcus dismissed with a wave of his hand. "You scared the crap out of me when you called me 'lieutenant'. I thought you were from the recruiting office."

Frank gave a short chuckle. "Where you headed?" He gestured in the direction the big man had been walking.

Williams nodded and resumed his shuffle. He regarded his older, shorter partner with what Campanelli judged to be a tired smile. The two made their way past closed doors of the other hospital rooms until they reached a small sitting room at the end of the hallway. Marcus grunted as he took a seat in a large overstuffed vinyl chair. His left arm was still immobilized in a sling and shoulder rig, making it difficult to lean back and be comfortable.

Frank stared at the diminished skyline of the city to the east. He removed his black fedora and sighed.

"Did they bring you in on that murder from Monday morning?" Williams inquired.

Campanelli knew better than to be surprised at his partner's intuition. He flashed his crooked smile once again. "Yeah."

"So...what's the big deal?"

"You looked up the victim's name in the CPD computer, right?"

"You know I did." Williams smiled. "Who brought you in?"

"Kirby McLain."

"Ah. So, what's the problem?"

"Rothgery's DNA modeler is blocked from coming up with an ID."

"Shit," Marcus grumbled. "Military man."

"Yeah." Frank dropped the old black hat to the couch across from his partner and took a seat next to it. He studied Marcus's face as he went on. "Werner was cut out of his vehicle and propelled into the air. He landed on his head from such a height that it fractured his skull, broke his shoulder, and a few ribs."

Marcus cussed in wonder, but did not seem overly surprised. He sat back in the thickly padded chair and ran his left hand over the stubble on his chin as his eyes lost focus.

Frank glanced up the empty hallway before continuing. "He was cut open and his heart and liver were removed and eaten."

Marcus looked back into Campanelli's eyes and nodded. "I saw the news that he had been bitten, but nothing about that."

"The media liaison left that out, thankfully." Frank leaned forward and lowered his voice to just above a whisper. "Lincoln and his people have noted several indications that the DNA was modified, military-style. But, the best the modeler can do is speculate to a degree. They can tell it's a male and heavily tinkered with. It gives them a different result every time."

Williams nodded in understanding and just listened.

"Werner's car was stolen after the assailant left him dead on the south end of the Ashland Avenue Bridge. It was found at the bottom of a foundation a few miles north."

"He ditched it?"

"No. It was driven at a high rate of speed when a tire blew. We think it hit the barrier at about eighty or higher and crashed onto the concrete floor, nose-first."

"And?" Marcus pressed after a moment a silence. Frank had gone quiet as he stared into his partner's eyes.

"No trace of the driver."

"No freakin' way," Marcus whispered.

"Yeah."

"Certainly not without being hurt, Frank," the retired SEAL insisted.

Frank nodded and sat back. "Oh, he was hurt. There was blood in the car. In addition to the victim's, that is."

Both policemen were quiet for more than a minute. They looked to each other, to the city beyond the window, and the hazy blue sky beyond that.

"Marcus, I need to know something," the Captain of Detectives said, and again checked the hallway. "As a former SEAL and an officer, do you have any insight...any clue...as to what this thing is?"

Williams looked back at Frank for several heartbeats. His eyes darted up the vacant corridor, but even then he hesitated. Clearly, he knew something, but for a moment, Campanelli was convinced that his partner would remain silent.

Marcus leaned forward and spoke in a near-whisper. "About four years before we, the SEAL teams, were formally retired, there were rumors that we were going to be replaced with a new kind of unit. It was supposed to be cutting edge in genetic technology."

"Well? What happened?"

"That's just it. I thought nothing happened. It was all rumor, Frank. Look, there's no way the federal government could have afforded any advancements and I doubt if there was anyone still Earthside that could have improved on us."

"So, you never saw any examples of a...well, person that resulted from this...program or whatever," Frank surmised.

"No. Never."

"Damn it."

"Perhaps there's other explanations for this crime," Williams said.

"Like what?" Campanelli wondered.

"I don't know...how about an ex-soldier traveling with a doppelganger?"

"An automaton with the strength to throw a man up into the air?" Frank scoffed.

"McAllen Industries had that military model...the, ummm...Model Eight," Marcus recalled with a snap of his fingers.

"What about it?" Frank asked, exasperated. He spread his hands in front of him and looked to his partner and friend with an annoyed expression.

"The Eight had the strength to do heavy lifting. That's what it was for."

"I'm aware of that model, Marcus," Frank added with both hands up. "That unit did not have the agility to do something like this."

"Are you sure?"

Frank tilted his head to one side and regarded Williams with barely contained anger. "Give me a little break, Marcus. I've only been in the detective business for two and a half decades!"

Williams held his right hand up. "All right, all right, Frank. Just let me think."

Campanelli sank back into the couch and ran his hand over his flushed face. The two went silent for a few moments while each considered the other's words. Frank stood from the couch and gazed at his city to the east.

"Kirby hopes that…whatever this creature or person is, that he's moved on," Campanelli spoke onto the glass, fogging it faintly.

"What do you think?"

"I don't think anything's that easy. I think that thing's still out there," Frank went on as he turned from the window. "I don't know. In any case, all we can do is wait. McLain's alerted units to its presence, but without a physical description…" He trailed off, shaking his head.

At that moment, one of the nurses entered and informed Marcus that his lunch was waiting in his room. As the three of them headed there, Frank and Marcus linked implants.

"*You should contact the FBI on this one, Frank,*" Williams transmitted in an audible message.

"*It may be a bit early for that,*" Campanelli replied in like fashion.

"*Perhaps, but if this is one of those super-soldiers, you could get someone on the Federal level a heads-up.*" Williams slowed his pace and studied Frank's face. His eyebrows were slightly raised as he locked eyes with his senior partner.

The nurse was a teenager, born too late to enjoy the benefits of bio-electronic implants, but she recognized the body language of the two older men and understood that they were conversing. She walked closely on Williams's right and helped him watch his step. To Frank, she looked like a large child's doll on a date with Frankenstein's monster. The disparity in height was almost humorous.

"*You may be right,*" Frank sent, then added vocally, "I'll see what I can find out about that. Have a good lunch."

"Thanks, Frank," Williams replied as he stepped inside his room. "Talk soon."

The man was recovering quickly, there was no doubt. The nurse escorted him inside without donning the anti-bacterial suit. Frank smiled as he walked away, happy to see his partner on the mend.

He placed his fedora on his head as he entered the elevator. He rode down to the lobby, thinking of his partner's fast healing. He knew that genetic alterations made that possible, and considered the fact that such things were old hat. Marcus's words rattled around in Frank's mind as he walked back to his cruiser. "Rumors", the man had called them.

Campanelli sat in his car, thinking for several minutes before leaving the facility. He imagined the genetic capabilities of healing had advanced since Marcus's time. The Captain of Detectives wondered what other advancements had been made and shuddered when he thought of the destroyed sedan. Marcus had used the term, "super-soldier", which sounded like something right out of a twentieth-century B movie.

Frank grunted in thought and ordered his cruiser to drive. Out of habit, he set the destination as a favorite Chinese restaurant not far from home. The car pulled out onto the street casually, leaving its driver to contemplate.

He wondered if the ex-SEAL was holding something back in the name of national security or some other outdated reasoning. Frustrated, he roughly tossed his hat to the passenger seat and shook his head. Frank Campanelli knew that it would be a restless night ahead.

***

As night fell, the hungry predator stepped from the empty office building in which he had slept for most of the day and stood for a long moment, watching, feeling and listening for indications of life. He inhaled the cool air through his widening nostrils deeply and soundlessly. The first thing he could discern from the intake was the aroma of cooking meat. Beef, if he was not fooled by seasoning. His eyes danced upon the apartment building directly across from him and, like most structures of Chicago, it was sparsely lit. The soft glowing electric light gave his prey's presence away, more effectively than a campfire in the wilderness.

He glanced in either direction and, noting the absence of vehicles, the naked male sprinted to the other side of the street. As most of the street lights did not function, his pale skin was adequate to do so with a low possibility of being spotted. After all the energy his body had spent in the healing process, he needed to be conservative. Changing pigment took calories and resting for a day could only do so much.

The mishap with the old and worn out vehicle had left him with a grocery list of injuries, most of which had been greatly improved upon since then. The broken nose had been set and was healing well. The hairline fractures in his ribs had mostly healed, though the yellow and purple contusions from his subcutaneous tissue on his face and chest would take a few more days. His headache from the concussion had faded that morning, though the skull fracture would take days to repair as would the broken fingers. All of this healing sapped much of his energy, and it would progress agonizingly slowly if he did not feed.

He had expected to be pursued further by the city's police force, but surprisingly, it had seemingly ended after he left the stolen vehicle behind. He had perused the old building only briefly before settling down to sleep behind a citadel of unused and dusty office furniture. The incessant hunger he felt had kept him from sleeping further. The rest of daylight had been spent meditating and being aware of the area around him.

Seeing no one to challenge him, he scratched his fortified claws into the small glass window of the apartment building. As his wrist twisted one way then the other, the grating, screeching sound echoed down the silent street. Quite soon, the outer layer of glass was ground away, ceasing the intermittent squealing. In just over a minute, the outer pane was cut free.

His pale yellow eyes searched frantically for signs of discovery, but there was none. He pulled the roughly shaped circle of glass from its place and silently set it upon the concrete slab by his feet. His claws worked on the next layer immediately, carving out another, similar circle. The task was delicate, making his limbs stiff with the effort of remaining as quiet as possible. With the inner layer cut free, he pushed it through. The glass struck the carpeted floor with a muted thump.

Reaching his arm inside to the elbow, he felt for the locks and undid them. He turned the knob and swung the door out of his way. Once inside, the aroma of cooking meat was maddening. The humanoid spat his excess saliva onto the rug and closed the door silently. Following the scent of food, he quickly deduced that it was coming from the apartment on the second floor. The other seven inhabited dwellings, if the telltale lights were any indicators, were on the third and fourth floors.

The foyer and stairway were unlit. Adjusting his vision, the hunter scaled the steps casually, though stealthily. The hall was equally dark, but a beam of light scattered against the carpeted floor marked his target. Adjusting further, he studied the light coming from under the apartment's front door. Though his augmented hearing picked up sounds of movement and an electronically generated voice, there was no shadow cast to disrupt the light. Taking a moment to listen through the wood, the predator quickly determined there was a great possibility that his victim was not within visual range of the door.

He flicked his long, black strands of hair from his eyes and gave the knob a turn. It was locked. Though he was ravenous with hunger, he called upon his calm to fortify him in his moment of need. He took a deep breath as he felt through one of his belt's pouches for his lock pick, a tool he had made himself out of a strip of an automobile's decorative trim, the design for which had been supplied in his implant's survival manual.

In the blink of an eye, the lock was disabled. He opened the door and gave it a nudge. It stopped after traveling only a few centimeters. He listened for signs of discovery, but there was none. Peering through the gap between the door and the frame, he found the problem and smiled.

It was only a brass chain. The predator pressed his weight against the door at intervals. The framework popped and gave a crack. He halted and listened again. There was nothing but the sound of a holovision program. More applied pressure stretched the mount from the doorjamb. Once he reached inside and pressed upon it with the heel of his hand, it came free.

He smiled over his exhilaration. The hunter loved this part of the game. He thought to spend a little energy to turn himself charcoal black as he scanned the living space. The majority of the light came from the living room's lamp, directly across from the door he had just breeched. The sounds of the occupant, the cooking meat, and the holovision emanated from the kitchen area some three meters in and to the left. A darkened hallway lay to his right, leading to the rest of the rooms.

His footfalls along the carpeted floor resulted in no sound, no vibrations, and very little disruption of the air. The victim was an old man of medium build and height, standing in front of his stove while he dutifully watched his miniaturized holovision set mounted on the east wall.

The predator lightened his color just a few degrees, for something as dark as night can be easily spotted in the light. Soundlessly, the bayonet slid from the hunter's belt.

Now, the fun begins.

"Hoo-aack!" the victim exclaimed and went rigid with surprise and pain. The sound was short, but sharp, louder than the predator had planned on when he decided to thrust the blade into his target's back. Being so far from another human's ears, however, the killer had decided there was room for such an error.

Blood pooled at the dying victim's spine and covered the murderer's right hand. More blood erupted from the triangular carbon fiber blade's exit at the front of the old man's chest. A metal spatula struck and rang crisply against the marble tile as the body went limp around the bayonet like a shrimp on a skewer.

The killer used his wounded left hand to keep the body upright, holding the dead man up by the collar of his shirt. He did not wish to get human blood on the cooking bovine meat. It would change the taste.

Tilting the tip of the bayonet, the dead man slid from it and dropped heavily onto the kitchen tiles with a splattering thud that shook the floor and the utensils on his table.

The hunter dropped his blade to the kitchen counter and grabbed up the filet mignon from the broiling pan with no regard for the sizzling heat. Madly, he chewed and savored the nearly forgotten flavor. Steam left his mouth as he chewed frantically. It was a fatty cut of the delicacy, but it went down ever so smoothly. Hunger persisted.

After moments of crude and frantic clawing and cutting, the heart and liver of the predator's victim lay on the broiler. He took a seat at the kitchen table, downed a glass of water, and casually watched holovision while he waited for the rest of his meal to cook.

He rose to give the sizzling heart a turn and as he did, the news show flashed pictures of the crime scene at the Ashland Avenue Bridge. The killer dropped the heart from the metal tongs and stepped back to take in the view of the holovision. His mouth dropped open in surprise, for he had not realized that such a small act would gather such media attention.

So enthralled was he with the broadcast of his deed, that the cannibalistic assassin failed to hear the footfalls of the other inhabitant of the apartment. As the room's relative calm was pierced by a female's scream, the killer's entire body spasmed and turned toward the screamer. The blood-covered tongs twirled into the air and clattered to the tile.

In the living room beyond the kitchen, some four meters away, stood the woman of the house. Approximately seventy-five years old, in the hunter's judgment, her wide eyes bounced from the horrible sight playing chef in her kitchen and the fallen body of her husband. Her hands clawed and covered her mouth in fright and horror. After the first scream, she stood upon shaking legs, unable to move.

With a sound similar to a dart striking a wooden wall, the beast's carbon fiber blade entered her septum and buried deep within her skull. The body dropped to the floor before the vibrations in the handle ebbed.

The skilled and efficient murderer silenced the HV set and became quite still as he listened and felt for a response to the scream. Slowly, he bent and retrieved the tongs from the floor near his feet and carried on with his grilling.

***

On the third floor, a couple had been slipping into their routine and predictable late night snooze in front of the holovision. The woman heard something beyond the sound of the program.

"Matt?" she mumbled to the man sitting next to her on the couch. "Matt?" She tried again, more urgently, this time with a smack to his thigh.

"What?" he blurted upon being struck. "Christ, woman."

"Did you hear that?" his wife asked with frightened eyes.

"Obviously not," he shot sarcastically.

"Smarty," she fired back. "It sounded like a scream."

Sighing heavily, he knew that Gertrude was not prone to panic. He muted the program with his handheld controller and listened to the silence of the night with her for more than ten seconds. He shrugged and shook his head questioningly.

"It sounded like it came from the Drakes' place," Gert explained and pointed to the wall. "I heard it through the vent."

Matt gave the slightest nod and continued to listen. He grumbled as he lifted his hefty girth from the comfortable cushions and crouched near the floor-level vent. He scratched his scalp through his thinning, greasy hair as he waited there in silence.

There was nothing.

"It was probably on the show."

"I don't think so," she answered, though she was now doubtful.

"Well, I don't hear anything," he answered and dropped himself back onto the sofa. In a matter of moments, the voice in the vent was forgotten as Matt and Gert dozed in front of their holovision set.

***

The killer moved through the apartment with the grace and aplomb of a ghost. He had realized that he had been so hungry that he had forgotten to close the drapes of the living room windows, the very ones that had allowed him to see the light into this place originally.

On his way back to the kitchen, he set his left foot upon the forehead of the unharvested woman and pulled his bayonet from her face. He bent and cleaned the blood from it onto her white nightgown before returning it to his belt.

Returning to the kitchen, he judged the liver to be done well enough, though it remained bloody. Out of a sense of humor rather than etiquette, the killer tore through the cabinets in search of a plate. Finding one, he set the liver upon it and deposited the plate onto the table. He located a large fork and a steak knife and sat in one of the kitchen chairs. Hungrily, he dug into the meat. He smiled at his circumstance and regarding the splayed corpse of the geriatric organ donor near his feet. The old man had been rather tall, the killer noted. He chewed his food and looked a little closer. Like himself, the victim appeared to have a lanky figure.

The hunter choked down the liver sloppily and used several paper napkins from the holder to wipe the mess from his face. He left the table and gave the heart another turn with the tongs. From his experience, that meat would be tougher and would take longer to cook.

In the meantime, he decided to search the closets for clothing.

Part Two

*F*rank's sleep was peppered with dreams of mass killings by a race of humanoid creatures that tore through the populace of his adopted home, leaving half-eaten corpses in their wake. He saw himself driving through the streets of Chicago, steering around discarded pieces of human flesh as he tried to get himself and Tamara out of the city.

Dozens of cannibalistic soldiers in green uniforms and old-styled army helmets eyed the car as Campanelli drove by, too busy eating what was already well in hand rather than to chase down the police car.

Frank drove on, fascinated by how quickly two of the huddled soldiers devoured a citizen their size.

"*Frank*!" Billingsley shouted from the passenger seat.

His head snapped forward in time to see that the road was blocked by a group of the uniformed monsters. Though he floored the accelerator, the cruiser came to a halt. Its computer had detected an impact and slammed the brakes on for him.

In a heartbeat, the automobile was surrounded and the blood-spattered creatures ripped into the car, tearing away body panels and shattering windows to get at the juicy treats within. Their open, fang-laden mouths uttered no sound as they came.

As Tamara screamed in pain and terror, Campanelli awoke. He felt as if he had been thrown a great distance, so disoriented he was upon waking into darkness. Frank was certain he had uttered a shout, but realized quickly that it could have been in the nightmare.

He thought about initiating his implant and giving himself sight, but he decided against it. From the peacefully rhythmic light snoring coming from his left, he could tell that all was well. He took several deep breaths before feeling for his RadarCane and making his way to the bathroom. The cane hummed and wowed as he swung it left and right, outlining the path the blind man needed to adhere to if he wanted to save his toes and shins from the furniture.

The nightmare haunted him as he went about his business. The cool of the night paired with the horror and he shivered so violently that he shook his head hard to push the memory of it away. He cussed as he washed his hands. He felt for the towel and dried them. He knew he was tired and should go right back to sleep, but the violent nightmare had been intense enough that Frank decided that he would not try for a time.

Campanelli returned to the bedroom and felt the surface of the nightstand for his pack of cigarettes and lighter. He dropped them into his robe's front pocket and followed his cane into the living room.

He stopped next to the glass patio doors and placed a paper tube of the tobacco between his lips. By feel and with much practice, Frank spun the wheel of his NYPD lighter and lit his smoke. He clicked the lid shut and opened the patio door as he expended the first puff into the cool night air.

Frank probed the night with his cane and found the short brick wall at his patio's far side. There he stood, smoked, and thought. The night air was driven by a steady breeze out of the north that gave him a sharp chill, so he cinched his robe around himself tightly and flipped the collar up to cover his neck.

Since being moved to the Sentinel Division, there had not been a case that had kept him up late at night since the Ignatola/DeSilva mess. A missing person was simply that, missing, and most likely, voluntarily. The citizens of Chicago were not prisoners, after all. They could move to another part of the country if they wanted. America was still a free country, freer than ever, perhaps, as the federal government's influence had been weakening for over two decades due to the loss of population.

This Werner murder case, however, gave Campanelli a deep worry. He could not imagine a military man like his partner being driven to cannibalism to survive. Any thoughts of the perpetrator being sane had left Frank as soon as Lincoln's findings came to light. He shivered to think that a man genetically engineered and built like Williams could be out there in his city, preying on innocent people, drilling into them a fear of living in the city and possibly driving more of them out.

Frank finished his cigarette and crushed it out on the cement. He yawned deeply and knew that he had to try to get some rest, even if he laid flat and remained mostly awake. He went inside and crawled back into bed.

Once he decided that he would bring in the feds, if Rothgery had not already done so, his mind felt enough relief to drift to sleep, where the nightmares did not return.

***

Frank awoke a few hours later, feeling every minute of lost sleep. He prepared himself for work, shuffling like a zombie from place to place. Once in the shower, the hot water invigorated him, though not as much as Tamara's coffee.

While he sat in a recliner in the living room, watching the holovision news, the phone rang. He lifted himself from the chair and snatched it from the coffee table.

"Campanelli," he answered and sat back down.

"Frank, it's McLain."

"Good morning," Frank greeted, but he could tell that it was not to be so.

"Mornin', sir," Kirby replied and quickly pressed on. "We've got quite a mess out here…an apartment building. I've been over it, Gherling's going over it, now. He's called Rothgery."

Campanelli squeezed the bridge of his nose and shut his eyes tight. "What kind of mess, Kirby?"

"We have three dead, here. The address is on the blotter. It was reported at six-thirty this mornin'.""

Frank accessed the CPD server and found the case. He read it over quickly and stood up from his comfortable chair. "Okay, got it. No one in or out of the building and no one talks to the press."

"Already done, sir."

"Good. Be right there," Frank said and hung up the receiver.

"What is it, Frank?" Tamara asked as she stepped to him from the kitchen. Her face had that trademark look of worry. Her eyebrows were up, her eyes slightly bugged out and her lips were clamped thin.

"Triple murder. Possibly our guy, again," he answered while putting on his overcoat. He kissed her goodbye and exited the apartment. Tam called after him to be careful as the door closed. He promised that he would.

Campanelli jumped in his cruiser and commanded it to take him to the crime scene. As the car zipped through traffic with lights and siren, he looked at the address on the dashboard monitor. 417 Jefferson Street. Frank selected a satellite imagery of the area, and although the picture would be almost thirteen years old, it would still be at least somewhat accurate.

"Damn it," Frank said and struck the seat next to him with his fist. The apartment building was right across the 290 expressway from the empty foundation where the perpetrator's stolen car had crashed.

While the cruiser made its way to the scene, Frank fumed over his failure. The car turned onto Jefferson, passed underneath the expressway, then carefully passed between two marked police cars that had blocked off the street. Frank took manual control and guided the car into the apartment complex's parking lot.

He met Kirby McLain at the front door. Immediately, the cut glass took his attention.

"Hi, Frank," McLain began. "He used some tool to cut these holes, reached in an' unlocked the door."

"Prints?"

"None."

Campanelli bent at the knees so he could inspect the holes in the glass. "Two panes. Not a perfect circle. Both are a little different."

"I noticed that. We've got both pieces in evidence bags…neither one is shattered," Kirby explained. "Handheld tool. It looked to me like there was a drop or two of blood on each one."

"Rothgery's on his way?"

McLain nodded. "Should be here any minute."

"Okay," Campanelli said. "Get those to him the second he gets here. He'll be able to test them on scene."

McLain called over another detective and passed the evidence with the instructions to him.

"Frank." Kirby spoke in a low tone once the other detective had moved on. "We've got a couple of witnesses this time."

"Oh?" Campanelli brightened a little.

"The wife of victim number three said that they both heard a woman's scream last night," McLain explained. "Didn't check it, 'cause she said they thought they were mistaken. It was late, so they went to bed. This morning, Gertrude Henson gave a call down to the Drake residence. No one picked up. Matthew, her husband, went down to check on the Drakes. Got jumped."

"Cut up?" Campanelli inserted.

"No. His head was twisted from behind. Broken neck," Kirby supplied and then took a step closer to Frank.

"Matthew Henson's a big man, Frank. Our killer must be extremely strong."

Frank took a deep breath then let it out. "Okay, show me."

Kirby opened the door and walked straight for the stairs. At the second floor landing, he left the staircase and turned right at the hallway. At the first door on the right, he stopped and gestured to the inside of the apartment.

Frank stopped at the doorway and took in the sight. Closest to the door was Henson, lying on his front with his head turned around and his feet stretched out toward the door. Beyond him was the mutilated corpse of an elderly woman. Her chest cavity was splayed wide and her face was distorted by some sort of injury. Campanelli walked inside, looked about the room and stopped to take in the sight of the deceased Matthew Henson. He figured the man to be just over six feet tall and at least three hundred pounds. He would have fallen face down had the perpetrator not twisted his head nearly off. From the stretched skin at the neck and the odd angle that the head lay, it appeared to have been accomplished with amazing force.

"Pardon me, Detective Campanelli," Dennis Gherling said from behind him.

Frank covered the fact that the young man had startled him by reaching up to remove his fedora. He turned to look at the young forensic technician expectantly.

"Looks like the killer showered and ransacked Mr. Drake's wardrobe. Umm, Mr. Drake is victim number one." Gherling pointed toward the kitchen.

Without comment, Frank looked upon the gutted corpse and took note of the smell emanating from the small space. From experience, he could tell that this man had not been dead long. The stench of decomposition was the one thing Detective Campanelli would never miss about being moved to Sentinel. He nodded at Gherling to have him continue.

"It seems that Mr. Drake was taken by surprise at the stove. He was run through with that triangular bayonet." The young forensic investigator, as resilient as he seemed on the outside, swallowed hard and went on. "Then he was...you know, dissected and had his heart and liver removed...as did Mrs. Drake, who was killed by the bayonet being...thrust into her face...with great force. Both sets of heart and liver are...missing." Gherling halted and placed his hand on the half-wall that separated the kitchen from the dining room. His other hand wiped the sweat from his forehead. "I've tested the...remnants of what was left behind in the broiler pan on the stove..."

"Dennis," McLain said lowly from the doorway.

"Blood traces indicate that bovine blood is...mixed with both Mr. and Mrs. Drake's blood."

"Dennis," Kirby tried again. "It's okay, son. Go for a walk."

Gherling nodded and forced a smile as he wasted no time leaving the place.

Frank moved into the kitchen, carefully stepping over Charles Drake. He inspected the countertops, the stove, the pan, and the table. Anger and disgust met in a crescendo.

"That filthy son of a bitch sat here, calmly consuming these people like he was at some goddamned diner!"

Kirby McLain stepped inside just enough to watch what Campanelli was doing. He had already inspected the kitchen as Frank was doing now. He could think of nothing to say.

"That son of a bitch," the Captain of Detectives repeated, fuming with his hands tightened into fists.

"Frank..." Kirby attempted.

"He was right across the fuckin' street, Kirby," Frank seethed and took a step toward the taller man.

"Frank, I know."

"Probably watchin' us from the roof, laughing at us!"

Kirby raised both hands, showing that there was no argument. "Would ya listen a minute?"

Frank nodded sharply and kept his eyes on McLain's.

"We had no idea what kind of animal we were dealing with," Kirby explained calmly as he stood between the bodies of Brenda Drake and her neighbor, Matthew Henson. "If we had a clue, we would have cordoned off the entire neighborhood and done a building by building search. We're both angry that we didn't listen to our inner voices on this. My instincts told me that something…beyond our understanding was happening. I'm sure yours did, too."

Campanelli nodded. He opened his mouth to speak, but could not.

"There's no point in blaming yourself, Frank. I was there, right along with ya."

"I know."

"Let's get outta here," Kirby said with a heartbroken expression as he looked over the bodies.

Both detectives stepped into the hallway. Kirby pulled the apartment door nearly closed and met Campanelli on the stairs.

"Hey," Frank called behind him. "Gherling said that the perp ransacked the closet for clothes. How does he know that?"

"Mr. Drake's clothes are tossed all over the bedroom," McLain answered him as he descended the steps. "He's assuming some items are missing. Oh, that and we have a ten-year-old boy who witnessed a man jumping from the roof of this building onto the balcony above his."

"What?"

"The building next door," Kirby explained and jerked a thumb to the east. "It's six stories tall. This one's five. The boy says that he saw a tall bearded man hurl himself from the roof and land on the balcony one level above him."

"Who took his statement?"

"Detective Lyman." McLain accessed the statement that had been logged into the CPD server and sent it to Campanelli's implant. "There's the report."

Frank opened the file, projecting the text to his lenses and read it. The interview was short, depicting only the time that it had occurred and a brief description of the jumper.

"This is it?" he asked of Lyman's boss with his palms outstretched. "This is one crappy report."

"Yeah," Kirby said, "I was going to talk to the boy myself later."

"Let's go," Frank insisted and headed for the door as he put his hat on.

"It's Wednesday morning. He's in school."

Frank stopped, looked to the ceiling, and sighed heavily.

"I know, I know," McLain said as he took the lead and opened the door for the Sentinel detective. "Let's go get 'im outta class."

"Now you're talkin'."

McLain led his impromptu partner to his cruiser and the two set off for the middle school nearly a mile and a half away.

"Damn fool," Kirby muttered as they pulled into a parking place across the street from the school.

"What?" asked Campanelli.

"Lyman. Neither he nor his partner, Davies, thought to visually inspect the balcony," McLain explained as he shook his head and opened his door.

"I know the both of them. They're good men, but they aren't taking this as seriously as they should," Campanelli commented as he got out of the car.

"Trust me," Kirby said over his shoulder. "They are now."

"Good."

The pair walked up to the main door of the red-bricked school and pressed the doorbell. A doppelganger sentry answered immediately by opening the door partway, but remaining in the way as it was programmed. It was a more recent model, Campanelli guessed, around thirty years old. It was in good shape and slightly less anatomically correct than its predecessors. Standing about five-foot, ten inches tall, it was given the dress of a school maintenance man, gray overalls with a white shirt. When not busy maintaining the premises, such a machine acted as an unarmed security guard.

"May I help you two gentlemen?" it asked in a gently masculine voice.

Both detectives displayed their badges and introduced themselves.

"Come in, please, officers," the antique machine bid and opened the door. It stepped to one side to allow them a path.

"Thank you," Kirby granted as he returned his badge to his sport coat's inner pocket. "We're looking for Martin Kilbourne. We need to speak to him about an incident he witnessed this morning."

"I see," the doppelganger replied. "I have signed you both in as visitors and am contacting the vice principal, Margaret Thames. Martin Kilbourne is in his advanced math class upstairs. Miss Thames will meet us outside the classroom."

"Thank you," McLain said as he and Campanelli followed the automaton into an elevator.

The machine was programmed for small talk, which bored Frank immensely. "Lovely day," it commented once it turned to face the detectives.

"For some," Frank said flatly. He had no love for doppelgangers.

"Oh, my," the machine replied. "That's a bit of a non-sequitur, I'm afraid, Detective Campanelli."

"I'm afraid that I don't give a good god…"

"Frank," Kirby interrupted with a hint of a smile.

Once on the second floor, the elevator doors opened with a loud creaking, nearly loud enough to trigger the noise suppression in both men's implants.

"How about a little grease, Otis?" Frank shot at the doppelganger. Kirby smiled.

"I am Calvin, sir. I maintain the electrical and lighting of the building. I will inform Otis, immediately," the automaton replied humorlessly, making it even more so for the detectives, who chuckled. It would be their only laugh of the day.

Calvin exited without acknowledging the humor he had caused and made a right turn. After several doors, he stopped and turned to them.

"This is Martin's class. Ah, and here's Miss Thames," Calvin announced.

Both detectives turned around to see a young woman in professional attire striding up to them. Her shoes were flats, making no more than a whisper along the tile.

"Miss Thames, may I introduce Detectives McLain and Campanelli of the Chicago Police Department," the doppelganger addressed as she shook hands with the policemen.

"Gentlemen," she nodded, not disturbing the perfect bun in her amber hair. "How can I help you?"

"Ma'am, we need to speak to Martin Kilbourne," McLain spoke quietly. "He was a witness to an unusual event this morning at his apartment building."

"Oh?" Thames replied and folded her arms in front of her. Apparently, she needed more information.

"Miss Thames," Frank took up in his normal tone with a sprinkle of impatience, "Martin may have witnessed the escape of a serial murderer. We need to ask him some important questions, in private and quickly."

"Of course," Margaret Thames responded. Flushed, she opened the door of the classroom, silencing the teacher within and causing all heads to turn to her. "Mr. Backstrom, I need Martin Kilbourne," she said to the teacher. "Come with me, please," she called to the boy in a shaky voice.

The ten-year-old approached the vice principal quickly, but warily. When he saw the two detectives, Frank in particular, he shrank back. Looking closer into the face of Frank Campanelli, he blinked and looked to Thames.

"It's all right, Martin," she said. "These are policemen. They need to speak to you about this morning."

"Hello, Martin," Kirby said once Thames closed the classroom door. "I'm Detective McLain. This is Detective Campanelli."

"Hi," the timid boy said. His eyes passed over Frank once again, curiously.

"There's an empty classroom at the end of the hallway. Everyone come with me," the vice principal directed.

Martin followed her with the two detectives close behind. Once the four were inside, Thames closed the door. "Have a seat, please, Martin."

The child took a front seat as the vice principal took the one nearest the door. Though it was a child-size school desk, the demure grown-up fit into it. She looked at the two detectives expectantly.

"Well, Martin, we just need to follow up with you on what you saw this morning," McLain began.

"I saw a guy jump. He landed hard on the balcony," Martin said in near-whisper as he again stared at Frank.

"What did he look like, Martin? How was he dressed?" Frank asked. He thought he knew what the boy would say before he said it.

"Like you, sir," he answered.

McLain blinked and looked over at his co-worker. His mouth had dropped open slightly while his eyebrows slowly lifted.

"Like me? How so, Martin?" Frank asked.

"Well, dressed like you. Black hat and long black coat."

"Did you get a look at his face?" Campanelli followed up.

"He was fast. I saw a black beard," Martin said and nodded.

Frank nodded and gave the boy a slight smile. "Is that why you got startled when you saw me? I'm dressed like him?"

"Yes, sir."

"How tall was he, Martin?" McLain interjected.

"Um, I don't know." The boy shrugged. "I guess, a little shorter than you, sir."

"So, a black beard. What color skin?" Frank inquired as he rubbed his cheek.

"It was very light."

"What brought you to the window, Martin? Do you just like the sunrise?" Campanelli asked gently.

"I heard sirens. Thought I'd see a fire truck. All I got to see was an am'blance and a cop car...um, police car."

"I see." Frank nodded. "So, we were already on our way when you saw this man jump. Now, did he jump from a standing position or did he take a running start?"

"Umm..." The boy stopped to think. "He ran first. He came flyin' and landed hard on the balcony above ours."

"Must've hit hard, huh?" McLain led.

"Yes, sir. The whole thing shook and, like...rang...like a bell, I guess."

"Did either of your parents see him?" Kirby asked next.

"No. Mom was in the shower. Dad leaves for work real early."

"Did this man see *you*, Martin?" Frank asked next.

"No, sir."

"How do you know for sure?" the Captain of Detectives pressed with a kind grin.

"He was too busy grabbing onto the rails so he wouldn't fall. Then he looked toward the alley to the street and then climbed up."

"He went *up*?" Kirby inquired with a tone of surprise.

"Yes," the young Kilbourne replied as if the fact was of no concern.

The two detectives shared a look that said otherwise.

"*Was the building swept?*" Frank sent to Kirby in text via implant.

"*Yes, except for the balcony, apparently,*" McLain answered.

"*I think you'd better order another. Apartment by apartment, even if they're empty. This guy's dangerous, Kirby.*"

"*Agreed. Doing it.*" McLain connected with the CPD server with the help of the school's system and ordered an armed detail back to the building.

"Martin, would you be able to identify this man?" Frank asked.

"I don't think so," the boy answered immediately.

"Why not?"

"I only saw the beard part while he was in the air," Martin answered nervously. "He looked away once he hit the balcony and then climbed up and he was gone."

"That's okay, kiddo," McLain said calmly. "We understand."

"Martin, I want you to think carefully," Frank said as he took off his fedora and spun it on his fingers. "You're sure about a black hat and coat. Like this?"

"Yes," he said and nodded emphatically.

"And he had a beard," Frank went on, all the while, Martin nodded. "And he went up, not down."

Martin kept nodding.

"Okay," Campanelli granted and replaced his hat with a smile. "Thank you very much, Mr. Kilbourne."

With that, the detectives let Martin go back to class and were escorted to the door by the vice principal. Before they took their leave, Frank turned to Thames.

"How well do you know Martin, Miss Thames?" he asked of her.

"Pretty well, Detective," she replied with some certainty.

"He's not prone to making things up...you know...to entertain others or to say, bring attention to himself?"

"Not at all, Detective Campanelli," she answered, not seeming to be offended by the question. "Martin's a very bright boy and I've never known him to be a fibber."

"Thank you very much, Miss Thames," Frank said and shook her hand. "I had to ask."

"I understand," she answered with a smile.

The detectives walked to the cruiser in silence. While McLain drove, Campanelli thought hard about what the boy had told them. Kirby mentioned that he added an official APB to the report using Martin Kilbourne's description and forwarded it to the men searching the apartment building at 420 Clinton Street. He received only a vacant nod as Campanelli stared ahead.

"What are you thinking, Frank?" McLain inquired as he turned onto Van Buren.

"I'm thinking I want to take a look at that balcony and the roof."

"I'm with you."

The entire apartment complex had been taped off by the time they returned. They identified themselves to an officer, who moved a wooden barricade to let them through. Kirby drove along Van Buren and, in doing so, were about to pass H. Lincoln Rothgery's parked mobile laboratory when the lanky forensic genius stepped from the rear of it.

"I wonder if Lincoln has something yet," McLain murmured and applied the brake.

Frank lowered the passenger side window and hailed Rothgery, who turned to the sound of his name and approached the cruiser, unsmiling.

"Frank, Kirby," H. Lincoln greeted more grimly than normal. "I've got some tests done on the pieces of glass. The blood matches the blood of we found in Werner's car. It's the killer's."

Kirby and Frank shared a look. Campanelli sighed. "Understood. What else, Lincoln?"

"I wanted to identify the type of cutter, so I put the edges of both samples into the electron-microscope. I took samples of the fragments left on the glass and found a strange substance, sort of an acrylic material, but it looks a bit like tooth enamel in the scope."

Frank took off his fedora and ran his hand through his gray strands. "Are you trying to tell me that our suspect chewed his way through the window?"

Rothgery let out a sigh of impatience. "Obviously not, Frank," he retorted. "I'll have to test this stuff more, but it's all along the edges of both pieces of glass. So is the blood, by the way."

"Interesting," mumbled Kirby, though Frank doubted that H. Lincoln heard it.

"Okay, Lincoln," Frank said as he replaced his hat. "Keep McLain informed on everything. Send a copy to me, too, 'kay?"

"Sure."

"Let's go, Kirby," Frank told the driver and cast a finger toward the world beyond the windshield.

Rothgery watched the departing cruiser for a moment and placed his hands in the pockets of his lab coat. "*Chewed,*" he scoffed and shook his head. "Ridiculous. Why would he say that?"

"Lincoln?" Teri Wilkins, the assistant called from the old van.

"That's not even funny," he mumbled as he turned toward the voice. "Is it?"

"What?" she answered, confused. She bent at the knees to look the tall man in the eye.

"Never mind." H. Lincoln waved her off as he shook his head. "What's up?"

"Are we heading back to the lab?"

"Oh. Yeah. Might as well," Rothgery said and nodded. He reached out to the open rear doors. "Get belted up front."

"Can we stop somewhere for lunch?" Teri inquired before she would move out of the way.

"It's not lunch time," he protested with a glance over his glasses at his watch.

"It will be." Wilkins smiled and tilted her head. She knew that if they went straight to the lab, the workaholic in H. Lincoln would burn away the day. She had gone home on many occasions so famished that she was dizzy.

H. Lincoln sighed. "Fine, but then we work on this stuff."

"Of course," she agreed and disappeared into the van as Rothgery closed the doors.

McLain made a right onto Clinton Street, where the front door to the apartment was located. They parked and went inside. They were met by Detective Hank Lyman, the man that had originally taken young Kilbourne's statement.

"What have you got to say for yourself, Hank?" McLain hailed without greeting.

Lyman looked from McLain to Campanelli and back. "I'm very sorry guys," he said. Frank knew the man long enough to know he meant it. "It just sounded crazy. I thought the kid made it up." He shrugged, out of excuses.

Kirby nodded. Frank remained silent, insisting on not looking pleased.

"Anyway," Hank went on, "we checked out the apartment above the Kilbournes'. *Something* hit it from above."

"Show us," Frank ordered.

"This way," Lyman said and headed for the elevator.

"Has anyone found a trace of this guy?" McLain asked of his subordinate.

"The apartment on the sixth floor, two levels directly above the Kilbourne residence, was entered. The glass door had a circle cut out of it, just like the one on the 417 Jefferson side. The stairwell to the roof was accessed and he exited there."

The elevator door slid open and Lyman took the lead down the hallway.

"How many families are in this complex, Lyman?" McLain asked as he followed.

"This place is more populated than most like it. We've counted forty-six families," Hank answered as he approached the open door to the apartment at the west end.

"Has the *entire* complex been swept?" Campanelli asked, standing inches from Hank Lyman's face. His expression was deadly serious. It was clear to the younger detective that he had not forgotten about the poor report. "Storage compartments in the basement, recreation facilities, the gym, *every* single unit?"

"Yes, sir, Captain Campanelli," Hank replied, thinking it wise to use his former boss's honorary rank. "He left a trail of footsteps in this place, open doors, and the hole in the glass. That's it so far."

"Very well," Frank granted and followed McLain inside.

The unit was empty. Not simply unfurnished, but devoid of everything including appliances, cabinets, and counter tops. There was dust everywhere, except where the suspect had walked directly from the balcony door to the front door of the apartment. Kirby and Frank kept to the walls to avoid disturbing the evidence. Other detectives had walked in before them and had been just as careful. The dust in the carpet at the walls was already well-traveled.

"Well, he's got shoes," Frank remarked with his hands in his overcoat's pockets.

"Big," McLain commented as he lifted his right leg and held the foot over it for a moment. "Looks like my size. Thirteens."

"Thirteen?" Campanelli exuded in surprise. "Where the hell do you find shoes, man?"

Kirby smiled. "They are few and far between, Frank."

"I'll bet," Frank murmured. "Show us where he accessed the roof," he directed Lyman, who nodded and bid them to follow.

The stairwell to the roof was located eastward, down the hallway. Detective Lyman took the stairs two at a time and popped out on the roof with no trouble. Both doors had their latches torn apart. Campanelli and McLain appeared next, walking out into the morning sun. Frank's eyes were shaded from light above by the fedora's brim, but the reflection from the light gray metallic roof was enough to trigger his lenses, dimming his view to a comfortable level in response. The bio-electronics of the other two men responded similarly.

"There are some scuff marks along the aluminum sheeting," Hank Lyman said as he pointed out the light creases and dents in the material. "I think these appear pretty fresh. There's no build-up of dirt in these crevices. He was running, not even trying to be quiet or careful."

Frank quickly picked up on which direction the new dents led and followed. Soon, he found himself at the edge of the roof, peering down upon the southbound lanes of Clinton Street and a few police cars, including McLain's.

"If you look close, you'll find that he apparently dropped from the roof and landed on the balcony. See the broken flowerpot?"

Frank and Kirby grunted positively as they followed what Lyman was pointing toward.

"I take it he descended to the ground, balcony by balcony?" Campanelli asked. Hank nodded. "Have you looked for witnesses in those apartments?"

"We've interviewed both families, sir," Lyman provided. "We had to track them down at work. Everyone left for jobs starting at seven this morning. That's around the time Mister Henson was killed and a few minutes later, Martin Kilbourne saw him land on the balcony above him."

"No street witnesses?" McLain asked.

"None as yet," his underling answered.

"He's out there somewhere, just walking the streets," Frank murmured as he stared into the windows of the mostly empty office building across the street.

"We'll get him, Frank," said Kirby.

"We'd better. Four dead in three days." Campanelli spoke through gritted teeth and adjusted his fedora as he stepped away from the edge of the roof. "We've got to get him, quick."

Frank walked with McLain to the ground floor, leaving Lyman to wrap up his final report and oversee a last sweep for evidence. He opened his cruiser's door and turned to the head detective of the homicide division. "What are you going to recommend to Treadwell?" Darius Treadwell was the chief of the Violent Crimes Division.

"A high-priority alert, force-wide," McLain informed him. "I'll see about recalling patrolmen from vacation. I don't want to underestimate this man anymore. Might even get the press involved and work for us."

"Hmm," Frank grunted thoughtfully and tossed his black hat to the passenger seat. "Dealing with the press can work both ways."

"I know that."

"Okay," Campanelli gave his friend a two-fingered salute. "Later," he said and dropped himself into the driver's seat. McLain waved and went to his own car.

***

Frank decided to pay his partner a visit earlier than planned. Marcus's reluctance was either real or imagined, but the killer had proven to remain a danger to the people of Chicago. If William's knew something, Campanelli would have to convince him to help.

As he guided his vehicle in manual mode around a right turn, the APB interrupted normal radio traffic with three long tones before the young female dispatcher spoke. "*All units. Updated APB for suspect wanted on four counts homicide. Approximately six feet tall with a dark beard. Wearing black hat and long black coat. Race unknown. Last seen at Clinton and Van Buren this AM. Presumed heading east on foot. Subject is highly dangerous, and is known to be armed with bayonet. Assume armed with firearms when confronting.*"

Campanelli cussed flatly when the broadcast ended. With all the evidence they had discovered at both murder scenes, there should have been an approximation of the physical description on the screen, but with the DNA reader blocked, they would be flying blind. *This must be how they did it in the old days,* Frank thought.

The Captain of Detectives parked and went inside the hospital. Surprisingly, he found Williams's bio-electronic implant within range of communication on the ground floor. He linked with it and was informed by Marcus that he was in the physical therapy department. After walking the maze, Frank located it and went inside.

Under the supervision of a male physical therapist, the ex-SEAL was seated and lifting a light barbell with his right arm. Marcus waved with his left as his partner walked in.

"Good morning," Campanelli greeted. Marcus and the trainer replied in kind. "Did you get the latest?" Frank asked of his partner.

Without a word, Marcus nodded and held his partner's gaze for a moment. Besides the therapist working with Williams, there were other patients around them and a couple of other hospital employees.

"Did you see that APB?" Frank thought and sent in an audible message.

Marcus nodded again. His face bore no trace of pain, though he exercised the bare arm and shoulder gingerly. The bullet wound at Marcus's collarbone was covered with a square adhesive bandage. He knew that the man was healing fast, but it had not failed to take Frank by surprise each day he visited.

"McLain sent that out and is recalling some officers from vacation," Campanelli stated in his next message.

Marcus listened to it carefully and thought his reply. *"The department's intensifying the search east of that area?"*

"Yeah. He's going to talk to Chief Treadwell about putting it on the air."

"Hmm," Williams grunted vocally and narrowed his eyes at Frank.

"It might help," Frank spoke.

"You're doing very well, Mr. Williams," the short, slim therapist said. "Think you can do that with a ten pounder?"

"Sure," Marcus replied and handed the small one to the man.

"Feelin' good?" Frank asked of him and took a nearby chair.

"Yeah. Tryin' to get outta here ASAP."

"Good man." Campanelli removed his fedora and fiddled with it in his fingers.

"You'd better hang that thing up awhile," Williams said and smiled while giving the hat a nod.

Frank grinned. "Yeah, don't want to be hassled by the man," he said and chuckled. "When does it look like they'll spring you?"

"Day after tomorrow," the therapist said as he handed Williams the heavier weight.

"Tomorrow," Marcus amended.

"No way," the medical professional said with a shake of his head. "You're healing fast, but not *that* fast."

"Tomorrow," Marcus repeated with his eyes on his partner.

The therapist chuckled. "We'll see."

"*Marcus, I need you to be as forthcoming and honest with me as you can be on this*," Frank sent in an audible. While bio-electronic implants did not emulate the emotion of the sender's voice well, there was no mistaking Campanelli's earnestness in his facial expression.

"*I understand, Frank*," Marcus sent back.

"*This killer is nothing like we've ever seen.*" Campanelli went on describing the murder scene and supplied Williams with the few pictures that Frank had the wherewithal to save to his implant. *"I've got to know all that you know about this creature or whatever he is."*

While he lifted the ten-pound weight with ease, Marcus stared into his partner's eyes, breaking on occasion just long enough to take in the pictures from Frank's implant. He grimaced at one point, making the therapist think that he was feeling pain.

"I think that'll be it, Mr. Williams," the younger man said as he reached for the weight.

"I've got it."

"You're in pain," the therapist protested with his hands out, ready to relieve the bigger man of the small barbell.

"I've got it," Marcus repeated sternly. He continued lifting the weight over his head and down repeatedly. The therapist backed away.

"Frank, I did keep some information from you," Marcus sent in an audible transmission. *"I'm sorry, but I had to be sure."* He looked back into Frank's face solemnly.

Campanelli pursed his lips in anger and tossed his hat onto a chair behind him. He leaned all the way back in the chair and crossed his arms expectantly.

The young therapist, sensing the mood between the two policemen change, strolled away.

"I believe this killer may part of a group called FROG. They were intended to replace SEAL and the standard Marine Force Recon. It means Force Recon Optimized Genetics."

Frank ran his hand over his hair and blinked while he listened to his partner's digitized voice in his ears.

"The Navy retired the entire SEAL program in anticipation of these Marines. They had no parents, only sperm and egg donators," Marcus went on as he placed the weight on the floor and stood from the chair to stretch. *"A*

couple of years ago, we heard that the Marines had put an end to the FROG program due to budget cuts."

Marcus hesitated, but could tell from his senior partner's expression that he was to continue.

"The FROGs are rumored to have high-bone density and extremely fast healing capabilities," Williams explained as he looked about the therapy room. *"This explains why there was no body in that car. He was inactive for a day, telling me that he hid somewhere, allowing his body to heal."* He halted and looked to Frank for a moment.

"Go on," Frank commanded.

Marcus crossed his arms over his big chest as he sent the next message. *"FROGs also have scaled skin and gills. The skin was supposed to be able to change color for camouflaging. They can make themselves appear like any race, short of changing the shape of their bone structure."*

"What else?" Campanelli pressed at the next hesitation.

"Their muscle strength was highly improved over a standard human without needing to be bulky," Williams explained and began to pace. *"The gills were to save on the cumbersome scuba equipment."*

"What else?" Frank asked aloud.

"Everything else truly is rumor," Marcus replied, keeping his voice down. "Or it's classified. I'm not even supposed to know this."

"Why the hell didn't you tell me about this yesterday?" Campanelli transmitted. While the voice in Williams's ears was mostly flat, the expression on the Frank's face more than made up for it.

"Frank, I told you. This is all classified information. Besides, there wasn't enough info to go on."

At this, the Captain of Detectives flew from his chair so quickly that it slammed against the wall behind him. The room silenced as all eyes turned to the two policemen, now standing toe-to-toe.

"*Goddamn you, Marcus. Four people have been killed by this creature,*" Frank sent as he stared up into the bigger man's face.

"*Frank, if this is a FROG, there's nothing you could have done to prevent it,*" Marcus replied.

"*Bullshit. We could have swept the area. Cornered him in that building and caught him by now,*" Campanelli sent as his face grew red and his eyes drilled into Marcus's.

"*That's a long shot at best.*"

"Why?" Frank asked aloud through seething teeth.

"*Look, just let me make a call to an old SEAL buddy,*" Williams said, keeping it in digital audio form. "*He's with the FBI now, but he has connections in the military.*"

"You're that convinced that this…" Frank whispered harshly, looking around for eavesdroppers, "…thing is that dangerous?"

Marcus nodded. "I honestly can't think of what else this could be, Frank."

"How many of these Marines were created?" Frank whispered.

"I have no idea," Williams replied in kind with a shrug. "I can't imagine that very many could have been made. There was barely a budget to keep the SEALs going."

Campanelli turned from his friend and partner, snatched up his black hat from the chair and paced. He was clearly agitated and Marcus knew from experience that the need to act immediately boiled within the man. It was what made Frank Campanelli a great hunter of fugitives, but a feisty, gruff human being at times.

"Frank," Marcus said gently and lowly, "if you had rushed into his hiding place, your first responders would most likely have been killed."

"You said yourself he was probably healing, sleeping," Campanelli said as he stood still, eyeing his partner's face with a trace of skepticism.

Marcus said nothing in reply, letting a slight shrug, a tilt of the head, and raised eyebrows do it for him.

"Do me a favor," Frank said as he stepped closer to his partner to whisper the rest. "Call your friend. Give him whatever reports he needs. Get his advice on this."

"I will just as soon as I return to my room."

Frank nodded. "Okay. See you tomorrow?"

"Yes, at the office," Williams replied with certainty.

With that, Campanelli left the hospital. Once in his car, he updated the APB that McLain had issued on the suspect that he was not to be confronted, but tracked until sufficient back-up arrived, which was to include the SWAT team.

***

After the morning's escape from the police, the killer was left exhausted. The burst of speed which he had required to hurl himself from the roof of the apartment building had been sizeable. The act was exhilarating and invigorating at the same time. However, it had been a long time since he had experienced such a rush of adrenaline.

Thinking about it as he walked, he smiled. Some of the pedestrians around him returned the smile, for other than the out-of-style hat, the man appeared to be nothing more than a handsome, six-foot-tall male. The façade he kept on his face, though it took energy, did smooth out his appearance. A happy chill went up his spine when he thought of his newly acquired clothing. He felt fortunate that he had acquired a hat and coat similar to those he had seen on the police detective that had shown up to investigate the wreck he had made of the stolen car. The murderer especially liked the hat, for not only did it intrigue him, it saved a little bit of energy. All he had to keep camouflaged was his face and parts of his neck. The shade provided by the brim helped his eyes as well.

As he traveled north on foot, he realized an increase of population and, therefore, police patrols. The last one was a marked cruiser driving southward, and as he strode across a street with no one near him at that moment, it had prompted the fugitive to make a sudden right turn. This soon brought him to an alcove of an aged building that, while not particularly tall, appeared to take up the whole block, as did the parking structure he had just walked past.

From behind a pillar, he looked back into the sunlit day for the police, but they were gone. He was trying to be careful not to shows signs of paranoia, but it was difficult for him, considering what he had done. The killer retreated into the shade and read the sign on the glass door: *Chicago Union Station Museum.*

He opened the door and went inside. As he did, he changed his face, approximating a light brown mustache, a shadowing effect on the chin that gave the impression of a dimple. He used a similar trick to make his eyes, now dark blue, appear more deeply set.

"Good morning. Are you here for a self-guided tour, sir?" a voice called to him.

Spinning too quickly, he found he had been startled by a short, middle-aged Caucasian female. She gazed at him with a steady smile. Confused as to how he had not detected her, he answered in the affirmative.

"Very well, welcome. If you are equipped with an implant, please link with the server labeled, 'Union Station Tour' and step to your right, following the red velvet ropes to the stairs. The tour begins in the Great Hall."

It was then he understood that the woman was a hologram. He had triggered the interactive playback by entering the building.

"Thank you," he said and proceeded in, not bothering to link with the museum's computer. He walked quickly down the marble steps to the Great Hall, a place where once tens of thousands gathered daily to meet trains that would take them to various places in the country. Union Station's tracks met underground, he knew from the encyclopedia of knowledge within his own memory. Projected upon his artificial lenses was the layout of the immense structure, above and below the surface.

Within the Great Hall, a few people wandered from exhibit to exhibit, scattered all around the massive wooden benches in the center. Ahead of him, an exhibit featured a train car, set atop a fixed piece of track placed on the marble flooring. A family of five boarded it from the west end for a walk-through.

The killer walked ahead into the Great Hall, bearing right as he headed for the terminals. He passed beyond a large set of sliding glass doors that were, for the moment, kept open and proceeded within, not paying attention to the other visitors to the museum. He rode up an escalator and looked about him. Where once there were restaurants, shops, and a bar, there was now only a cafeteria, not yet opened, and a gift shop. Most of the other places were not in use, and served only as more exhibits.

It was all very interesting, the cannibal decided, but all he required at the moment was a quiet place to rest. He walked aimlessly for a time until he came to a terminal. Through the windows, he could see a train, this one complete with a diesel engine and what looked to be four or five train cars attached to it. Stepping toward the glass, he found that it was nonresponsive. Withdrawing a pale right hand, he tugged at the separation, trying to part it.

"Pardon me," someone said from behind him. This time, the trained killer was not startled, for he had heard footsteps. "I'm afraid access to the terminal part of the museum is only available for the guided tour," the automaton said. It was male, short and dressed like a conductor.

"Oh, I see," the killer said and activated his device hacking program. The automaton was called a Model Six by the manufacturer, the McAllen Corporation, but their software security had been outdated since the company lifted off for the colony planet. He was able to obtain access to the machine's computer and communicate his will directly.

In a moment, the glass door slid out of the way. As it was done in front of a security doppelganger, it was given little notice by a few of the passing patrons.

The killer slipped inside, allowed the glass doors to close, and released his connection with the doppelganger. The machine's memory of the incident was wiped, so it strode away on its beat.

The murderer's hopes for a cushy rest on a train car's seat were dashed by the presence of a few security cameras, easily spotted from their mounts. Instead, he climbed down onto the tracks. Hunkering down, he tucked himself within the shadows of the platform and promptly went to sleep.

***

Marcus Williams became restless that afternoon. The possibility of a FROG running loose through the city should not have been alarming, but this one had clearly gone insane. While FROGs were intended to be the ultimate in aggressiveness and self-sufficiency, they were certainly not intended to run rogue and turn cannibal.

Even though it would run up his hospital bill, he made a couple long distance phone calls. The first was to the FBI office in DC that his friend had last been known to work from. The second was to the office in Texas, where he had been reassigned. Williams had left a message for him and stewed for hours in his hospital bed or the slightly more comfortable lounger, waiting.

The sun went by his window as the hours rolled around, reinforcing Marcus's angst. Another nice sunny day was wasting away in front of his eyes.

At 5:55, the phone rang while he sat watching the holovision and waiting for the 6 o'clock news to start. Marcus picked it up before the tone had a second chance.

"Marcus Williams," he answered.

"Marcus!"

"Hey, Jerry!"

"How the hell are ya?"

"Getting better," Williams provided, knowing full well how much press that he had received over saving Mayor Jameson's life. "Probably getting out tomorrow."

"Good to hear, man!" Agent Jerry Quinne called. "I'm sorry I didn't check on you, but you looked fine on the news."

"I did, huh?"

"Oh, yeah. Other than being flat on your back, that is."

"Cute," Williams commented. "Listen, Jerry. We've got a situation going on here in town. It should be on the local news tonight."

"Oh?" Agent Quinne said while the sound of him turning and rolling in an office chair came through. "Do tell, old buddy."

"I know we're not on a secure line…" Marcus led grimly.

"Really. That bad, huh?"

"Possibly. We're not sure yet. We've got a crazy running around attacking and eating people. He's killed four, so far."

"Holy shit," Quinne said through a cringe.

"Yeah. Can you get online and watch our local news? My partner said that it was going to be announced tonight."

"Already on it," the agent said. "The internet's getting spottier every week. Wow. You guys are down to three local channels, huh?"

Marcus chuckled. "Yeah. Only two have any news broadcasts."

"I see that," Quinn mumbled absently. After a moment, Marcus could hear the same audio feed through the phone that his holovision was receiving, though Jerry's was a few seconds behind.

"Wow," Williams said. "They aren't kidding around. It's the first story."

"*The bodies of three people have been discovered this morning in an apartment building at four-seventeen Jefferson Street,*" the young male anchor began. "*The names of the victims have not yet been released by the CPD, but this triple homicide is apparently related to the killing that occurred near the Ashland Avenue Bridge last Monday morning. A brief interview with Homicide Detective Kirby McLain took place this afternoon near the crime scene,*" the anchor finished and disappeared, allowing the video of the interview to replace him.

"*We do have a witness that saw a person of interest leaving the crime scene,*" Kirby said to the two microphones in his face. Behind him sat a police cruiser and a brick building, taped off by the familiar thick yellow 'Crime Scene' tape. "*This individual is around six feet tall, lean, possibly Caucasian with a darkly colored beard. He was last seen wearing a black hat, possibly a fedora, and a black overcoat.*"

"*Detective McLain, a question,*" a reporter interrupted, "*were these three new victims eaten like the first one?*"

Kirby looked to the sidewalk he was standing upon and cleared his throat before answering. He was clearly surprised that the detail had leaked. "*Let me stress that this is a partial consumption of the victims' bodies, but yes, some...cannibalism is involved."*

The reporter holding the other microphone spoke next. *"What is the next step that the department needs to take to find this man?"*

"The entire department is on high alert, looking for this suspect," McLain spoke deliberately, measuring his words carefully. *"This man is to be considered highly dangerous due to the violent nature of his crimes and he is not to be confronted. I can't stress that part enough. If someone sees this man, we need to be contacted immediately. All we ask is that if seen, do not approach. Call the police immediately and leave the area."*

"Jesus," Agent Jerry Quinne said when McLain was done speaking.

"Quite a dangerous individual," the anchor stressed when he reappeared next to a crude drawing of the killer. *"So, please, if you see this suspect, keep your distance and call the police immediately."*

"Oh, hell," Marcus grunted. The picture was bordering on the ludicrous, placing a shadow over the man's eyes as provided by the wide-brimmed hat. The mouth was wide open in a snarl, and the teeth were drawn with fangs.

Quinne laughed at the sight. "Well, that's a bit much."

"Maybe."

"Seriously?" the agent grunted.

"Yeah." Williams allowed the silence to accentuate his sincerity.

Jerry Quinne cleared his throat. "Okay, can you get to a computer? Maybe you can email some details to me."

"It may take some time to find a terminal, but give me your email address." Marcus's implant acquired the data from the man's voice and saved it to the memo file.

"I'll look for that, Marcus," the agent promised solemnly.

Williams smiled, happy that his friend and former service buddy did not give him any nonsense about security. They said their goodbyes and ended the call.

Marcus walked to the nurses' station and inquired about access to a computer. With charm and the knowledge that he was a police officer, it was no problem.

***

"Holy crap, Frank," Tamara Billingsley uttered after the news story had ended. She did not take her eyes from the creepy caricature.

"Yeah," he replied and took another bite of his dinner. "They can really overdo the artwork."

She turned to him, looking for a sign of humor, though there was none. "That's not what I mean. That guy sounds absolutely ruthlessly...evil."

"It looks that way," he agreed, and chewed while staring at his plate.

The news broadcast switched to another topic, but the killer remained at the forefront of Frank's mind. That fact was clear to Tam, as he was quiet for most of the evening and kept the telephone close by while the two of them tried to relax for the evening in the living room.

"Damn it," he muttered as they watched the holovision.

"What?" Tam asked without removing her eyes from the images.

"That's it for HV for me tonight," he explained with a tap to his temple. His implant's main battery was depleted.

"Already? It's not even eight-thirty," Billingsley marveled as she rose from the couch. "Where'd you leave it?"

"Coat pocket...I think," he replied.

"It's a little early in the evening for that to happen, isn't it?" she asked over her shoulder as she searched his overcoat's inner pockets for his RadarCane.

"It is," he agreed glumly then ordered the holovision set to mute. "I couldn't help it. I kept checking my work email."

"Frank!" she called with disdain on her way back. "Why? If there was something urgent, someone would call," she said as she placed the cane in his hand and retook her seat on the couch.

"I know," he said and turned his head toward her voice. He tapped the white folded cane on his knee.

Tam hated to look at Frank when his implant shut down. He was no less handsome as his eyes, unseeing, but constantly searching for light, seemed to beg for something. Perhaps they sought an answer to a question that remained unasked throughout the time that she had known him. Maybe the reason for it was the uncomfortable darkness over which he had only part time control. Unconsciously, his orbs swung to and fro, his eyebrows lifted from the center, while the outer corners of his eyelids angled ever-so-slightly downward. Whatever the cause of the subtle change in his expression, the appearance conveyed despair and chipped pieces from her heart whenever she saw him in such a state.

"Well, it's not your case, anyway," Tam said softly. She angled her eyes away from him and back to the mute HV. "You're second in command of the Sentinel Squad, anyway. You have other business."

"There's not much on our agenda that the boys can't handle," Campanelli dismissed. "I told you the caseload's been lighter since Ignatola 'n' DeSilva were put out of business."

"I know," she said bitterly, more so than she had intended. She crossed her arms and pouted, knowing what he would say next.

"I've always been a homicide detective, Tam," he quipped. "I can't help that."

"Well, forgive me if I don't want you in the middle of this one," Billingsley said harshly. "This creature is...an...animal!"

The frown that had appeared over Frank's face retracted quickly, shifting beyond the doleful, questioning blind man's expression on its way straight into humor. He chuckled before rolling into unrestricted laughter, disarming Tamara Billingsley's concerns for his safety.

She laughed with him and slapped her knee as her heart lifted. Tamara believed this man in front of her, laughing, showing his teeth while his body trembled with humor, this man was the *real* Frank Campanelli. Or, at least he had been once.

"That creature *is* an animal, Tam," Frank rephrased and laughed once more.

She fought for a breath in between her gales. "Shut up!" she howled gleefully before making the effort to stamp out further laughter. "Okay, listen. What I mean is..."

"I know what you mean." Campanelli nodded and likewise, quieted. The humor disappeared as fast as it had struck. "I'm just consulting with McLain and my old squad."

"Yeah, well, maybe," she conceded. "But I know how you get when you become obsessed over a case. You're either at the department until late or, because you can't stop thinking about it, you end up like this...without the use of your lenses for the evening." She made an effort not to say the word "blind." She never understood why.

"I have a bad feeling about this one, is all."

These words sent chills throughout Tamara Billingsley's body and she studied his face closely. His unseeing eyes steadied upon her face. Two people stared while only one saw. Tam shivered violently and gripped her knees with trembling fingers.

"Are you all right?" he asked.

Tamara blew out a breath that she had been holding. "Oh, not at all. I don't think I've ever heard you say something like that, Frank."

"No?"

"No."

"Well, I do. I believe that more people will die before we can catch up to this thing," he opined while unfolding the cane. He stood and let the humming, beeping cane guide him toward the kitchen.

She watched Frank for a few moments as he felt his way into the cabinet for a short whiskey glass. He sidestepped to his left and retrieved his bottle of bourbon. With well-practiced precision, he poured, stopped when he felt he had poured a few fingers then replaced the bottle's cap. He turned and sipped the deep amber liquid, remaining in the kitchen, standing at the counter.

Tamara turned off the silenced HV and walked to him with her arms crossed. Her thoughts at that moment were hopelessly scrambled. She knew she was not over the shock of being brought into Frank's last case. The bruise around her left eye socket was still present, though it faded a little every day. She stepped next to him as he took his second sip, wrapped her left arm around his hip, and kissed his cheek.

"Why, thank you," he responded and smiled.

Billingsley sighed and placed her head on his shoulder. "Frank," she said in her leading way.

"Yes?"

"You ever think of leaving Chicago?"

"Sure."

"Well?"

"Well...what?" His right arm encapsulated her shoulders.

"Any reason why we can't?" she whispered.

"What about your diner?"

"I can...maybe, do that somewhere else."

"I don't know, Tam."

She sighed once again as she tried to bring her thoughts into line. "I just don't want to see you hurt again. Last time was a close call, Frank."

"I know, but Chicago needs good cops."

She withdrew from him slowly after planting another kiss. "There are other cops, dear."

"You need to understand something here and now, Tamara," he said as he set down his drink. His blind eyes searched for her in his darkness. "There aren't many new recruits these days. No academies, no criminal justice courses at the local colleges. Nothing but veterans trying to teach the young ones the ropes."

"I know, Frank, but Chicago's shrinking," she retorted. "The mayor keeps closing districts. How long will it be until you're out of a job?"

"I can't allow that to happen," he shot with agitation.

"*You* can't?" Tamara questioned with her arms folded over her chest. Her eyes searched his face. "You can't stop it. This...society is degenerating, Frank." She bit her tongue before spilling the next words on her mind. *When are you going to see that?* Instead, she closed her eyes and turned away.

"Maybe," he conceded. "But we will come to a day where the people of Chicago will refuse to leave, and *they* will need protection. *They* will still need police."

The two of them were silent for a long time. Campanelli sipped his bourbon until the glass was empty. He poured himself another and followed his cane to his recliner, next to the couch. Not knowing what else to say, Tamara abandoned the conversation and picked up her Sherlock Holmes novel. She read it on the couch and watched Frank drop into the chair from the corner of her eye.

"What would you have me do, Tam?" he asked of her after another sip. "Quit?"

"Just forget it," she murmured. "I don't know what I'm asking you to do."

"I understand it, if it helps," he replied and stood up. His restlessness was not abating with the alcohol.

"I think it does," she said with an audible smile.

Frank nodded. "I'm gonna get some air 'n' try to relax."

"Okay." Tamara watched her love walk away until he was out of sight. She listened as the cane sounded its way to the closet, where he took his overcoat from the hanger. With another topping off of the whiskey glass, the troubled Captain of Detectives slid the patio door open, stepped into the cool night air, and closed the glass panel behind him. With a thoughtful sigh, she went back to her book.

Campanelli popped a cigarette into his mouth and felt his way to the plastic patio table. He set down the bourbon and pulled out his lighter. His deft fingers flipped it open with a click and spun the wheel. Sensing the heat, he lit the tobacco and shut the lighter.

His first puff was let out with a loud sigh. With it, the night air worked a chill up his spine which set his muscles trembling involuntarily. The RadarCane let out a *"wow"* to let him know that he had found one of the chairs. Pulling it closer, he sat down. He folded his cane and placed it inside his coat to give himself a free hand. In the complete darkness that was his blindness, he felt for the glass and brought it to his lips.

Frank Campanelli had no choice but to think about the current case. As a longtime inspector for the NYPD and a detective with the CPD for the last few years, the thought process had become instinctive.

He settled into the flexible chair, took a puff of the cigarette and balanced the glass on his knee. The images of the murder victims of the past couple of days tumbled into his mind. He thought of Werner, the Drakes, and Matt Henson, imagining how each met their fate. Frank then thought of young Martin Kilbourne, the only one that had, so far, laid eyes on the creature.

Creature, he thought and smirked. Campanelli had to stop thinking of the psychopath that way. He hoped that this government issued and trained killer was not as dangerous as Williams had alluded to, but time would tell. *I wonder where he is and what he's doing*, he contemplated with another puff and another swig.

With these thoughts and more rattling around in his head, Frank's exhaustion pressed upon him. Unnecessarily, his eyelids drooped.

***

From less than twenty meters away, the Captain of Detectives, Frank Campanelli of the Sentinel Squad was seen exiting his apartment and taking a seat on the patio. He did not wear his hat, but the coat was present. The hunter became perplexed with the noisy device in the policeman's hand. In the darkness, his night vision studied the white stick with its red tip and wondered about its function.

The FROG sat upon the quiet L tracks next to the Campanelli residence and contemplated his quarry. He had retrieved Campanelli's identification and address from an active CPD squad car's computer, which his military-grade implant had easily hacked into. With the trains being only part time, the electricity was shut down to conserve energy, making it extremely easy for the Marine to make his way along them.

He inhaled the air a moment after watching the detective light his cigarette. A Turkish blend, it was clear, grown not very far away. A second sniff brought the traces of alcohol to his olfactory senses. The FROG turned his nose up in disgust. His body was engineered to detest alcoholic beverages and reject the fluid with violent consequences if it was ingested.

A gust of wind lifted the brim of his stolen hat and threatened to remove it. Quickly, he mashed it upon his head with a hand and continued to watch Campanelli with interest. He was not sure why the man interested him, but it was clear given his service record that he was an intelligent man.

"Ah," the cannibal hissed as he reread the report on the man. As the District One Station was just across the street to his back, the CPD computer was now well within range to be hacked into once again. "*Blind?* How interesting," he whispered as the wind pressed against his back once again.

The FROG reached out with his implant, but found that he was unable to find Campanelli's device. At once, it became clear. The detective's unit was deactivated, which was the explanation for the white cane. *A blind man's cane.*

"Of course," he whispered. He stood and stared across the expanse between the tracks and the policeman's patio. The FROG marveled at the rarity he witnessed before him. A policeman so revered that even blindness did not stop him from doing his job. It was no wonder that Detective Kirby McLain had brought him in on the case.

The Marine grinned darkly as the wind flittered through the tails of the overcoat.

***

A gust ran through Frank's patio and lifted the right half of his unfastened coat. The movement forced him abruptly awake as his right hand shot out to catch the glass that was on its way to the tile. His fingers saved the majority of the drink, but he felt some splash onto his hand.

"Damn," he muttered, which dropped the inch-long stretch of ash onto his coat and shirt. This he did not notice, let alone prevent.

A whisper on the wind froze him in place.

It was only for a moment, but he swore that he heard the hint of a voice. Nonchalantly, he took a puff of the burned down tobacco, noted the nearness of the heat and squashed the butt onto the floor of the patio with his foot. He switched the glass to his left hand and gave the other a lick before wiping the remainder on his pant leg.

Another gust, another whisper.

What the hell? This time he stood, turned to the north, and listened hard. He wondered how long it had been since the implant had shut down. He thought the command to activate it.

"*Intriguing,*" the wind seemed to say.

"Come on," Frank grunted through gritted teeth. The implant failed to boot, which meant that it had not yet achieved fifteen percent of its total battery capacity.

***

The FROG watched as the policeman's eyes searched the darkness. Though the man saw nothing, his expression portrayed fearlessness. He decided he would not attack this man, as it seemed undignified, at least for the moment. The Marine knew he would have decided differently had the detective's implant been activated.

He remained still as the detective, clearly deciding that his ears had betrayed him, unfolded his white cane and disappeared into his apartment.

Smiling, he turned from the residence and walked over the tracks. He stopped and crouched for a few moments, regarding the police station across the street. The facility was well-lit and he watched a police cruiser drive out of the parking lot with mild interest. The grumbling in his stomach spurned him into action. Looking about the street below, he waited for an eastbound vehicle.

Five minutes went by with only the occasional passing car. To commandeer a coupe or sedan so close to a police station would be unwise, he felt. A few minutes later, the perfect vehicle approached. A large gray van was rolling east at a nice, easy pace. With precision, the killer launched himself from the L platform and landed upon its roof with his hands and feet splayed to minimize the sound. Despite his care, the uneven road surface jarred the van and caused his entire body to flatten loudly against its metal surface. Fortunately, since the cab was separate from the cargo section, it dampened the blow enough so that the driver took no notice.

The van drove on into the night with its deadly passenger undetected.

***

Thinking himself overtired, Frank turned and tapped the cane against the glass door. He picked up his glass and lighter from the table and went inside. He closed the sliding door behind him and shivered.

"Chilly out?" Tamara called from the couch.

"Yeah."

"Are you okay?"

"Huh? Sure, why?" he asked as he made his way to the kitchen.

"You looked confused, frowny-face."

"I did? Sorry," Frank said over his shoulder as he hung his overcoat in the closet. "I think this damn case is getting to me."

"Noooo, really? You?" Tamara giggled over her sarcasm.

"Cute."

Frank prepared himself for bed and turned in. It was early for him, but as his implant was recharging, he had nothing better to do. He lay in bed for a long time, it seemed, and though he was exhausted, his thoughts were a cyclic storm of restless turmoil that turned to nightmare when consciousness finally released him.

When Tamara Billingsley finally came to bed at past two in the morning, she noted Frank's conflicted sleep with a sigh. She knew better than to wake him as he often could not get back to sleep. She slipped under the covers and felt the bed tremble with his jittery arm and leg movements. In time, she slept.

***

Kirby McLain was awakened from an uneven sleep by the telephone's electronic warble. He sat up and set his feet to the cold wooden floor as he reached for the cordless handset.

"McLain," he croaked and cleared his throat. He listened to the voice of Detective Daryl Davies, Hank Lyman's partner, for a few seconds and slapped his knee with his free hand out of deep frustration. "Is it on the blotter, yet?"

He stood and reached into the open closet for the next suit in line. He tossed it on the bed and dug through a drawer as he continued to listen.

"All right," he said while reaching into the shower stall to turn on the hot water. "I'll get there soon. Tape off the area and get Gherling over there. You did? Good. Okay."

McLain ended the call and set the phone on the vanity. He cursed the cold water as he jumped in the shower. There was no time to wait for the hot water to make its way up to his floor.

He finished washing quickly and dried himself off with hurried abandon. He strode into his bedroom and began to dress. With his white shirt partially buttoned, he put his legs into his pants and pulled them up. A metallic click from the living room paralyzed him. The distinct sound of his door being closed pressed him into movement. He zipped and buttoned his fly as he turned and snatched his nine-millimeter from the nightstand while he accessed the building's security computer with his implant.

There was no record of his door being accessed this day. The portal remained locked.

Kirby released the handgun's safety and, barefoot, stepped into the hallway. From his bedroom's doorway, he could see his kitchen and front door. It was closed. He had begun to think that he was mistaken when the sound of his floor creaking came to his augmented ears.

"I don't know who the hell you are," McLain said calmly, though his heart was pounding, "but you've just broken into a cop's apartment."

Silence.

Kirby brought the handgun's sights to eye level, but kept it close to him with bent elbows.

"And I don't think you're gonna make it outta here alive," he added in his most intimidating baritone as he took a few steps toward the room. Behind him was the den, truly a second bedroom, but the door was shut. He stopped to listen anyway with his bio-electronic audio receptors turned up to maximum.

"You've one chance," Kirby called again. "Show yourself with your hands up. I'm armed and I will shoot your ass."

Instead of silence, his ears picked up a passel of cars on Indiana Avenue and a hint of white noise that could have been breathing.

As he stepped into the living room, he caught movement from his left. Before he could turn, his recliner flew up from the floor and struck him hard. The force of the hit threw the big policeman back and his trigger finger involuntarily flinched. A round fired next to his head, but the blast was partially muffled by the cushion of the chair which was now in his face. His receptors reacted to the gunshot, but his left ear rung anyway as it could only react, not prevent the sound from doing harm.

The weight and force of the flying piece of furniture carried him into the kitchen and, off balance, he landed hard on the tiled floor. The back of his head and shoulders struck the cabinets, darkening his vision as pain exploded and reverberated throughout his skull.

For a full second, McLain laid there underneath his ruined recliner, too dazed and shocked to think about his next move or even comprehend how the heavy item could have been propelled so hard.

In an instant, the chair disappeared. It crashed against the far wall of the living room, breaking several items. Kirby saw a dark figure of a man standing above him, smiling wickedly with horrifically sharp off-white teeth and eyes of orange and yellow that stood out from the unnaturally gray scaly skin of the face around them.

With a slashing motion from his attacker's left arm, Kirby's firearm flew from his fingers, which flared in intense pain. His thumb and forefinger had been broken.

Without hesitation, McLain struck back. The heel of his hand collided with the intruder's nose, sending him back and away from Kirby long enough for the tough detective to scramble to his shaky feet. Immediately, he pursued the man in the black overcoat and hat, who had turned his back to nurse his broken nose in one hand.

Among the sounds of combat, there was laughter. Raspy, deep, sinister, the intruder exuded amusement.

Infuriated, Kirby carried his attack to the man, back turned or not, and tackled the gray-skinned freak of nature. The two combatants impacted with the balance of the living room furnishings, ending with the holovision set's plastic cabinet, which shattered into hundreds of pieces.

McLain landed on his attacker's back and pummeled his head with lefts. His right hand could do nothing more than hold the squirming intruder down. Blow after blow landed squarely, bending the brim of the black hat and impacting upon the cheek and left ear of the man pinned to the remnants of the broken HV.

The growling, menacing laughter continued.

As Kirby's fist drew back for another strike, he found that the creep was far from done. With great strength, the prone figure lifted himself and McLain from the floor and managed to spin, throwing Kirby from his back and dumping him into the bare spot where his recliner had once been. His already concussed skull struck the wall, stunning him and leaving him lying on his left side, wincing.

"That was great!" the intruder howled delightfully through a face full of blood as he removed the hat and tossed it to the floor. "You know, that's the second time in the past few days my nose has been broken! How *fun!*" he screeched gleefully and smiled in grotesque delight, showing his blood-stained teeth.

Kirby stared into the face of the enigma in front of him as he struggled to regain his feet. Underneath the flowing blood, the grayness of his skin fluttered and transformed through a mosaic of colors. At first, McLain thought the knocking on his noggin was causing a hallucination, but after seeing the intruder's skin tone settle into a light brown, he discarded it. The transformation seemed too real. The creature's eyes transformed from the harsh mustard yellow into an emerald green that caught the light of the sun flowing into the apartment from the front windows.

"You're also the only one that's been able to land any blows to me since my hand-to-hand training," he or it continued in the same tone. "Congratulations, Detective McLain, you're doing quite well, indeed!"

"What the hell are you supposed to be?" Kirby managed to say through wheezes. "It's a little early for a Halloween freak show." The policeman stood at his full height and found little solace in the discovery that he was at least four inches taller than his assailant. He thought the command for his implant to connect to an internet server in the den. He needed help and reached out to the CPD server.

The intruder threw his head back and laughed. It was all McLain needed. He charged, though with his shortness of breath, he realized it was not as robust as his first tackle.

Catching the detective's movement well in time, the Marine crouched slightly and flung out his right leg in a flying roundhouse kick. His foot landed squarely on McLain's jaw and had the added benefit of moving him to the right of the man's charge.

Kirby, sans a few teeth, landed on his couch with a frame-breaking crunch. The room spun and spun while he tried to deal with the rolling fields of pain his body had been dealt. Somewhere in that passing few seconds, he discovered his implant was unable to connect to anything.

"Good for you, Kirby McLain!" the FROG commended as if the man had won a prize. "This has been most entertaining!"

He moved to the detective and loomed over him triumphantly, only to receive another blow from McLain's left fist, followed by a right, which was far less potent given the broken appendages. Kirby howled in pain after that strike, but still managed to give the intruder a hard kick in the abdomen which drove the nutcase to the other side of the room with an audible crack of his ribs.

Like a drunk on a Friday night bender, McLain scrambled clumsily from the couch and fell more than leaped onto the floor of the small foyer. His blurry vision caught sight of his nine-millimeter, which he was able to pick up with his left. With a great amount of pain flowering in his chest and back, he spun to take aim of the freak and he fired three times.

The first round looked to have found its mark, but he could not be sure. The target was incredibly fast, and had tumbled to Kirby's left and out of the way of the next two.

At some point during that tumble, McLain felt something strike him hard and deep, though he could not comprehend what it was, considering the distance between himself and the man in the black overcoat. A wave of fresh pain erupted in his upper chest and left shoulder, resulting in his pistol falling from his fingers against his will. His suddenly powerless arm dropped, too, but struck something on the way down, which cranked up the pain to never-before-experienced levels. Kirby's world dimmed when he screamed until his breath ran out. He rolled and fell back against his foyer closet's door which only added to the agony. Looking down, he solved the mystery of the new pain. The intruder had somehow thrown the bayonet into him. It had entered his side just below his armpit at an upward angle, given McLain's prone position. The blade had done something to his shoulder from within, ending the usefulness of his left arm.

"Now, *that's* shooting," the intruder remarked while searching for the place he had been hit. "Damn fine work, Detective McLain!" he mocked.

Kirby watched, defeated, as the intruder removed the newly-holed black coat and patted the tan pullover sweater which bore a patch of fresh blood at his lower abdomen. Laughing, the attacker flashed a winning smile as he shook his head and winked at Kirby.

"Who...who are...you?" McLain could only whisper.

"You know something," the other answered. "You, my good man, truly deserve to know." Wearily, he took a couple of steps toward the fallen policeman and dropped to the floor in front of him with his legs crossed Indian-style. He patted his knees and took a few deep breaths. "My given name is Elliot. I don't have a surname, per se. The military gave me a number. Imagine that shit. A fucking number for a name."

Elliot's eyes, now light blue, searched the ceiling for something, perhaps a memory. His skin paled before Kirby's widening eyes. Together with the greasy, curly black hair, which so far had not changed color, Elliot's appearance became that of a teenager. Young and perfect in its porcelain finish despite the blood trickling from the nose. The youthful blue eyes gazed into Kirby's own. A thin smile crossed his lips, mercifully hiding the predatory teeth.

"What...," McLain started, but was interrupted by a watery cough. "What are you?"

"Elliot Three-dash-Seven," the young man continued while he tilted his head up and snorted blood back up into his sinuses. He turned away and spat the bloody mess across the room. "The dash is silent." He cackled insanely for a brief second before turning solemn once again. "I *was* a Marine attached to Force Recon. Part of their Optimized Genetics squad."

Abruptly, Elliot Three-Seven popped up on his feet and closed the distance between himself and McLain. He scooped up the pistol and tossed it to the hallway, placed his left foot upon the detective's chest and yanked the bayonet free.

Kirby screamed, though it was short and weak. Heat washed over his chest and lower abdomen.

"Ooo...yuck," Three-Seven commented through a faux grimace. "That doesn't look good, Kirby, old buddy." A laugh overtook him while he wiped the blood from the triangular blade onto a couch cushion. "You should get that looked at!" He gave a short, wicked cackle.

Kirby groaned and grunted in pain. He discovered he was unable to move, save for his legs, but even that caused pain.

"Oh, but there's good news!" Elliot called brightly after returning from the kitchen. He had retrieved an apple and was devouring it as he came near Kirby and crouched. "Becawza yer can'her," he said while chewing, "I'm not gonna eachoo. I ha'e a phobia." He swallowed and continued. "Don't want cancerous meats."

Kirby stared at his killer and the killer stared back. There was no animosity in the face of either man, only fading strength in one and childlike curiosity in the other.

"You're so funny," Elliot granted with a chuckle as he flung the core away to the sink. "You're trying to figure out, even now, as you lay there dying, how the hell I got in here, how I found you, and why you can't seem to use your 'plant."

McLain gave a brief, weak nod.

Three-Seven tapped his temple. "It's all up here. State-of-the-art-type shit, old bean. I hacked the CPD computer and matched up your face and that of Detective Frank Campanelli's. Saw him last night."

Kirby squirmed and grunted in pain. He squinted with renewed anger at the mention of his co-worker.

"Oh, no worries," Elliot provided as if he had been asked. "I didn't kill him. You know, that's one interesting motherfucker. A blind cop...a detective, no less. Now, I've seen *every* fuckin' thing, huh?" He cackled high and loud again while his eyes turned from blue to black. "I was watching you two when you came to check out the car I wrecked. He's got an interesting style about him. An air, if you will. Luckily, I was able to procure similar stylish threads the other night. Kinda wish you hadn't put a hole in the coat, though. Not nice, Kirbinator." He wagged his finger and feigned fatherly disappointment.

As the world became darker, Kirby's heavy chest turned his breathing into raspy wheezes.

Elliot's ears perked up. He was listening to something that McLain no longer had the ability to hear.

Kirby tried to speak again, but failed. Only a weak moan escaped his cold lips.

"Hmm. Sounds like it's time for me to go," Elliot said regretfully. "Methinks the nosy neighbors doth ratted us out, eh, Kirbs? Anyway, it's been fab." He stood and gracefully scooped the overcoat from the floor and stepped back into the kitchen.

He returned as Kirby's eyes closed for the last time with a white kitchen towel held to his left side under his coat and a paper bag of miscellaneous food. It did not account for much, but it was better than nothing.

"Oh, damn," Elliot oozed with phony regrets. "I forgot to ask if you had any last words." He shrugged and walked away. He retrieved his black hat, reshaped the brim and put it on.

The sirens from at least three police cruisers were quickly approaching.

"Well, it's now or...slightly later than now, Kirby McKirberson," Three-Seven said cheerfully and chuckled.

As if he had no care in the world, Elliot stepped into the hallway, ignored retreating footfalls and at least two slamming doors, and briskly walked from the scene.

***

Frank wakened to the sound of sirens. At least two squad cars were leaving District One in a hurry, tearing the silence of his darkness to shreds as they screamed off.

"Time," he croaked.

"*Six-twenty-two, a.m.*," the voice clock reported.

Campanelli initiated his *CAPS-Link* and crawled out of bed. Sirens at that time of morning were never good, but lately had proven to be far worse than normal. Without bothering with his cane, he felt his way to the bathroom, making it just in time for his lenses to come online and light up his world.

Frank cranked the hot water handle in the shower and went about preparing himself for the day. He accessed the CPD server and read the blotter. He sighed and grunted a profane response to what he had suspected. Another victim of the psychopathic cannibal had been found on Michigan Avenue. It was the owner of an antique electronics shop, found dead just feet inside the open shop door.

He read the rest of the report as he dried himself. Units en route were listed at the right of the data screen as well as the units requested. It accounted for the two marked squads that had awakened Campanelli and homicide detectives, Jorge Chavez and Charles Morgan, men he knew well, were already on scene. The coroner, Dennis Gherling was on the way. One other bit of data caught his eye.

"Head of D1 Homicide Requested" it read, with the tag, "En-Rte", meaning that Kirby McLane had been alerted and had acknowledged that he was on his way. Frank continued to dress as he stared at the up-to-the-moment report. He expected "En-Rte" to be replaced by "On-Scn" any second. A minute went by with no change. Two minutes turned into three. Kirby did not live that far from the murder scene and Frank wondered what was taking the man so long. The man could have jogged there, one diminished capacity lung notwithstanding.

Campanelli looked at himself in the bathroom mirror as he put on his tie. He watched the "En-Rte" status stubbornly refuse to change. A feeling of dread washed over Frank as he stepped out of the bathroom and into the kitchen to prepare the morning coffee.

As he dumped coffee into the filter, an alert came through his ears. The tone was not overly loud, but as the morning was quiet and Frank's concern grew, it might as well have been a squad's siren next to his ear. The repeating medium to high-pitched double tone directed him to a fresh report on the blotter. With a focus on the button and a thought, the dispatcher's voice was fed to his audio.

"Any units in the vicinity of Twenty-twenty-five South Indiana. Callers, two, report a four-fifteen. Possible fight. Units responding, acknowledge," she narrated calmly. Two patrol units answered her call and declared themselves en route.

Campanelli poured the water into the old coffee brewer and set the pitcher down hard. "Shit!" he shouted in recognition of the address. Frank scampered for the bedroom and retrieved his shoulder holster rig and pistol. As he strapped it on, he contacted the dispatcher through the implant and advised her that the address was that of Detective Kirby McLain.

Frank snatched his coat and hat from the closet and, taking no time for a word to Tamara, he rushed through the door of his apartment and flew down the stairs, nearly careening into the glass doors of the lobby. He had ordered the dispatcher to roll additional units and upgrade the four-fifteen to an "officer needs assistance" call. The fact that Kirby was overdue to the murder scene just a third of a mile from his apartment while a fight was happening in his building was too much of a coincidence for the seasoned detective to ignore.

As he set his cruiser to Condition Three and slipped it in reverse, driving it in manual mode, the dispatcher upgraded even his report.

"Shots fired...caller reports shots fired at Twenty-twenty-five South Indiana. Roll code three all responding units."

"Goddamn it," Frank muttered as he pulled out of the parking lot. Pressing the accelerator near the floor, the four tires of his car screamed and puffed white smoke as the turbo-charged engine whistled and whined amongst the wailing double siren.

"Unit five-one-six-two," he called to the radio over the noise of his automobile. "En route to shots fired call!"

"Roger, five-one-six-two," the dispatcher replied.

Even though it was less than a half mile to McLain's residence, Campanelli drove like he was chased by a demon. The turn from Eighteenth onto Indiana was made with tires smoking and the car's rear end kicked out wide. He found relief in the fact that he looked to be fourth on the scene, but it did nothing to quell the feeling that they were all too late.

He brought the cruiser to a sideways stop, blocking the northbound side of the street along with the three other marked cruisers. Frank snatched his fedora from the seat and mashed it on top of his head without conscious thought. He pulled his eleven-millimeter from his holster and charged into the familiar building, bolting directly for the stairs. With his ears peeled, he noted a significant and heart-stopping silence within.

Bounding onto the second floor, he found the six uniformed officers milling about the hall. Their guns were in their holsters and two of them were speaking to residents. The rest looked glum. The youngest officer among them had removed his cap and appeared pale.

Frank Campanelli's heart sank as his sprint fell off to a sullen shuffle.

The sergeant among the gathered uniforms spoke as Frank approached the open apartment door. "It is Detective McLain, sir. He's gone."

Campanelli nodded and forced himself to peer through into the apartment. The place was destroyed. It was obvious that Kirby had fought hard by the wreckage and the bruises on his face. He noted two spent brass casings, one on McLain's lap, and the other on the floor, between the man's knees.

"The caller says dat a guy, six feet in height, black coat, black hat," the sergeant, whose name was Marx, went on, "walked outta here like nuttin' happened. I've called for backup units to comb the area."

Frank cleared his throat. "Anyone been through the place?"

"Yes, sir," Marx added. "No one's inside. There's a nine-mil lying in da' hallway. Probably McLain's."

"Okay," Campanelli said and took a deep breath. "Forensics?"

"Just called 'em, sir."

"Thank you, Sergeant Marx," Frank replied and cleared his throat several times. He looked down upon the body of Kirby McLain, with his head and shoulders propped up on his foyer closet door. Incensed, Campanelli wanted to scream with such intensity the officers around him would label him mad. He wanted to be free of this and every responsibility, to be taken to a home for the mentally broken and dysfunctional. He wanted to be somewhere else, anywhere else at all, so that he could scream, kick, and cry like a child. All at once, he decided there had been too much pain and misery in this mankind-forsaken world and selfishly, foolishly, he wanted it all to go away. He wanted to shut down his implant and never reactivate it, condemning himself to a world of darkness for the remainder of time. Blindness is freedom. Frank's fists clenched tightly, so much so that they trembled. His teeth were clenched hard enough that his jaw ached all the way to his ears and his eyes bulged under stress.

Frank was unaware, but he had begun breathing heavily through his nose.

"Detective Campanelli?" the sergeant attempted quietly. He looked around and found that his other officers remained outside the apartment. This was a good thing, he decided, because the detective on scene looked as if he were either going to break down and cry or go on a shooting spree. The man shook with anger, setting the brim of the fedora aquiver and leaving the large handgun to rattle within his grip. "Sir," he tried again.

Frank blinked several times, aware that someone was speaking. "Yes, Sarge?"

"Can I do somethin' for ya?"

Barely under control, the Captain of Detectives made himself think before he spoke. "This animal likes to head to the rooftops, Sergeant," he said in a raspy, forcefully subdued tone. "Have your men find the access to the roof and check it. I'm requesting a helicopter."

"Yes, sir," the patrol sergeant replied and was off.

Frank knew the possibilities of spotting the killer were slim, but it was a possibility that needed to be covered. Perhaps he was becoming sloppy.

He stood over his colleague for several minutes, simply looking down upon the broken and beaten man with a flood of thoughts and memories running through his mind.

It's not supposed to end like this...for any of us.

Campanelli stepped back from Kirby McLain, replaced his eleven-millimeter to his shoulder holster and accessed the CPD server from McLain's computer network, one that the man had put together himself.

Frank entered the helicopter order into the blotter and the dispatcher acknowledged.

Looking about, he began piecing together what had happened. Somehow, the murderer had found out McLain's identity and had walked into the apartment. Frank shook his head when he pondered the possibility that Kirby had simply let the man in. The door and its frame showed no signs of being forced. He bent to pick up the top half of the recliner, which had separated from the base and had fallen next to the half wall of the kitchen. The base lay broken in the northwest corner of the apartment, next to the couch.

Carefully placing the back of the chair on the floor where he had found it, Frank stepped toward the ruined holovision set. He stopped short and found blood spattering on the living room's southern wall. Looking down, he found that he had nearly stepped on droplets. Watching his footing, he went to the ruined HV and bent over it. He adjusted his vision to compensate for the shade and zoomed in on the ruined electronics and cabinet. It appeared that one or both of the combatants had fallen on it, or perhaps been thrown into it.

Campanelli stood up straight and looked over his right shoulder. Kirby had some cuts among the bruises, but no tiny cuts, like the sharp plastic of the cabinet or unmachined metal framework would have caused. The wall behind the unit was gouged deep, proving to Frank that it was hit with great force before the cabinet failed.

A thought occurred and he moved to McLain's body to verify it. He grimaced at the discovery that the thumb and forefinger on the right hand were both broken. The knuckles on the left hand were puffy and bruised.

"Good for you, my friend," he whispered. The man had landed a few before being skewered by the large blade. Remembering that the sergeant had mentioned the presence of a pistol, Frank looked to the hallway floor. He walked to it and found a mark on the far wall. The nine-millimeter had been flung there, probably removed from Kirby's hand by the killer. Campanelli deduced from the blood spatter and the proximity of the casings to McLain's body, that the murdering cannibal had been hit at least once. He looked to the wall with the blood spatter again and found a hole to the left of it.

"Hi, Frank."

Campanelli looked up and saw H. Lincoln Rothgery and Teri Wilkins in the doorway. Their expressions were somber and reverent. Frank wanted nothing more than to reply, but he was temporarily out of words. He nodded and Rothgery entered.

"The report says there was a gun?" Teri asked of Frank. He pointed it out. "Ah," she acknowledged and went to it with her hand scanner/camera device.

Campanelli remained crouched there for a moment. A big hand dropped to his right shoulder and he noticed that he had been joined by the lanky forensic genius. He looked over and into the man's face. The expression was that of deep regret and understanding.

"Frank, why don't you take off? We've got this."

Campanelli nodded. "Help me get this fucker, Lincoln." With that, he stood and walked out.

He took a deep breath once he stepped outside. The brim of the fedora shaded his eyes from the morning sunlight above, while his lenses adjusted for the reflected orange light from the concrete at his feet. Frank reached for his lighter and a cigarette. He connected his *CAPS-Link* to his automobile's booster and accessed the file for the other murder that morning.

Campanelli let out a cloud of white smoke as he sauntered to his cruiser. He read the report and noted that the body had already been packaged up and moved to the morgue. Gherling's report reflected the usual missing heart and liver. For the moment, Frank saw no reason to visit the scene.

Frank got behind the wheel of his cruiser and sat for a moment, reading over the details. There weren't many, as there had been no witnesses to that killing, unlike the show that had gone down when he went after McLain. The victim was an antique electronics collector, dealer, and refurbisher by the name of Bart Stauros. He lived alone and owned the building on Michigan Avenue. His only other possession was a sixty-year-old gray cargo van.

"Hmm," he grunted as he put his car in reverse. The report said the van was missing. As he turned the car to the north and began to leave, his eyes scanned to his left. "Shit!" he cried out and brought the car to a jerking stop.

Campanelli found himself parallel to a gray cargo van, parked on the west side of the street. He put the car in park and jumped out. With his hand on his gun, he stepped across the street and waved a uniformed patrolman over.

No driver was visible, but with his free hand, Frank grabbed the door handle and found that it was unlocked. The van's cabin was empty. He quickly stepped to the front of the van and matched the license plate number to the one on the report. This was Stauros's vehicle.

"What do we got?" the uniform inquired with trepidation. His hand was on the butt of his handgun.

Frank told him and sent a message to Lincoln and Teri that Stauros's van was outside and was to be given a looking over. Considering what they had found so far, he knew there was little to be gained by an in-depth search of the vehicle, but it was evidence, and evidence needed processing.

Frank watched two uniformed officers tape off the van and decided to head to Bart Stauros's shop after all. The drive was short, as Michigan Avenue was only one block west and the crime scene, two intersections south. He parked his cruiser on the west side of the street and walked across, noting that one unmarked cruiser remained in front of the shop. There was little pedestrian traffic, and the few who passed gave the tape a cursory glance and kept moving.

Campanelli unhooked the tape from one side of the open doorway and replaced it as he passed through. The shop was larger than it appeared from the facade, being very deep with a high ceiling. It was also dimly lit, despite the sunlight spilling through the windows. The walls were finished with darkly treated wood paneling, covered by an impressive collection of audio equipment and computer technology manufactured by a variety of long-defunct manufacturers. Counters to his right were full of these components, all of which appeared to be no newer than thirty years of age. All had ridiculously high price tags, in

Frank's opinion, but he was not in the market for such things and the value of the dollar seemed to plummet daily.

A large pool of blood stained the dry wooden floor several meters from the front door, lit by a single light bulb hanging by a cord from the ceiling. Frank noted streaks of blood on the wall and on some of the items on a shelving unit there. Where the body had fallen was taped off as well.

"Hi, Frank," Detective Charles Morgan called from the wooden stairs at the southeast corner of the shop. The man's dark suit and the low light virtually guaranteed that he would not have been seen unless purposely searched out.

"Charles," he replied. His voice broke halfway through the man's name.

"We heard about McLain," Morgan said with a thumb thrown back toward the stairs he had just come down. Frank deduced his partner, Jorge Chavez, was still up there.

Campanelli nodded and looked about the shop, unsure of what to say.

"Was he...well, treated like the other victims?" Morgan inquired with a whisper.

"No," Frank answered. "He fought like hell, though. I don't think the bastard had time to do anything but get out of there once he heard the sirens."

"Is it true that McLain got a shot in?"

"Yeah," the Captain of Detectives provided. "Shot 'im once before he died."

"Jesus," Morgan mumbled.

"Anything interesting here?"

Charles Morgan shook his head. "We can't tell if the murderer had time to rummage through the place or not. If he stole anything, we wouldn't be able to tell short of dust patterns on shelves and such. Stock primarily consists of clocks, audio equipment, some computers, automaton parts, miscellaneous high quality wires, and other junk. If

Stauros had an inventory list, he must have kept it up here," he finished with a tap to his temple.

"I see." Frank sighed deeply as he looked about the heavily stocked shop. "Did you know that Stauros's truck was found outside McLain's?"

"No way," marveled Chavez, who was just coming down the creaking steps.

Frank just nodded.

"Well, that fits," Morgan surmised. "He found this guy, killed him and took the truck to McLain's. The only thing is, how did he know where to look?"

"I've been thinking that over," Campanelli admitted. "Maybe the killer saw Kirby make that announcement on HV. Then he must have hacked into the CPD computer and looked over the personnel files."

"Great, a computer-savvy cannibal," Jorge commented with widened eyes.

"Anything unusual upstairs?" Frank asked.

"Nah. Nothin'. Stauros kept it a bit neater up there than the shop down here." Chavez looked about the area as he spoke.

"Was the door broken in? Jimmied?" Campanelli asked even as he walked back to it for a look himself.

"No. We're not sure how he got inside," Charles answered. "Stauros might have left the door unlocked."

Frank read the report submitted to the blotter by Hank Lyman and stifled his next question. There had been no witnesses and the time of death had been approximately ten to eleven o'clock the previous night. This timeframe was beyond the shop's posted hours.

"Do us all a favor," Campanelli said wearily to the two detectives. "There's as much as eight hours between the time of Stauros's murder and the attack on McLain."

"Yes, sir?" Jorge Chavez agreed, but appeared confused.

"I want to know what that monster was doing for those hours," Frank said more forcefully. "Look hard for anything in here that appears to have been moved recently. Did this bastard steal anything? Did he sleep here? We need to know," Campanelli finished more softly. He knew that it did little good to display his frustration, let alone take it out on his fellow detectives.

Chavez and Morgan nodded and said nothing. It was clear that they felt as terrible about the death of a fellow officer as Frank. Campanelli thought of Lyman, who was the one that had called McLain that morning. While he and his partner, Davies, were here clearing the building and waiting for backup, their lead detective was in a losing battle for his life.

Frank shook his head. "Look, you guys know what yer doin'. Don't mind me." With that, he turned and left.

***

From the rooftop of an apartment building, Elliot Three-Seven watched Frank Campanelli enter the antique shop and, some minutes later, exit. He smiled to himself over the expression of despair veiled by anger upon the old detective's face. As much as he wanted to laugh out loud, however, the pain in his lower abdomen was too bothersome to do so.

His body was working overtime to stop the bleeding, but the creation of scar tissue threatened to drain him of energy right then. Already, his stomach growled with uncomfortable hunger and his hands shook with impending exhaustion. Despite consuming three apples, a package of ham, and a half-full bag of Swiss cheese, the need to feed was great.

Elliot knew he had been lucky to escape from the detective's apartment building. He was fairly confident that he had left no blood trail. A long rest is what he needed now. He could hunt when the sun fell.

He watched Campanelli's dark blue cruiser pull a U-turn and head northward as he stood up. A sound from far away froze him in place. He augmented his hearing and, identifying it, searched the sky. In the distance, he could make out a low flying helicopter of silver, white, and blue. It was heading toward his general area, so he knew it was time to get out of sight.

Elliot yanked open the door and descended the stairs to the top floor of the building. He emerged from the stairwell to find an empty hallway. With his ears fully augmented, he could hear a helicopter approaching the area and at least three voices emanating from the apartments ahead of him. He stepped stealthily along the thinly carpeted floor and halted near each door, listening hard for sounds of life within each residence. Halfway down the corridor, he stopped. Two of the three voices were a couple from down the hall. They were talking to each other about random, daily, dull things. The third, as he suspected, was the sound of a holovision, which was now behind him.

Three-Seven pressed his head against the door and, hearing nothing from within, tried the knob. It was locked. He retrieved his pick from his tool belt and easily defeated the lock in absolute silence. He tried the knob again and pushed the door gently out of his way. As his ears had told him, it was an empty apartment. Further, it was devoid of any furnishings whatsoever.

The door from the couple's apartment suddenly clicked open and the voices of the two occupants became louder. Without glancing in their direction, Elliot moved inside the apartment and closed the door behind him. He hoped the two young people had not heard the thump, but he had lost his balance in his exhaustion and had dropped to his knees as soon as he stepped inside.

With his hand on his bayonet's handle, Elliot listened. The voices headed away from him. The man laughed at something the woman said. An elevator door slid open and their voices were swallowed up, silenced altogether as they descended.

Three-Seven let the doorknob slip back to center, locked it, and took to his feet. His heavy legs propelled him reluctantly from one room to another, finding each empty until the master bedroom. There was no bed, but a wooden chair and a tall coat rack were set against the far wall. With his eyes half closed in anticipation of a long nap, Elliot dragged the coat rack to the front door. He opened the closet door and set the metal feet against the doorjamb. The top was pressed against the front door. There would be no way for anyone to get in without delivering a great amount of violence to the door.

He would have been much more comfortable putting more distance between himself and his second most recent crime, but like the incident involving the crashed automobile, he realized that he could not get far without being seen on the street. Sleep would get him past the hunger, he hoped.

He peeled off the ruined overcoat and dropped the crumpled hat to the bare wood floor. With a hand pressing against the bloodied towel at his wound, he lay on his back in the sun, which would work to recharge his color-morphing scales.

Elliot tucked the folded overcoat under his head and hoped that the police did not put themselves through a building search. The logic within him told him they would do exactly that, but he was too exhausted to run. His body was too committed to healing itself.

Just a little rest and then...the hunt for something to eat.

Helicopter blades beat incessantly overhead as the Nighthunter drifted to sleep.

***

Frank drove for a couple of hours, patrolling the area right along with a concentration of marked cars, from block to block, down this alley and that, with no success. The helicopter had caught no sight of anyone on a roof anywhere, and had spent a full load of fuel doing so until it needed to return to base.

Campanelli had recommended to the Chief of VCD, Darius Treadwell, that a building-by-building search was the next step. Treadwell had agreed and Frank attached himself to a group of uniforms assigned to the block where McLain's apartment was located. Another similar squad was doing the same to the entire block, two blocks west of them. An empty lot lay in between, where once had been a large apartment building, so another squad began one block further south.

After two hours of searching the buildings around McLain's now former residence, there was nothing.

He pressed on with the same group, moving to the next block to the south. Again, there was nothing. The next possibility was that the maniac had nestled within the remnants of the facility known as McCormick Place, once a vast convention center and hotel complex that had been the pride of Chicago. Now, with bits of the multi-structure facility burned out or collapsing from disrepair, the sprawling eyesore represented a daunting task and was a known hideout for gangs. Mayor Jameson had proposed a demolition of all the buildings in the name of public safety, but the plan was still in the works when last Frank heard. The complex was a giant source of angst for law enforcement.

Still, the patrols continued in the apartments and commercial structures around the neighborhood, in the hopes of at least eliminating the possibilities of the killer hiding in the residential buildings.

Instead of tackling McCormick, Captain Campanelli led the squad of thirteen men to the block east. On it was one tall condominium that had been placed next to the foundation of what once was a commercial high rise. The tired squad sealed off the exits and searched floor by floor. Due to the size of the building and the fact that many residents were not at home, which required the cooperation of the building's security staff, hours passed before the clearing of the building was complete. It was late afternoon by the time the patrolmen exited the building and milled about the sidewalk, waiting for further instructions.

"Where to next?" Frank casually asked Sergeant Louis Marx, with whom he had spent the majority of the day.

"Um, that's it, Detective," Marx answered apologetically.

"What?" he barked.

"Orders, sir," Louis added. "Check the blotter. We've been called off."

Campanelli cussed harshly as he brought up the report to his lenses. The orders were directly from Chief Treadwell.

"I'm sorry, sir," the sergeant went on. "Look, most of these guys are off shift in a couple hours and we're spread pretty thin."

"Yeah, yeah, yeah," Frank uttered and waved him off. He sighed heavily and looked into the lightly clouded blue sky. "Okay, I understand, Louis. Forget about it. Orders are orders."

"Take care, sir," Sergeant Marx granted as he moved off to tell his men to return to regular duty.

Frank plodded to his cruiser, exhausted. He had to admit defeat, which left an awful taste in his mouth. He dropped into the driver's seat, yanked the fedora from his matted hair, and chucked it to the passenger seat.

Campanelli became aware that he had not eaten lunch. His head swam and his stomach grumbled. Since Tamara's place no longer existed, only one place came to mind, so he told the cruiser where to take him.

***

Frank ended up in Chinatown at a place that had become semi-regular to him. The Mellow Monkey was a Chinese restaurant that had started out as a massage parlor, but had recently expanded into the suite next to it. The result was a larger bar and a kitchen. The drinks were cheap and the food above par. The owner, Xiao Chan Wu, was a former informant for the goings on of Chicago's Chinese gangs, including the Tong.

The stout, diminutive Asian brought Campanelli another bourbon and beer, taking the seat across from him. Wu could tell there was something out of sorts with the man. He was drinking fast, eating slow, and not saying much.

"Well, Frank," Xiao said once he placed the fresh drinks on the table, "what's been going on with you?" He stared at Frank expectantly with his implanted lime green lenses.

Campanelli glared back at first, not pleased with the unsolicited interruption. After a moment, his expression softened. He sighed heavily and shifted his gaze beyond the window on his right, which overlooked the stone-tiled path and the stores on the other side of the marketplace.

Xiao leaned forward. "Does this have something to do with that cannibal?" he asked while he stroked his white Fu Manchu, a habit of his whenever he whispered.

Frank emptied the older glass of bourbon, dumped the remaining ice into the new one and sipped it. He followed that up with a long draw from the pilsner glass. His eyes wandered over the somewhat busy establishment before he answered with a nod. Campanelli went on eating his kung pao shrimp without another word.

"What's happened?" Xiao inquired as he sat back.

"The bastard killed a friend of mine, Xiao Chan Wu," Frank said in a steady tone once he swallowed. His voice, though not particularly loud, had a full quality that carried for several tables, quieting some of the conversations going on around them.

Wu sighed and his heart sank. The informant was privy to the difficulties that the CPD was having retaining and recruiting new men. Despite the drop in crime once the Tong and the Ignatola crime family had both been rendered impotent, largely due to the man sitting across from him, Chicago was still a dangerous place in desperate need of lawmen. Campanelli was one of the most respected in town, and if he was hurting, so was the city.

"My sincerest apologies, my friend," Xiao offered. He caught the eye of the waitress serving Frank's table, tapped the table with his left hand while holding up the index finger of the other. She nodded and went to the bar.

"We got there in time to keep him from being eaten, so I suppose that's something," Campanelli commented grimly before taking another deep swig of bourbon, then beer.

Wu fought a grimace. He knew he could never handle the alcohol that the Sentinel detective routinely put down, let alone match the plan of attack happening before him. The two men sat quietly for a time, allowing the conversations in English, Mandarin, and Cantonese, among other dialects to continue around them.

The waitress, a short Asian beauty in a double pony tail and a blue cheongsam, set another bourbon and beer in front of Frank, a tall glass of plum wine for Wu, and cleared the table of empty glassware.

"Thank you, Mindy," Campanelli said, sounding perfectly sober. He reached for the bourbon that Wu had brought and, not realizing that the waitress had moved it slightly, missed it completely.

"Sure thing, Frank," Mindy replied. "The one you're working on is here," she whispered and slipped it into his hand.

"Ah, thank you," he said. She patted his shoulder and walked away.

"Frank?" Xiao nearly stuttered. "Just how many of those have you had?"

Campanelli was taken aback for a moment, confused. Then he understood and gave a harsh chuckle. "No, Xiao. I shut my implant down when I came in."

Wu laughed. "You are getting quite good. I thought you could see me this whole time."

Frank's eyes met Xiao's, but the proprietor of The Mellow Monkey could see that the man was just a little off the mark, not noticeable unless one knew the man was blind. The alcohol was plain in the eyes, however, having turned them red and watery.

"I was wondering why you had not commented on my attire," Wu said as he watched the detective eat. "With the expansion, I figured it was about time to look a bit more professional."

"Don't tell me you've got one of those awful Mao suits, Xiao Chan," Frank's tone was jovial, though he could not bring a smile.

Xiao chuckled. "No, no. Just a nice suit with a Mandarin collar. Light gray."

Frank nodded. "Sounds great. It's about time you tried classin' the joint up." He took another drink.

"So, tell me, Frank," Wu pressed in a voice just above a whisper, "is this man going to be caught soon?"

"Dead or alive, Xiao Chan Wu. Dead or alive." Campanelli said this with great conviction and more than a hint of anger. His face turned rose and the hand holding the fork clenched it tightly. His unseeing blue eyes met with Xiao's perfectly.

"Can I join?" a voice from Frank's left called.

"Marcus," Campanelli blurted and set down his fork. "Please sit."

Xiao slid from the booth, shook Williams's hand, and let the big man take his place. "It's good to see you, my friend!"

"Hello, Xiao," Marcus greeted and took the offered hand and seat. "Nice suit."

"Thank you. May I get you something?"

Marcus took a look at Frank's small collection of glasses and the man's watery eyes. "Uh, a lager, please."

Xiao motioned for Mindy to return and relayed the order. He sat next to Marcus and the both of them shared a brief glance.

"You heard about Kirby?" Frank asked then took down the older bourbon and started on the remaining.

"Couldn't miss it," Marcus answered glumly.

"It's all over the news, I imagine."

"Yeah."

Mindy brought Marcus's beer and removed another empty.

Frank felt for the pilsner glass and lifted it to his mouth. "Treadwell send you? Sebastian? Tam?"

"No. I called Tam and she told me where you were."

"How's your collarbone?" Campanelli inquired and set the glass down.

"Good," Marcus answered and took a sip of his beer. He looked to Wu expectantly.

Xiao took the hint and picked up his wine. "I will leave you two to talk. See you later."

Williams watched the stout proprietor head away. "Rothgery's been trying to reach you."

"Yeah? What's he found?"

"It's confirmed that McLain was killed by that damned bayonet."

"I figured that," Frank agreed and took a bite of shrimp. "I saw that he broke a couple of fingers on the right hand."

"Yeah, he fought hard. The blood on the wall and on the floor was a match to what he got out of Werner's car."

"Good," Campanelli said and nodded. "I hope the son of a bitch is dead in an alley somewhere."

"That's doubtful."

Frank sighed and a flash of fresh anger swept over his face. His eyes came close to meeting Williams's, but missed. Marcus knew even before he arrived that Campanelli's implant was shut down as he had been out of communication for a couple of hours.

"That FBI friend of mine is arriving tomorrow. He's bringing a doctor with him."

"A doctor?"

"Yes. A Dr. Mitchell Ruger. He worked on the FROG project."

"Oh? Is he the designer of this damn monster?" Campanelli asked after another swig of bourbon and beer.

"Not quite. But Ruger's worked closely with the project for the duration," Marcus explained. "He's an expert on this thing and, apparently, once he took a look at the reports I sent Quinne, my friend, he was on board. We'll soon be able to tell if this is a FROG or not."

"Good."

The two were quiet for a time as Frank finished off his food. Mindy took the plate, leaving the two policemen to their drinks.

"Are you all right, Frank?" Marcus asked finally.

The Captain of Detectives nodded and his blind eyes found Williams's face. "Oh, shit!"

"What?" Marcus saw Frank's face go white.

"Last night. I was on the patio, waiting for my implant to recharge. I was having a drink and just lounging on the chair when I thought I heard something...or someone, that is, speaking."

"Talking to you on your patio? From where?"

"I never found out. I couldn't turn the implant on. It was recharging. Marcus, I thought I was tired and hearing things." Frank thought the command to initiate his implant's start-up sequence.

"Well, how the hell does he know where either of you live?"

"I'm not sure," Campanelli said and shook his head. "I think he got access to the CPD computer somehow. How did you get here?"

"I took a cab," Marcus explained, then took a long drink of his beer when he realized Frank was preparing to leave. "Tamara thought you could use a ride home."

"Perfect," Frank commented and blinked as he searched for some bills in his wallet. "Come on, get me home. I think Tam might be in danger."

Frank and Marcus left in a hurry, Xiao noted as he waved. He hoped their haste was due to a break in the case.

Williams slipped behind the steering yoke and Frank, who was now able to see, but too inebriated to function behind the wheel, dropped anxiously into the passenger seat.

In moments, they arrived at the apartment building's parking lot. Frank bolted out of the cruiser and into the building with Marcus Williams right behind.

Campanelli burst into the apartment, startling Tamara, who shot to her feet from the couch.

"Jesus, Frank!" she shouted. He returned his embrace and waved at Marcus. She and Williams shared a glance of concern. "Wow…you smell like a Chinese distillery."

"Sorry," Frank offered and looked into her face. "You haven't heard anything out of the ordinary tonight? Any funny phone calls, knocks on the door, anything weird?"

"No," she insisted. "What's this about?"

Frank planted a hard, passionate kiss on her lips. It was brief, but effective. "Okay," he said as he turned to Marcus, who had remained just inside the front door. "Last night, I thought someone was out there," he said and gestured northward. "I don't know for sure, maybe he *was* out there, standing on the L."

"*What?*" Tam all but shrieked.

"That's the direction I heard the voice come from."

"What voice, Frank?" Billingsley begged to know.

"I thought I was hearing things...exhausted," he explained, "I disregarded it. But considering what happened to Kirby...I think this FROG came here first...last night."

"But how does he know where you and Kirby lived?" She asked with her arms crossed.

"Kirby and I figured that the son of a bitch was watching us Monday morning when we were looking over the wreck," Frank said slowly as he processed his thoughts. "We were investigating the murders that happened Wednesday morning. They occurred right across the highway from the wreck. He was injured and didn't get far."

"So, he recorded your faces to his 'plant and then what?" Marcus asked, but discovered the answer before he finished. "Your thought was that he hacked into the CPD computer and matched up the pics to the personnel profiles, but there would have been an indication."

Frank nodded. "That's not beyond the realm of possibility when we're talkin' about military implants. Is it, Marcus?"

"I don't think so. I mean, the best that I'm capable of is guessing at passwords like the rest of you civvies. These FROGs were supposed to be a step ahead of us in every way," Williams explained as he shook his head.

"Shit, Frank," Tam groaned in fright and wrung her hands. "Are you saying that cannibal knows where we *live?*"

Campanelli nodded and stepped quickly to the phone. "Tam, if I'm right, we have time to get some protection, maybe move to a safe place temporarily. McLain shot him, so he may be resting a day to heal." He picked up the receiver and punched numbers into it quickly.

"Calling Treadwell?" asked Marcus.

Frank nodded. "It's almost seven, but he may be in." A moment later, it was clear that he was not. He hung up the phone and accessed the CPD server across the street. "He signed out for the day. I'm calling him at home."

***

Elliot was rousted from his healing slumber by the sound of heavy footfalls beyond the front door of his borrowed abode. It had only been a few hours, so the wound promised to be a problem. He got to his feet, snatched up his hat, and popped open the patio door. It creaked loudly, so he moved quickly outside and closed it with haste. Three-Seven climbed the ramped brick which led to the roof and stepped fleetingly and as quietly as he could manage to the northeast corner of the building. Sprinting at the end, he flung himself into the air and, with his powerful arms outstretched, grabbed onto the aged and rotting wood of a telephone pole.

He collided hard, as he expected he would. Further, the gunshot wound was reopened and bleeding once again. For a moment, Elliot clung to the pole and gathered the breath that had been forced from his lungs. As was his training, he did so without an utterance of pain.

Holding tightly, he descended the pole far enough to kick himself off, arching his body into a backward somersault, which carried him to the building across the alleyway. He coiled his body and landed on the roof of an aged sedan with a metal-bending *whump!* This was followed by the brittle tingling of shattering glass. Quickly, he jumped to the roof of the car next to the one he had just ruined, dropped to the paved surface of the raised parking garage roof, and ran off the edge of that structure as well. He landed gracefully on the concrete alley, crouched upon his hands and feet.

Elliot stood and looked about him, giving his body a moment to shake off the bone tingling impacts and his lungs a few passes at gathering much needed oxygen.

From above, he heard voices, so he broke into a stride southward as he tugged his black hat down over his eyes. He glanced to his left and smiled in recognition of the building where he had harvested the antique store owner. The smile faded when he looked forward again.

A police car turned into the alley and headed for him. In a flash of thought, Elliot broke into a blurring sprint to his right, toward the apartment building that he had just escaped from. Here, the structure recessed to accommodate the elevator shafts and joined two buildings into one. Three-Seven found several hiding places to choose from behind three large garbage receptacles. He crouched low and listened as the vehicle rolled on by him.

Wasting not a second, he moved to the edge of the wall and watched the cruiser turn onto the next street to the north. With it out of sight, he left his hiding place and ran southward. He kept to the wall and moved quickly, again sprinting across the street. He angled toward the first structure he picked up in his peripheral vision. As he sped toward it, he glanced upward and noted its relatively small size, peaked roof, and spire. Not bothering to slow himself, he raised his arms across his face and burst through the rear door, which disintegrated into long planks of rotted wood and strips of thick paint.

Elliot sidestepped into the shadows and listened with his hearing augmented to its full potential. Wind, creaking wood underneath his weight, and the movement of vehicles in the distance were all he could pick up.

He set his audio receptors to a few steps above normal and brushed the dust, paint chips, and splinters of wood from his overcoat. Three-Seven sauntered from the room he had just exposed to weather and found an interior door, which he treated with more respect by turning the knob and shoving it out of his way. He stepped up to a platform that he decided must have once been a stage. The floor was covered with an aged, dirty, and tattered maroon carpet. His footfalls thumped against the time-worn wooden framework, which creaked loudly with each step.

Ahead of him and below the level of the stage was row upon row of great wooden benches, covered in dust and mold. Some had been dislodged from the floor and either tipped over or carelessly shoved askew from the rest. The wind whistled through the tall colored windows that featured bits of translucent artwork, none of which could he discern due to breakage or fading. All he could pick out was a face here or a star there. As it was of no consequence, Elliot dismissed it and stepped amidst the benches. Choosing one at the front, he sat down, unconcerned for the layers of dust which covered it.

In doing so, he sat facing the stage that he had walked across, only now noticing the back wall had once been painted a myriad of colors and reached high into the air, approximating the shape of a tower, which tapered to a point at the top. Like any other abandoned structure he had ever wandered into, Elliot knew that he was experiencing only a shadow of what the building had once been. The purpose of this one was lost on him, as it did not resemble any theater he had ever seen. Its stage was too small and there was no backstage area that he could find. The benches were too upright for a movie theater, which he had only seen once before. He catalogued the experience, just the same as he was doing now.

At once, it came to him. "A church!" He slapped the bench and smiled widely. "This is a church." His mind had subconsciously run the items he was seeing into a search of his implant's encyclopedia. He shook his head, amused that it had taken so long to come up with the answer. It had been a long time since he had seen such a place, and never from the inside.

The time was nearly five-thirty and Elliot Three-Seven knew that sundown was not far off. He closed his eyes and lay across the bench. He smiled as he realized that the item was properly called a pew. In seconds, he had descended into a light, healing sleep.

It was dark when he awoke to the sounds of a passing storm of various types of engines. His military implant instantly began analyzing the individual sources.

"Motorcycles," he whispered in the dark, and got to his feet. He smiled and strode to the back of the church. He approached the open doorway cautiously and peered into the young night. Inhaling deeply, he detected an oncoming rainstorm. The air was clean and sweet.

He caught the view of a pair of receding red taillights to his left, heading east. Looking about, there was no sign of police cruisers or pedestrians in the area. Intrigued by the sounds of the antique vehicles, though some were of the more recent electric drives, Elliot stepped out of the church and walked in the direction that the sounds led him.

Three-Seven briskly walked past an abandoned commercial building and read the street sign as he crossed Michigan. It was Twenty-Fourth Street. Checking that against the map system of his *FROG-Servlink*, he deduced that the motorcyclists were heading for the sprawling convention center known as McCormick Place. The pack turned southward, so Elliot broke into a pursuing run, and turned onto a vacant Michigan Avenue. As he pumped his arms and legs, he was reminded of the gunshot wound in his lower left side. He gritted his teeth, too focused on the motorcycle gang's doings to care.

Elliot came to a building covered in vines and bookended in tall weeds and skinny trees which waved at the behest of the evening's damp breeze. Casting his eyes east, he glimpsed a flash of red lights. The bikers entered the parking garage area through what used to be an exit.

He walked on, exhilarated by the promise of feeding that emptiness inside him that begged for nutrients. Healing took its share of his body's stores, and Elliot could swear he was becoming thinner by the hour. The pants he had stolen from the old man the other day seemed looser. The black running shoes flopped slightly, as if even his feet had shrunk, though he knew it was in part, due to the laces coming undone.

This area of the city had been long ignored, it appeared. There were no street lamps for quite a distance to the north and south and, together with the cloud cover, made the night seem almost indefatigable to the unaided eye. His night vision cut through it as if it were daytime.

Elliot followed the paved roadway into the depths of the parking garage, mostly featureless save for a mysterious door and a multitude of round columns. To his right and beyond this part of McCormick Place was a highway, an interstate his map system labeled, I-55. At the moment, not a car or truck was in sight.

The sounds of the motorcycle engines echoed against the concrete structure. A few of them were being pushed hard for some reason. Their engines raised in pitch until they screamed. He approached a corner, slowly moving around a column. His heart pounded when he saw that the facility opened up to his left. From within, the glow of electric light and fire ripped through the darkness, forcing Three-Seven's lenses to compensate.

He smiled as he bent into a crouch and ran toward the glow. The hunt was on.

***

The showoff of the group held his front brake solidly, while his right hand worked the throttle of the ancient, gasoline-fueled motorbike. With practiced skill, his body nudged that of the bike, creating a curved black streak in the porous concrete floor. Abruptly, he let the brake lever go and balanced forward as the front wheel came up from the surface. The motorcycle screeched off for many meters with the front still in the air until the rider hit the brake.

The other riders, most of which having dismounted their rides, clapped or shouted sarcastic words of encouragement or nonsensical shouts and howls. The headlights of the motorcycles lit the area in electric blueish white, while fires set in large metal drums of black and rust spat yellow flickers along the concrete ceiling.

One by one, the motors silenced and the voices of the riders rose up to fill the void. As Elliot stepped forward, he bathed his face in a mask of dark gray, dulled his eyes to brown, and counted the different voice patterns. There were twelve of them, with two being women. He reached out with his *FROG-Servlink*, giving the group a 'ping' to see how many, if any, were equipped with devices. He found one, but it was a device of someone else in the building, not part of the group. Surrounded by such concrete and steel, the equipped individual had to be on the same floor.

Elliot Three-Seven smiled and pulled his bayonet from his belt. *Thirteen*, he thought and grinned. *With two females for dessert!*

***

Steed Yarborough was the leader of his pack, of which only a few had come out to ride in the ensuing poor weather. Others had packed it in alongside the road someplace, either stopping for repairs or to dodge the storm. Steed, his woman, Nan, nine members of the Warlocks and one recent addition, a younger woman named Trish, were the only ones to make the ride all the way downtown. They had beaten the rainstorm by minutes, watching the dark clouds and lightning strikes in their mirrors the whole ride from central Illinois.

"Asshole," Steed grunted and smiled as he watched the showoff, nicknamed Blades, fill the expanse of the parking garage with tire smoke. He waved the whiteness away from his face.

The others near enough to hear him chuckled, including Nan. She had just taken off her helmet and hung it on the back of her bike. Nan was one of two females in the gang who had their own bike. The others rode with their men.

Steed watched Nan stretch, taking in the sight of her lithe body in the orange flicker of the young flames in the barrels. Her hair was matted from the helmet and her light brown skin shone with light sweat, making her quite attractive to him.

"Hey, Steed, Nan," Gopher called just before tossing cans of beer to them. Gopher was one of the younger, shorter men of the gang, therefore, he rode the slowest, heaviest bike which carried their provisions in large leather saddlebags.

"Gimme one, ya lil' rodent," Ironman snarled. The tall black man had grown to like the newer guy. For weeks, his demands would be laced in unrestrained, curse-laden contempt. In contrast, "rodent" was a compliment.

Gopher obliged and handed Ironman a can, then tossed a few more to the other riders.

Steed watched Gopher's eyes linger upon Trish, who clearly had taken a liking to Maxx, a little too long. "Hey!" he called and motioned the new guy over to him.

Gopher quickly moved closer to the gang leader. "Yeah, boss?"

"A word of friendly advice," Yarborough growled.

Gopher nodded nervously. He had been caught staring and he knew it. His smile disappeared, but he watched Steed's face intently.

"Don't stare at other people's women," Steed warned and grabbed Gopher's t-shirt and vest in one large gloved fist. Though the men were only around five years apart in age, Yarborough's sheer size and weathered skin made him more intimidating. "Maxx catches you doin' that, ain't no one here's stoppin' him from guttin' you, boy."

"Yessir," Gopher answered resignedly.

Steed let him go and smacked his cheek with that same heavy hand. "Good. Now, go get the grill set up. I'm fuckin' hungry."

The new guy turned and hustled to his bike for the cookware.

Nan took a deep gulp of her warm beer and moved closer to her man. "He needs to watch himself, huh?"

"You bet your sweet ass, he does," Yarborough answered and wiped the excess beer from his blond horseshoe mustache. With one bare arm, he gave her leather-covered rump a playful swat and gathered her close.

It was then the screaming began.

Steed watched Maxx drop to the cement, clutching at something in his back. His new girl backed away with her hands over her mouth. Her scream covered the sound of her fancy, high-heeled leather boot heels as she retreated.

"What the shit?!" Yarborough howled as he gave Nan a tug to get behind him. He dropped the half-consumed can of brew to the floor and pulled the handgun from the inside of his vest. His first assumption was that Gopher had tried to prove himself by taking out Maxx, but that would have been a deadly mistake. Maxx was Steed's friend. But something did not add up. Maxx dropped forward, toward Gopher, who stood behind his provision-laden motorcycle. The man was staring dumbfounded.

Gopher's hands were full of the pieces of the grill and whatever struck Maxx had done so in the back.

As the group turned to gather around Maxx, another man shouted in pain and dropped. It was the oldest man in the group, Chappy. The thin man gushed blood from somewhere high up on his neck. His beard-covered face, normally a dirty white, turned maroon as Steed watched. Pappy Chappy fell dead almost immediately.

"Everyone, get him!" Yarborough screamed, even though no one knew who "him" was as none had seen the attacker.

***

Elliot grinned as he ran in a wide circle, having ditched his stolen boots, overcoat and hat. Stealthy and fast, he sized up the gathering of tough guys and flung his black steel throwing knives at the largest or closest of them. He had thought twice about taking out the older man, but he had the largest weapon Three-Seven had so far seen among them. The submachine gun struck the cement floor just before the dead body.

He ran a large circle counterclockwise around the group, which was reacting as he thought they would. In their panic, they were beginning to make a tight circle around their motorcycles, seeking comfort amongst friends while taking cover within the steel.

It would not help them.

With a mighty warbling shout that Elliot had learned resembled that of an ancient Apache warrior, he encircled his prey at his best running speed.

The bikers were beginning to panic. They shouted at one another in frightened voices. "Everyone, get him!" the leader bellowed. Another followed up with, "Where is he?" A third yelled that he did not know and others simply cussed in fright. One of the two women was screaming, being by far the most irritating to Three-Seven, who was tempted to make her target number three for his four throwing blades.

Instead, he focused on the black man with the short shotgun as that firearm could really do some damage up close. He screeched out in his mock Apache war cry and threw the third knife, striking his target in the throat, just to the left of the Adam's apple. In seconds, that man would be dead.

He maintained his full speed in his tight, continuous turn. His efficient lungs kept enough oxygen in him to more than do the job. His right hand tightened on the fourth and last throwing blade as he searched within the group for the next likely target.

***

Yarborough felt an object disturb the air near his right ear. It struck Ironman in the throat and wavered there as the man's blood fountained around the weapon. The big man's body dropped to the cement floor the second his meaty hands pulled it free. Steed's realization that the black blade had nearly hit him made his knees quake. He spun the wrong way, searching eastward into the depths of the dark parking garage and saw nothing.

"Oh, my God! Steed!" Nan screeched from his left. Her eyes were wide and her own pistol had been drawn, but like himself, she had no target.

"Shut the fuck up!" he thundered and yanked her to him by her hair. "Get on your bike and get the hell out!"

Nan had zero argument. Without bothering to don her helmet, she threw a leg over the machine and pressed the starter button. The motor cranked, but only coughed.

"Shit! Steed!" she screamed as he turned in a circle in a search for his target. She was familiar enough with her motorcycle to know that it had a hard time restarting when it was hot. She caught his eye as the starter whined with no result and shook her head, sending her dirty blonde hair flying.

"Well, run, goddamn it!" Yarborough yelled.

Nan did so in mindless terror, dropping her beloved bike to the floor in a crash. She chose to leave the group in the opposite direction that they had all entered, and sprinted for the northern exit. In her haste, she collided with one of the other Warlocks, not knowing which one other than it was a man. She peeled herself up from the cement and tried to resume her run for the gray sunlight spilling into the exit, but she had twisted something in her left leg. She howled in pain and hobbled instead, madly waving the pistol at nothing as she went.

***

Three-Seven let loose of the fourth knife, which took down another big male target, the biggest yet. He could tell his hit was not as immediately fatal, as this man, like a couple of the older ones in the group, wore a heavy leather vest. His blade struck him in the upper chest, near the collarbone. The thickly bearded thug dropped and writhed in pain upon the dusty floor.

The second to largest of the group was coming up again, so he grasped his bayonet tightly. As he turned in to strike, he noted that one of the women was attempting to escape to the north exit. In passing his initial target, he slashed at him across the back of the upper left thigh. This sent the man spinning to the ground counterclockwise, the same direction Elliot was running. Certainly, the struck biker would be looking behind him for the culprit.

At his full speed, he ran into the limping female, striking her in the upper back with a raised forearm. The blonde let out a short cry of surprise before again collapsing to the floor, sliding to a stop after a couple of meters.

Elliot hoped he had not hit her too hard. He was not done with her by a long shot. He continued running in a tightening circle and searched for his next target.

A gunshot filled the cavernous parking garage. The flash indicated that it was wasted in an entirely different direction. From within the embattled circle, one of the bike's motors came to life.

***

Steed roiled on the floor and felt the hot blood oozing freely from his left leg. He fired his gun more in frustration than anything else. In the flash, he saw only more emptiness, a few abandoned vehicles, and rows of cement posts.

A frightened Yarborough realized that numbness in his leg was not a good sign, so he crawled to his bike and felt for a saddlebag. He needed to tie off his leg.

***

Gopher saw Ironman take a blade to his throat and drop dead. He did not bother trying to figure out where the attacker was coming from, but all he knew was that there was only one. He had seen the blurred black figure dash along at the edges of the light emitted by the barrel fires. Not thinking, he bent and picked up Ironman's shotgun and looked for Trish.

In a moment, he found her, whimpering and lying face down in between Maxx's and Ironman's motorbikes.

"Hey! Get up!" Gopher called to her and dropped to one knee.

Someone to his right managed to start his bike. Right then, he realized that the gunshot Steed had let fly had impeded his hearing. Her response went by him unnoticed. Gopher grabbed her shoulder and shook it, hard.

"Fuck off!" Trish screamed shakily and placed her head to the floor.

Gopher checked to see if a shell was in the chamber. "You've got to run!"

"You got a gun! Shoot 'im!" she commanded. In the flickering light, he could see the fright and anger in her face.

"Yeah," he whispered and began looking for the black blur once again. As he lifted the barrel higher, a flash of gunfire erupted at his left. His ear rang instantly and he dropped on top of the woman, who squirmed violently in protest.

Gopher was aware that one of the other bikers had been hit by the shot. The screaming man sounded a lot like Slasher, but he could not be sure. Gopher had never heard any of these men cry out in pain or terror before and it frightened him to the core.

"Get the hell off *me!*" Trish shouted and punched at him.

"Sorry!" he retorted and rolled from her and onto his knees. He peered into the orange light and was determined to take their attacker down. Turning to his right, he saw the black blur again. He spun his upper body to the left and fired the shotgun.

For a moment, all Gopher could see was the flash of the shot and all he could hear was ringing. Disoriented, he dropped to his knees and pumped another round into the chamber. He saw but could not hear the empty shell as it danced along the floor.

Another gunshot sounded from behind them and another of the group responded in pain and terror. Gopher could not even begin to guess who it was this time. He checked Trish again. She remained on the floor with her hands over her head. Her bare legs trembled against the cement and her black calf-high boots knocked together. He was relieved, as he thought perhaps she had stood as he spun and took some of his shot.

Tires screeched at that moment and Gopher could see that Blades had gotten his machine in gear. It tore off toward the north exit.

"Go, Blades! Go!" Gopher bellowed as loud as he could.

As the motorcycle headed away, its headlight passed over the walls of the garage. At that moment, the black blur entered Gopher's field of vision from the right. The attacker fired another round after the retreating Blades.

Gopher lifted the shotgun to fire another blast at their mysterious attacker, noting that the shot must have missed because Blade was still accelerating. The bright white light narrowed and disappeared out of sight as the machine was shifted from one gear to the next.

Gopher's world lit up as the attacker surprised him with another shot. He was pressed backward into Ironman's motorcycle and, out of control, the young biker took it down with him. Pain exploded in Gopher's chest and his ability to breathe was immediately taken.

A mighty bellowing howl filled the concrete structure. The remaining members of the biker gang turned their attentions toward where it seemed to be the loudest.

"Some...body...kill this ass..." Gopher tried to say. Shot and stabbed in the chest, the remaining air in his lungs was forced from him as his attacker placed a foot on him and pulled the long blade from his body. Almost immediately, the youngest member of the Warlocks died.

***

From the dark depths of the garage, another watched the spectacle through his *CORPS-Link* implant. His lenses had fully adapted to the darkness and he saw the madman sprint in a tight circle, apparently supplied with an infinite supply of oxygen. He ran around and around, flinging throwing knives before knocking the gang leader's woman unconscious and relieving her of her handgun, all while barely slowing his pace.

The bikers, big and tough guys that he knew from afar, fell one after the other. He could not make his feet move, let alone run. He could not blink, let alone look away. The old Marine was transfixed upon the horror unfolding in front of him.

The lone attacker seemed to be wearing a tight black bodysuit, a facial mask, and a pocket-laden belt of a military design. His hair was long, slick with oils and quite dark. The eyes seemed to glow yellow in the greenness of the old man's night vision.

One by one, the Warlocks fell. The Marine felt little pity for them, for they were a violent pack, but when the leader's woman had been knocked hard to the cement floor again, he winced and found himself hoping she was all right. He had seen her often and had become infatuated with the woman. Normally, he would flee from the garage when the Warlocks or other gangs entered the parking garage, but after a time, he remained to watch her. Now, as he looked upon her crumpled form, he feared the worst.

The attacker continued his circular running rampage and fired the last round from the woman's handgun into the young biker who had been firing the shotgun at him with no apparent effect. The old Marine felt a chill arrest his spine as the dark garage was filled with the madman's howl. The black-clad figure retrieved his long blade from the body and tore into the last two men standing. In a flash of flying kicks and punches, he ended both of them with slashes to the throats. Neither man had fired a shot.

The assassin leaned over the prone body of the leader after kicking the gun from his hand. He seemed to say something to the young thug before ending him with a stab to the chest.

The old man crossed himself and whispered a prayer. His body trembled violently as the chill washed over his entire existence.

"Ho...holy sssssh..." His whisper trailed as the attacker's color changed from black to a light gray right before his eyes. The old man's heart pounded and he realized that if he had not already been leaning against the cold concrete wall, he would have fallen.

The other woman in the group shot to her feet and began to run. In a flash, the gray enigma was on her. The vicious animal tackled her to the cement, tore away her clothing, beat her until her sobs quieted, and proceeded to rape her with animalistic urgency.

The retired Marine looked away. Had he a firearm, he would have intervened. The thought occurred that he should try to approach the group of dead men and grab a gun. There were quite a few lying about. He imagined himself taking this monster by surprise and saving the women, at the very least. Using the wall, he lifted himself to his feet.

The beast let out another chilling howl as his use for the young lady had reached its inevitable end. Just as the demonic voice faded away, a loud crack echoed. He had broken the girl's neck.

"Son of a bitch," the Marine hissed as his eyes teared. Such cruelty he had never witnessed. Powerlessly, he slipped down the wall and settled upon the cold floor.

Stunned, he watched the mysterious monster drag the leader's woman by her beautiful blonde hair to the center of the body-strewn camp. Leaving her for the time being, the creature, for the Marine could not regard the thing as human, tore open the chest cavity of one of the male victims and went about cutting through the flesh and ribcage with the long black blade.

Upon this sight, the old man did faint.

***

Elliot Three-Seven stood watching the fresh meat sizzle on the grillwork set upon the burning barrel. He shifted his eyes to the broken female that he had used to death and smiled. She had been more pleasurable than he had anticipated, but was glad he spared the unconscious one for the moment.

He turned the cooking heart with his bayonet and remembered that there had been someone in the building with an implant. Elliot reached out for it by broadcasting another ping. This time, he held it, hacked away the security software, and read the identification tag.

"Semper Fi, Marine!" he called into the fire-flickering darkness. "Master Gunny Sergeant Nash Ferris...front and center!"

Elliot looked about him for the appearance of the older serviceman as he turned the delectable liver on the grill.

"Ah, there you are," Three-Seven called as the old man shuffled within the ring of orange fire light.

For a moment, the old man just stared. He came a little closer before stopping next to the body of the biker gang leader. He dared not look down, for he feared that the monster in front of him planned to pounce. Why he had even come closer, he was not certain. At first, he thought he might drop to the ground and pick up a weapon to remove this crazy man, but he suspected that he had zero chance of pulling that off.

Elliot stabbed a heart and used one of his recovered throwing knives to slice off a piece. "Want some?" He cackled and smiled crazily.

Nash shook his head and gave a grimace.

"Very well," Three-Seven replied and took a big bite of the heart in his hand.

Ferris groaned in disgust and looked away. In doing so, his eyes found a semi-automatic pistol at his feet, lying in a pool of its dead owner's blood.

"Now, now," Elliot chided as he chewed. "No bad thoughts, Ferris. I'll wish you out to the cornfield!" The maniac let out a high-pitched chortle. It was clear that the reference was lost on the older man, which surprised Three-Seven slightly, though he dismissed it. He had watched a collection of twentieth-century two-dimensional entertainment videos that he had found at the Drake residence and had thought them to be commonplace.

Master Gunnery Sergeant Ferris remained still and cleared his throat. "Okay, no problem."

Elliot Three-Seven attacked the heart ravenously. He checked on the fellow soldier as he ate mouthful after mouthful. Thinking the command, he hacked his fellow Marine's implant further. "What was your nickname?" he asked, once he found that he could not seem to discover that information.

"Nickname? I don't have one," Ferris answered.

"Sure you do," Elliot insisted once he picked the last of the meat from the heart and tossed it behind him. "I've been told my predecessors had amusing names for one another."

"Umm, well, I did have a training officer call me 'Slaw'," he answered and thought back. "I used to grab that in the mess hall whenever I could."

"Really? Weird," the FROG replied and gorged on a liver.

Ferris watched the perfectly honed, strangely inhuman teeth and blade-like fingernails tear into the human flesh and felt his head swim. "What are you?"

Elliot glanced to the Marine and flashed a bloody smile as he dropped the pigment of his skin to his default pale pink. Instead of answering verbally, he sent an identification file implant-to-implant. The information displayed immediately upon the older man's lenses without waiting for permission to link.

"What the...?" Nash uttered. He read the unsolicited file, deeply concerned that this cannibalistic monster had the ability to get into his mind and was further revolted to realize that this Elliot Three dash Seven, was indeed a fellow Marine. He mumbled the meaning of the FROG anagram and all at once, understood the creature in front of him. The information packet described the entire FROG program and outlined an individual's qualities and physical features. Under any other circumstances, the old sergeant would have been impressed.

Three-Seven turned from Ferris and went about cracking open another chest cavity.

This time, the older man could not keep from fainting. He turned from the horrific scene and braced himself from the fall.

Some seconds later, when Nash recovered, he realized that the FROG file was gone. He had not the chance to copy it to his *CORPS-Link*. He turned back to his tormentor and grimaced. He could hear the knife cutting into the next body. Nash looked about nervously, figuring he was next. As if his mind were being read, the psychotic FROG spoke.

"There's no reason to fear, brother," Elliot told him as he remained focused on his butcher work.

With that, Nash Ferris quietly stepped away, heading for the exit into the hard rain of the night rather than simply heading for the abandoned structure above them. He was not sure whether this FROG was just setting him up for a hunt or not, but he knew that he would rather meet his death outside than become just another dead body in an unused building. He would likely rot beyond the point of identification before he was found and Nash had always wanted the decency of a proper burial.

Ferris could not help but continually throw glances behind him as he walked up the entrance road. He had not gotten far when the sound of a woman's terrified scream overpowered the thrumming of the falling rain.

Nash stopped and stared into the dark cavern. His night vision caught only the orange of the fire light reflecting from the metal surfaces of the now riderless motorbikes.

Again, the woman screamed. Her cry for help ended with an abruptness that could only mean unconsciousness or death.

Nash turned and broke into a run. It quickly became clear to him that he had not tried running in a long time. After some blocks, his lungs burned, as did every muscle in his legs. A few passersby stopped and watched him go by from underneath their umbrellas or wide-brimmed hats.

Lost and exhausted, he turned into an alley, leaned up against the closest brick building and vomited. His heart pounded dangerously fast and hard. As his left arm became engulfed in pain, his legs failed him. Nash crawled back toward the sidewalk he had crossed.

"Hey, man!" a voice called out from above him. "Holy shit! Don't worry, man! I'm callin' da' medics!"

Nash Ferris's world went dark and he lost consciousness on the sidewalk, face down in a puddle.

**

In the dead of night, with his gullet full of the hearts, livers and the bits of muscle and other flesh he had decided to try, Elliot wiped the blood from his body with the sweat-stained white shirt he had torn from the older of the two women. That one had put up more of a fight than the young one, who had resigned to her fate all too easily. He felt the scratches the second one had gouged into his cheeks and smiled while he dressed.

The meat on the grill sizzled and smoked as he walked into the darkness to retrieve his hat and overcoat. He hurried back to his cooking liver, as it had begun to blacken. Thinking quickly, he skewered the meat and dropped it into a saddlebag attached to one of the larger motorbikes once he had dumped the contents within. He repeated this several more times, hoping to store enough meat for a few days.

Three-Seven's body made immediate use of the intake of calories, allocating much of the energy to healing the bullet wound. The bleeding had all but stopped some minutes after his assaults on the woman had finished.

Elliot stared at the motorbike he had planned on taking. Matching its physical appearance and manufacturer name to his *FROG-ServLink*'s encyclopedia, he verified the placement of the gear shift, clutch, accelerator, and the brakes. It was a large motorcycle powered by an antique internal combustion design. He had always wanted to try one.

He took his time going through the deceased gang's belongings. The weapons that he came across were rather crude and worn, ranging from revolvers like the one he had taken from the older woman, to a mismatched pair of compact sub-machine pistols. He left the shotguns behind as he did not favor them over his blades. Elliot shrugged as he chucked the firearms into the saddlebags, one on either side. The extra magazines he stowed in his coat.

Three-Seven grinned as he inspected one semi-automatic pistol in particular. His implant identified it as a rare model and chambered in a powerful fifty-caliber round. He had to pry the large handgun from the grip of the gang's leader. Upon inspection, its finish had been weathered, worn, and heavily scratched, as if it had been dropped to the pavement a hundred times. Elliot removed the magazine, cycled the action, and caught the ejected round in his palm. The pistol seemed to function well, so he reloaded it and stuffed it in his waistband.

Elliot considered staying in the garage for a time. He was enjoying the warmth from the barrel fires, but his interest in the motorcycle gnawed at him. He turned the key to activate the gauges and found the fuel tank was not but half-full. He fished around the other bikes for a syphon, for certainly there would be at least one amongst the group.

Three-Seven was in luck. From the motorcycle belonging to the now very deceased and partially digested young biker who had nearly filled him with buckshot, he pulled a hand pump with two rubber hoses connected to it. In a matter of a half an hour, he filled the tank.

Though it was raining rather heavily, Elliot yearned to ride the motorcycle. He straddled the machine and flipped the kickstand up with his foot. He gave the key a turn and was rewarded with the nearly instant ignition of all four cylinders beneath him. They settled into a pleasantly uneven idle that, after some revolutions, made an intoxicating rhythm.

In his excitement, Elliot emulated the sound of the engine vocally and smiled like a child as he slipped the bike into first gear and let it roll forward. Immediately, he understood the need to open the throttle in his right hand. He guided the motorcycle beyond the gathered corpses and took a tenuous left turn. With hardly a miscue, Three-Seven mastered the balancing act and quickly shifted into second gear. He gave the throttle a few sudden twists and felt the powerful accelerations.

The powerful white headlight allowed Elliot's night vision to relax and, with one last look and pass around the carnage he had created, he launched himself and the motorcycle through the south exit. He pulled to a stop just outside the garage and gazed beyond the concrete overhang. It was raining hard and he had never ridden a motorcycle before. He smiled over the challenging prospect and throttled up as he let out the clutch. The rear tire spun against the pavement and squealed loudly, giving Three-Seven a strong feeling of satisfaction that he had never experienced.

Elliot changed into second as the bike went from dry to wet cement. The tire lost traction for a moment and the rear end slipped to the right. Quickly, he shifted his weight and let off the throttle until the bike regained traction.

He was engulfed in the heavy rain by the time he reached Michigan Avenue. On a lark, he hung a left, carefully balancing his weight and the throttle to keep the bike under control. In the rainstorm, even his best ocular setting could see hardly further than a normal human could. Despite the danger, he laughed maniacally into the night as he pressed the motorcycle beyond one hundred kilometers per hour. The spray of the rain covered his face and he drank from it.

As the blocks rolled by, the pavement became more and more neglected. Elliot held the speed, nonetheless, daring the conditions to throw him from the machine. Weaving with quickly learned care, he made it around most of the potholes, but a few jolted the big, powerful bike. Still, he maintained ninety-five KPH. As the black hat caught a gust of wind under the wide brim, it was forced from his head. Elliot's laughter continued hyena-like. He realized that he was having too much fun to care about the loss of the stolen hat.

His greasy black hair was cleansed by the torrent of rain and the assault of the wind. His ears were filled by the thrumming engine and the continuous collision with the air.

A shocking jolt halted his laughter mid-gale. He had struck a gaping hole in the street, which seemed large enough to swallow a small child. The tires lost contact with the pavement for less than a second, but the rear end was sent askew when it returned, as he failed to lessen the throttle. His heartrate increased immediately, and for the briefest of moments, Elliot Three-Seven felt something beyond exhilaration.

Fear!

Elliot let the throttle snap to idle, counter steered, and balanced to keep upright. He closed his fingers around the clutch to disengage the power from the wheel and found that he had to counterbalance in the other direction. The tail end of the great motorcycle wagged like a dog's. His right foot met the brake for the rear as his right hand grasped the brake lever for the front. Together, he was able to slow the bike and bring the back wheel under control, just in time to keep himself from striking another hole.

"Fear! Yes!" Elliot shouted gleefully. He remembered it now. It was the emotion he had originally discovered during his first parachute lesson. It had melted away quickly, but it had happened upon his stepping out of the airplane. Three-Seven smiled as he recalled the reaction of his recent victims. "I gave fear to you! To them!" he called into the rain. "I am…the giver of fear. Fright," Elliot confirmed for himself and nodded vigorously.

The FROG's mind was flooded with the sudden and complete understanding that he had been guided to this failing city. Whether it was by a god or some unknown and untapped form of telepathy, Elliot understood that he had been sent to Chicago to dispense his gift of terror.

"They will relearn their fear!" he cried out above the din of the machine he straddled. "I will give them the gift of myself…and they will worship me! Fear and respect me!"

Three-Seven took the motorcycle out of gear and placed both feet upon the ground. He remained there, accumulating rainwater as the engine grumbled out its strangely beautiful rhythm.

"Pa-cha, pa-cha, pa-pa-cha, pa-cha, pa-cha, pa-cha, pa-pa-cha," Elliot emulated in a childlike voice, over and over until he fell into lighthearted giggling.

As he sat thinking, he looked about the landscape he had ridden into. He realized that, at some point, he had left the large apartment complexes and the commercial high-rises behind. There were small trees and overgrowth in the center islands of Michigan Avenue and larger trees on either side of the road, but the buildings scattered among them were small, decrepit, and appeared uninhabitable. Still, he noted flickering orange light in the windows of a few of them.

Elliot adjusted his vision to its maximum magnification of six times, but was still defeated by the rainy gloom. This intersection was missing its street sign and he had not counted the blocks he had ridden.

There was not a vehicle in sight that was not an abandoned hulk lying on an empty lot or left at the curb. There was no sound beyond his engine and the weather, even though the sky to the southeast flashed with lightning. Thunder was still too far away. He had wandered beyond civilization.

Elliot put the bike back in gear and guided it eastward. He rode on and on, passing over intersection after intersection until the seemingly endless gray of Lake Michigan loomed ahead of him. He slowed and turned north onto a multi-lane highway that he knew had to be Lake Shore Drive. At a more reasonable pace he rode, noting the improvement of the pavement as he came closer to the city's center. Lightning lit the gray to a brilliant white and Three-Seven heard the thunderclap just over the sound of his motor. The heart of the storm was still approaching.

I will teach them all. One after the other.

He rode on and on, pushing the bike to higher speeds as he found himself returning to McCormick Place. Much of it lay on the left side of the road, while the remains of the Arie Crown Theatre and vast convention halls took up the right.

Though the rain stung his face and forced him to squint to see, Elliot decided to ride on. Soon after, however, a looming, half-dish shaped structure appeared ahead of him. He slowed as he checked his *FROG-ServLink* to discover what it might be.

Ah. Soldier Field.

Part Three

Agent Jerry Quinne stepped out of the terminal with his baggage trailing behind him in the grip of one hand and a briefcase in the other. He walked to the curb ahead of his reluctant and much older companion.

Quinne was about to raise his arm for the cab when he heard his name called from his left. Looking toward it, he could see Marcus Williams standing next to his unmarked police cruiser.

"Come on, Professor," Jerry said over his shoulder. "It's an old friend of mine. The reason we're here, really."

The older man sighed. "I am not a professor, Agent Quinne. I'm a doctor."

Jerry Quinne rolled his eyes unobserved by the man behind him and strolled to the dented and faded gray sedan. He and Williams shook hands and the luggage was placed in the trunk. The three men jumped inside the car to get out of the mist of the gray spring shower.

"Marcus, this is Dr. Mitch Ruger," the FBI agent said in a professional tone. He gestured to the elderly man in the rear seat. "Dr. Ruger, this is Detective Marcus Williams."

"Nice to meet you, sir," Williams replied and shook the old man's hand gently. He was a small man with white wispy hair and thin, bony appendages. The doctor's hand felt especially fragile.

"Same here," he returned somewhat reservedly and with only a hint of a smile. Once his hand was released, he retreated to the comfort of the back seat.

Quinne and Williams shared a quick glance. His agent friend made his eyes bug out slightly in mock frustration. Marcus smiled and manually drove the cruiser away from the curb.

"So, what's new on the case, anything?" Jerry Quinne asked.

"Well, last night, we had a wanted man drive himself to the hospital, claiming that some sort of monster had attacked his gang. He was shot in the back with a small caliber revolver," Marcus explained while merging onto the interstate that would take them downtown.

"What did he say, then?" Quinne pressed.

"He passed out in the ER before he said anything further," Marcus continued and set the cruiser to automatic. He turned to Quinne and could see Dr. Ruger in the corner of his eye. "He was rushed into surgery, where they removed the bullet and patched him up, but it appears to have nicked a kidney pretty good. Frank Campanelli is with the uniforms guarding the door."

"But that could be anything," the doctor piped up. "What makes you think that he's talking about one of my FROGs?"

"Dr. Quinne, the man I'm talking about is Scott Kabel, a.k.a., Blades." Marcus expectantly watched the doctor's face for signs of recognition. There was none. "He's wanted for murder in two other states besides ours. He's got an extensive arrest record for A and B, armed robbery, and a few counts of murder."

"Career criminal," Jerry grumbled.

"Yes," Marcus nodded and again watched the doctor's face for a reaction. "He's a badass that would never turn himself in to the police unless he was legitimately frightened over something."

"Most likely, it was one of his own people," Dr. Ruger inserted with certainty. "A FROG can use any number of weapons, but if this man was shot in the back, it was one of his own."

"We can't be sure of that until he regains consciousness, Doctor," Williams answered.

"I suppose," Ruger mumbled.

"Anyway, we're on our way to the hospital," Marcus stated.

***

Campanelli sat in the hospital room with Scott Kabel and contemplated the thirty-eight-year-old in silence. Blades was the epitome of a tough biker. Somewhat taller than Frank and muscular, the man's predominately black hair was salted with white, both at his temples and in his beard.

From what was pieced together from the rambling wounded man, the Warlocks had been on a ride and then had returned to their frequent hiding place only to be slaughtered, if what Kabel said was true and not some symptom of being a quart or two low on blood.

Normally, this man would be in the hands of a homicide detective, as Kabel was wanted for murder, but since his last words before collapsing in the ER indicated that the Warlocks had encountered the serial killer they were looking for, he appointed himself for the duty.

Kabel stirred. The oxygen mask covering most of his face fogged up fully and the man's head began to thrash from one direction to the other. As Blades's eyelids remained closed, Frank deduced that the biker was having a nightmare.

Campanelli stood up and stretched. He had been sitting there waiting for nearly six hours, having been awakened by a phone call by Detective Lyman at a quarter of two in the morning. He had offered to do the waiting in the room for him, but as Frank's sleep was light and restless anyway, he had volunteered to go. Campanelli had drifted in and out of sleep in the recliner, listening to the beeping heart monitor and the hissing of the oxygen machine.

Frank stepped to the side of the bed and tightened his tie from habit. Kabel's head went from one side to the other and a groan of despair was muffled by the mask.

"Mr. Kabel," Detective Campanelli called. "Scott Kabel."

The wounded biker grunted in response to his given name. His eyes fluttered open and searched the white tiled ceiling.

Frank repeated the biker's name, following it up with his Warlock nickname. Kabel's eyes followed the voice. He blinked his eyes to focus and as he did, tried to move his right arm. The handcuffs kept Kabel from moving it very far. He looked from his right to his left. Both wrists were linked to the bed frame. Scott gazed into the face of the detective staring down at him.

"Thank you," he croaked.

"Thank me? Thank me for what, Mr. Kabel?" Campanelli inquired and placed his hands in his pants pockets. "Thank your surgeon."

"I will," Scott said in a tone of promise. "But you're arresting me, right?"

"Sure." Frank shrugged with a smile on his face. "I'm Detective Frank Campanelli and I'd like to know why you have this change of heart and want to turn yourself in."

"Well, that thing was yours, right?" Blades asked through the mask. It was clearly an obstacle to conversation.

Frank leaned over and tugged the oxygen mask to the man's chin. "What thing, Mr. Kabel?"

Blades chuckled and put on a weak smile. "Yeah, good one."

"Does it look like I know what you're talking about?" Campanelli pressed and continued quickly. "An ER nurse said that you were running on about some monster."

The door to Kabel's room opened and Williams, Quinne, and Ruger entered.

"Yeah," Scott Kabel confirmed. "That thing moved so fast...in the dark. I couldn't see the fuckin' thing, but he…whipped knives into the group. You're telling me that he didn't belong to you?"

"That's what I'm sayin', Kabel," Frank answered with a nod.

"Jesus Christ!" Blades went on and pulled at the cuffs. "He was everywhere…just running around us in a blur, just outside our campfires."

Frank turned to Marcus and raised his eyebrows.

"Frank, this is Agent Jerry Quinne and Dr. Mitchell Ruger," Williams said and stepped to the side.

Campanelli shook hands with both men. "Glad you're here. He just came 'round. Nice timing." Quinne nodded. Ruger was a painting of a man not happy to be where he was or what Kabel had just been saying.

"If that thing's not yours, you've got a big fucking problem in this town," Kabel said with great agitation. He shook the bed with further futile attempts to free his arms.

"Knock that off!" Frank commanded and leaned both hands on the rails. "Tell us what you saw and where this all happened."

Williams stepped to the left of Campanelli, giving his friend and the doctor a clear view of Scott Kabel.

"Okay." Kabel took a deep breath and tried to calm down. "We just rolled into town ahead of the storm. Me and the rest of 'em went to camp at McCormick's garage."

"That's a known hangout of yours," Frank informed him and acted as if he was becoming impatient. "What else?"

"Just after we lit the fires to get warm, this…whatever fuckin' thing…attacked." Kabel's voice rose in volume. He noted a stern look from Campanelli and the muscular and taller Williams behind him. Scott took another deep breath and went on. "He started with knives…throwing 'em into the crowd of us as he ran in a circle around the camp. Then he knocked Nan flat to the floor. She didn't move after that. This monster...picked up her gun and started firing into us."

"Still running in a circle?" asked Agent Quinne.

Kabel nodded frantically. "He was incredibly fast. Couldn't see him. I got on my bike and got the fuck out of there!"

"At what point did he shoot you?" Campanelli asked.

"Um...I didn't even know I was hit until I was outside. It must have been on my way out."

"Did you get a look at him? His face?" Quinne asked next.

"No, he was just a...black blur, running around us. Never seen anything so damn fast."

Williams noted Quinne giving Dr. Ruger a look. Ruger's eyebrows rose slowly and he crossed his arms in front of him and casually wiped his bearded chin. Marcus could not tell whether the two were having an implant-to-implant conversation, or if it was just a knowing glance, but he did not like it.

Kabel quieted for a moment, but continued when he thought of another detail. "And the damn thing howled," he said excitedly while his eyes teared with fright. "It let out this noise. It was so damn loud. So loud, I couldn't hear the rain anymore."

"Which garage at McCormick Place?" asked Frank.

"Uh...it's at the corner of Indiana...southwest corner, next to that old expressway."

"We'll check it out, Mr. Kabel," Campanelli said in a calming tone. "Don't go anywhere, we'll be talking again."

Blades lifted both arms as high up as he could make them, making the cuffs clink loudly. "You're funny."

With that, the four men stepped out of the small hospital room and walked slowly down the hall toward the elevators.

"We've got to roll there right away, Frank," Marcus opined as the door closed behind them.

"Yeah," Frank agreed, and linked with the CPD computer, using the hospital's server. He brought up an overview of the abandoned facility and located the garage of which Kabel spoke. "What do you think, Dr. Ruger?" he asked, while sending the orders.

Mitchell Ruger shrugged. "A FROG is definitely capable of such an assault. They are extremely well coordinated and can sprint for longer periods of time than we can. Their heart and lung capacity is double the efficiency of ours." He said this with a faint trace of pride.

Campanelli requested a SWAT team, though he was all but certain their maniac would be nowhere near the scene. The men stepped onto the elevator and descended to the ground floor. Once in the parking lot, Williams connected to his cruiser and granted access to Agent Quinne. He walked with Frank to his car and dropped into the passenger seat with a stifled grunt.

"How you doin'?" Campanelli asked as he started the engine.

"I'm good. Let's go."

Quinne and Ruger followed Campanelli's cruiser with lights and sirens once they were away from the hospital.

"So, what's with this Dr. Ruger?" Frank asked as he guided the car manually. He was not in pursuit of anything, so he kept the pace sane, much to his partner's relief.

"Quinne told me he was a genetic engineer."

"Was he part of the team that created these damn FROGs?"

"Yes, but I don't know just how involved. It's all classified stuff."

The Captain of Detectives grunted in response. As he guided the cruiser through a right turn onto Indiana

Avenue, he reviewed the orders he had created for the mission.

"Unit five-one-six-two to dispatch," he called out to his dash radio.

"*Five-one-six-two. Go ahead*," the dispatcher replied immediately.

"Revision to orders for McCormick location," he continued. "I want three or four squads covering the north entrance to the parking garage. SWAT commander is to meet me at the garage exit. We're going in through the out door."

"*Roger five-one-six-two. Will amend.*"

Frank gave Kirby McLain's apartment building a glance as they drove past. He felt a flash of anger and the lust for revenge rise up in his chest. He drove on, and, despite slowing to check for traffic at the intersection at Cermak Road, his cruiser overrode him and stopped. The police car that Quinne was driving pulled alongside and did the same. The cause for this was immediately apparent as the sound of warbling sirens filled the air. Two marked squad cars rolled through the intersection in response to Campanelli's orders.

In his rearview mirror, Frank could see the SWAT van, a little more than a block behind. The danger clear, the cruiser continued on. Impatient, Campanelli mashed the accelerator and shot down the street, leaving Quinne and Ruger well behind.

Frank silenced the siren and drove on to the dead end, where Indiana Avenue was interrupted by the Stevenson Expressway. He turned left, entering the parking garage of McCormick through the exit. Not wanting to venture too far inside, he guided the car up the curb at his left and parked. As he and Williams climbed out of the car, Quinne turned in, and was followed by the SWAT van.

Campanelli walked to the van as the SWAT team filed out of the back. "Who's the commander here?"

A SWAT member pointed to the driver, who was hopping out. "I am."

Frank noticed the stripes on the man's sleeve and his name tag. "Sergeant Frohm, I'm Campanelli, Sentinel Division. I'm on loan to homicide."

"Pleasure," Frohm smiled and shook Frank's hand.

"This is my partner, Marcus Williams," Campanelli said.

"Pleasure," Frohm repeated with Williams's giant hand in his. "Jesus, you should be on my team."

Marcus chuckled. "Naw...waaay too dangerous for me."

"This is Agent Quinne and Dr. Ruger," Frank went on, gesturing to the two men standing behind him. The men all shook hands.

"FBI, huh? Just what do we have here, guys?" the SWAT commander asked while readying his automatic rifle. His joviality faded into stern professionalism.

Frank looked over the assembling half dozen men. "We have a suspected crime spree inside the parking area," he said as his hand pointed toward the innermost depths of the structure, "courtesy of our serial killer. Heard about 'im?"

Frohm nodded and ran his hand over his curly white hair before placing his black helmet over it. "Oh, yeah."

"A witness has stated that his biker gang was jumped at this location. We're here to check it out and I'm taking into account that our suspect may still be here. Probably isn't."

"Gotcha," said Frohm. He turned to his squad, all of whom were young men and not equipped with implants. "Break out the goggles."

A marked car rolled into the garage and parked, adding to the blue flashes that kept the shadows at bay. Campanelli had not asked for it, but it was understood that other units that were not occupied could assist. Frank recognized the driver. It was Sergeant Louis Marx, whom he had met at McLain's apartment.

"We'll follow your men in," Campanelli said and pointed to the elderly doctor. "Except for you, sir. I want you to stay here."

Ruger nodded. To Frank, the man appeared to be quite nervous. He was looking all about the area, as if in search of an escape.

"Sergeant Marx!" the Captain of Detectives called over his shoulder.

"Yes, sir!"

"Watch this man for me. He's a civvie."

"You got it."

Frank turned to Frohm. "Ready when you boys are."

The SWAT commander nodded and ordered his men through their weapons and gear check. A moment later, they headed further into the parking garage with Frohm in the lead. Equipped with an implant, he needed no additional visual aid.

Frank watched as the SWAT team walked along the wall to their left. He followed with his eleven-millimeter drawn. Marcus Williams and Quinne kept close to Campanelli with their own handguns at the ready.

Frohm reached the corner, crouched and peered around it. He could see motorcycles, metal drums and the body of a male. He stood, stepped back, and relayed his findings to the team and the others.

Frank and Marcus sighed. Both men were relieved that the tip was not bogus, but the prospect of another murder scene removed any joy from it.

Frohm moved in with his team closely behind. Frank and company followed with their guns up and eyesight adjusted for darkness. The only light to be found within was from the entrance on the far side.

The SWAT team cleared the immediate area and encircled the gory crime scene. One of them let out a string of profanity over the horror.

"Can it," Frohm ordered.

For several tense minutes, the nine men searched and listened for signs of any live occupants within the garage. It was soon clear they were the only living creatures within the dark structure save for insects and rats, some of which had long before discovered the bodies. They scampered away with the approach of live humans.

Frank stared down into the face of a young woman. Her clothes were torn from her body and she had been beaten. Her body had been assaulted in almost every way possible and left with her legs splayed far apart.

"Son of a bitch is a rapist, too," he grumbled.

"Nine men, two women, Frank," Williams informed him. "Looks like he raped both females."

"I'm calling for Rothgery and Gherling," Campanelli said as he connected to the cruiser's computer. The signal was weak, considering the location, but the order went through.

Quinne returned his pistol to the holster under his suit jacket and kneeled next to a body lying near one of the drums. "You were right about that cannibalism, Marcus," he said to his friend. "Heart and liver cut out. Crude and fast."

"Yep," Marcus agreed. He was not yet ready to stand down. He kept his nine-millimeter in his hand and his eyes wandering about the garage.

"Looks like there's remnants of meat on this grill over there," Frank said from his place near the other. "Watch your step, there's blood everywhere." He moved from it as the other two came to inspect his finding. His eyes passed over the bodies as he sauntered around the kill zone. "He only took from five."

"What's that, Frank?" Williams asked and walked over to his partner.

"He killed all these people...and only chose to feed on five," he reiterated and pointed them out. "Quinne?"

"Yeah."

"What might this Dr. Ruger be able to add to this?"

The FBI agent stepped closer to Campanelli before answering and kept his voice low. "Well, from what Marcus described to me, we were thinking this was a FROG. Dr. Ruger was part of the team that designed them from the DNA up. He's not convinced that one of them would turn this...psychotic."

Williams walked up to the two men, listening with interest, though his eyes never stopped moving.

"Great," Frank muttered. "What's your analysis?"

"I've seen some training video of these FROG guys," Quinne said as he looked over the carnage in the circle of abandoned motorcycles. "There's no way these bikers were unarmed, so they must have put up a fight."

"I'm calling Marx. Telling him to bring Ruger in here," Frank announced and connected with the officer.

Quinne nodded and moved off, observing the scene, but being careful not to disturb anything. His stomach churned from the sight and the smells that had begun to emanate from the corpses.

The SWAT team formed a loose circle around the sight. None of them wanted to come any closer, but as experienced officers, they knew that the crime scene needed to be inspected by a forensics team. Frohm approached Campanelli.

"The area's clear."

"I'd like you boys to stick around awhile," the Captain of Detectives directed. "Your role is one of security now."

"Sure thing," Frohm agreed. He moved off and called out orders to his squad.

As Frank sauntered around the sight, he noticed a blood trail. Looking closer, he noted that it was, in fact, tire tracks that had rolled through the blood. He followed it around and saw that it faded halfway around the circle of dead.

"What is that? Oh. Tracks," Marcus said.

"Looks like he can ride," Frank said lowly. "Stole a big one, too. Wide tires."

The two of them noticed Ruger and the two uniformed patrolmen approach them. It was dark for the doctor, as he was without bio-electronics. Marx touched his elbow to keep the old man from stepping into the blood pool at his feet.

"Dear God, what is that smell?" Ruger asked the moving shadows around him.

"Thought you might need this," Sergeant Marx spoke up and handed the doctor a flashlight.

"Good thinking, Sarge," Campanelli commended then turned to Mitchell Ruger. "That is the stench of eleven dead people, Doctor."

Ruger reluctantly searched out the light's switch and gulped as he pressed it. Immediately, the ripped open chest cavity of a young biker was lit upon. Mitchell covered his mouth and gagged within a few seconds.

Quinne guided the old man away. "You okay, Professor?"

Ruger could not speak. With his back turned and well away from the crime scene, he released his breakfast.

Frank turned to Marcus. "This may take a while."

Williams nodded, unsmiling.

After a couple of moments, Mitchell Ruger returned to the corpse and lit it up with his borrowed flashlight. To his credit, the initial reaction seemed only to strengthen him.

Holding his white handkerchief to his mouth and nose, the old genetics expert walked around the entire crime scene. Frank followed him closely with Marcus and Jerry Quinne just behind.

When Ruger discovered the body of the younger of the two women, he stopped and let out a sympathetic groan.

"You okay?" Campanelli asked of him.

Mitchell nodded. "Looks...looks like my daughter...a little."

"This girl was raped by the suspect before he ran his bayonet through her neck," Campanelli stated flatly, but not unkindly. He pointed out the entry wound, located on the right side of her neck, just under her jawline.

"Triangular," Ruger muttered and gagged. He stood and took a step back. "That fits."

"How so, Doctor?" Campanelli pressed as he studied the man's face.

"That bayonet was standard equipment for the FROGs' assault weapons," the old man said. "Carbon fiber, eighteen inches long, with a short handle."

Frank nodded, but studied the old geneticist's face.

"What I don't understand is this...cannibalism," Ruger nearly whined as he looked to Quinne.

"Do you consider it an impossibility?" Campanelli pushed.

"They weren't designed for it," Ruger explained. From behind him, H. Lincoln Rothgery's van entered the garage, halting at a SWAT member's guidance. "For that matter, neither was this rape. They've been taught to respect noncombatants. This...all this...took rage. They weren't supposed to be capable of this."

"This one's learned new tricks, Dr. Ruger," Frank said accusatorily.

"We haven't even proven this is a FROG yet, Detective," Quinne interjected in defense.

Campanelli ignored the FBI agent and turned to the approaching Rothgery. "Lincoln. Good morning."

"For some," the tall man replied as his eyes passed over what he could see by the light of his and Terry Wilkin's flashlights.

Frank introduced Ruger and Quinne to his forensic scientists.

"Lincoln, Dr. Ruger requires some kind of proof that this...*thing* is his or not," Campanelli said.

"Certainly. I have something to show you, Doctor," H. Lincoln said as he set his toolbox down upon the cement floor. Opening it, he retrieved a manila folder. From within that, he removed an eight by ten print and held it out to the elderly geneticist.

Mitchell placed the light on the picture, angling it so that it did not glare. After a moment, he nodded, reluctantly. "These pictures are of a FROG epidermis. I recognize it."

"Taken from the Drake residence, this matches the sample we retrieved from Detective McLain's body," Rothgery said to the group. He turned to Wilkins and pointed to the dead female near them. "Check her fingernails, would you?"

"Sure," Wilkins responded and removed a handheld device from the box. She stepped to the dead woman and looked her over with the flashlight in her mouth. After a moment, she straightened to her full height, well shorter than Rothgery, and held the scanner up to him. He nodded. She turned the device so the geneticist could inspect it.

"I...just..." Ruger looked about, uncertain. He nodded at Wilkins and Rothgery, confirming the pattern was identical. It was clear he had much more to say. "Not sure why...this," he finished with his arms outspread. The man was close to tears.

"Let's go somewhere and talk," Campanelli more than suggested. "Lincoln, a full report, when you can."

"Yep."

The Captain of Detectives led the other three out the way they came in. He and Marcus got into his cruiser and left the garage with Quinne and Ruger once again in the car behind them.

"Incoming call," the car's computer piped over the speakers. *"Detective Lyman."*

"Answer," Frank directed.

"Frank. We've got another witness. One that was in McCormick during that attack on the Warlocks. He said he spoke to the man," Lyman chattered excitedly.

"Get outta town!" Marcus blurted.

"Honest to crap, guys," Hank went on, *"Nash Ferris, sixty years of age. He says that the man told him his name was Elliot and they exchanged ID's via implant. This guy saw the whole thing."*

"Did Ferris call this in?" Frank asked.

"Yeah, from a hospital bed. He said he was so scared he ran from the place until his heart gave out. He's here in County Hospital."

"Do you have his complete statement, Hank?" Campanelli inquired as he gave his partner a glance.

"Yes, sir. Me and Davies left him to rest. He's not in good shape."

"Meet me at my office, pronto."

"On the way!" Lyman agreed, and ended the call.

"Yes!" Frank exclaimed. "We're getting closer to catching this bastard!"

***

Campanelli led the group from the parking lot of the District One Station into his office on the second floor. Lyman and Davies were there waiting. He introduced Quinne and Ruger to them. The doctor and FBI agent were invited to sit. Williams and the two homicide detectives remained standing, fanned out behind the chairs.

"Okay, Lyman," Frank opened as he took a seat behind his desk, "give us the details of that report from this Nash Ferris fellow."

Hank Lyman nodded and began to read off what he had entered into the statement. His implant had taken it all in via audio receptor and placed it in a text file. The statement took nearly ten minutes to get through.

"Doctor?" Campanelli prodded. "Your thoughts?"

"It checks out...it all does," Ruger answered as his shoulders sagged in surrender of his disbelief. His eyes teared thickly. "Elliot Three-Seven is one of mine."

"Tell us about these FROGs, Doctor," Campanelli directly gently. "We need to stop him."

Ruger nodded. "Yes, quite so." The old man recovered his composure and looked over the faces of the men in the room. He was quiet for a moment before continuing.

"Well, I was part of a group of geneticists that were put into the FROG Development Group. Most did not know the end product they were working on. What I mean is, some created the ears, others the eyes, some the olfactory devices, and so on. I was in charge of the epidermis layer. Those pictures that your forensics man showed me, he's probably perplexed over their matrix. See, the FROGs are...were...capable of changing the pigment of their skin for camouflage. This collaborates with Nash Ferris's statement. A FROG can also heal very quickly, if he has a source of calories. This explains how he keeps walking away from incidents like the car crash and being shot. The body begins healing immediately."

"Are you telling me that this FROG is invincible, Dr. Ruger?" Frank interjected and dropped his fedora to his desk.

"No, not at all," Mitchell answered. "His skeletal density kept him from incurring a fatal blow during the car crash. He crawled away and healed himself. Had your

Detective McLain shot him in the heart, Elliot would certainly be dead."

"What about the head?" Williams put in. "You're saying that the skeleton is reinforced somehow."

"That would depend on the range and type of weapon, but the skull is bullet-resistant. The bone is made up of concentrations of everything that makes up ours. Calcium, vitamins, K, D, what-have-you, but they're also mated with titanium."

"Jesus," Davies muttered from his place near the door.

"Yes, it was quite successful," Ruger said, turning to the man's voice. "The titanium would eventually leach into the layers of the bone and get stronger over time if it were properly managed."

"Doctor," Campanelli interrupted. "This is fascinating. To the task at hand, please."

Mitchell Ruger nodded. "Yes. Well, your detective shot Elliot, but he was able to heal quickly once he got some rest and later," he swallowed, "the protein and calories from those…poor victims."

"So, to kill him, he has to be dealt a fatal blow from the start?" Agent Quinne asked next.

"Well, yes, Jerry," Ruger answered. "If he were to have a major artery opened and he bled out quickly, that would kill him. Give him time to stop the bleeding, the artery could repair itself in minutes."

"How the hell is that possible, Doctor?" Campanelli asked.

"Nanites," Williams guessed.

"Yes! Exactly, Detective," Ruger answered excitedly and pointed to the ex-SEAL. "But unlike the nanites that are inserted into the human body that assemble the bio-electronic devices, these are *living* entities. A cybernetic nanite, made of human cells with computerized brains. They move to the site of the wound and become part of the flesh. Then, the computer brain in every cell removes itself from the area and rejoins the healing collective. It was so exciting to watch in testing."

"And the more he eats…the more protein-rich the food, the faster he can heal," Frank surmised.

"Well, there is a point where the healing can't progress any faster, but yes. I've witnessed a nine-inch long slash with a surgical knife, deep into the dermis layer, close and heal in under fifteen minutes."

Lyman and Davies looked to one another and cussed softly.

Frank Campanelli turned his eyes to Quinne, then to Williams. Both men appeared impressed, but unsurprised. Mitchell Ruger fell silent, though his expression indicated there was much more to tell.

"His name is Elliot Three dash Seven, right?" Frank asked next.

"Correct."

"That doesn't mean there's thirty-seven of these things out there, does it?"

"No, Detective," Doctor Ruger replied with a shake of his head. "The three is the squad number and the seven indicates his place in the squad. He is the seventh member. There are ten per squad and four full squads were created."

"Jesus," exuded Quinne. "There are forty of these things, Professor?"

"No, not any longer, and that's Doctor, not professor, Agent Quinne."

"Just how many are left?" Frank inserted.

"Elliot is the last, Detective Campanelli," Ruger answered with certainty.

"How do you know this for sure?"

Ruger took a deep breath and slowly let it out. He shifted uncomfortably in his chair. "Because I was there when the directive to eliminate the FROGs was carried out."

Quinne and Williams shared a hard look. Both ex-military men knew what that meant.

"Explain, please," Campanelli pressed in a quiet voice. He did not wish to, but needed to hear it.

"Well, the government decided that they were too expensive to maintain and too dangerous to let out into the population. They hadn't been socialized with any standard human beings other than the doctors and technicians...and the Marines on the base."

"So, you and your team were ordered to kill them," Williams added. He was seething as he leaned against the mostly empty bookshelf behind him.

Ruger swallowed and nodded sharply. "Yes. Their barracks were sealed and flooded with ether one night as they slept. Elliot was one of the strongest and most intelligent in the group. He rarely slept and, when he did, it was never deeply. He woke a few of his squad members and they broke out of the barracks. He and two others then succeeded in leaving the base. They were chased down and killed, save for Elliot."

"What base was this, Doctor?" Williams asked.

"I have to tell you that's classified, Detective," Ruger answered apologetically. "It's also not germane to our situation."

Williams looked to Campanelli and rolled his eyes.

"Can you at least tell us when this event occurred, Doctor?" Frank asked as he leaned forward on his desk and intertwined his fingers. He looked at the old man with a hard gaze.

"Not specifically, I'm afraid, but I can say it was within the last eight months."

"So, these FROGs had no parents, just donors, correct?" Williams asked.

"That's right. They are incubated and grown at an accelerated rate and awakened at a post-pubescent state. Their education and military training began immediately, and their rate of growth would continue until young adulthood. It stabilizes there."

"Stabilizes?" Campanelli's eyebrows lifted.

"Yes. They were not supposed to age in order to serve for an indefinite period. However, that wasn't achievable. The best we could manage was to slow it significantly." Ruger fell silent and looked to the Captain of Detectives.

"Okay. So, Doctor, what is your opinion of Elliot's next moves? Where can we look for him?" Frank asked and sat back in his chair. It sighed and creaked.

"It's difficult to say," Mitchell Ruger answered and formed his fingers into a steeple. "He is most certainly fully healed by now, unless the biker gang was able to injure him."

"That's not evident in the eyewitness's statement," Lyman interjected. "Ferris indicated that they couldn't lay a finger on him."

"And he's able to ride a motorcycle," Campanelli added. "Two bikes left that garage. The first was Kabel's and the second left a blood trail around the kill zone before it left."

"How did he learn how to ride a motorcycle?" Detective Davies asked from his place at the closed door.

"All he had to do was study the machine, let his implant discover the model and show Elliot where the controls are and how to ride it," Dr. Ruger answered. "FROGs were intended to be able to use any type of vehicle they came across nearly instantly."

"So, Doctor, what do you think his next move is?" Campanelli asked. "Will he try to leave the city, knowing that the search for him is intensifying?"

"Detective Campanelli," Mitchell began and shifted in the chair, "I couldn't even have predicted his fall into psychosis. He's turned into a serial murderer, a rapist, *and* a cannibal. I can't account for any of it, let alone predict what he might do next."

"Great," Frank muttered and thumped his armrest with a fist.

"I will be happy to help," Ruger added. "I mean, if I get a chance to talk to him, maybe I can get him to surrender."

"Doctor..." Quinne shook his head doubtfully.

"Jerry, I know Elliot pretty well," Mitchell said and turned to face the FBI man. "I knew all of those boys, quite well. Maybe I can get through to him."

"Dr. Ruger," Quinne interrupted and waved his hand. "This is not a man. We're not out to arrest him."

The four CPD detectives in the room looked to one another quickly. To Frank, Marcus appeared unsurprised. Lyman and Davies, in contrast, dropped their mouths open in shock.

"Jerry!" Ruger shouted.

"Doc!" Quinne returned. "This is a creature! A dangerous one. This is not a manhunt. We cannot put such a...murderous....*thing* in prison!"

"Detective Campanelli, you can't subscribe to this," Ruger blurted and stood.

"Dr. Ruger," Frank shot back, "you can't expect us to contain Elliot. It's likely that he would be turned over to the Marines for final disposal."

Mitchell Ruger froze with his mouth wide open and staring back into the face of Frank Campanelli as if the career policeman was a demon. All were silent for nearly half a minute while Ruger's turmoil boiled, then seemed to simmer and cool. He sat down, sighed heavily and nodded.

"You're right, of course, Detective," the elderly doctor said lowly. "I guess I've been too close to the project to be objective."

181 • Campanelli: Siege of the Nighthunter

"Will you stay on with us and advise?" Campanelli asked him. "Now that we've positively identified the suspect, I suppose you could return home, if you choose."

"I'll remain," Ruger said solemnly.

"Good," Frank commended. "All right, I'm going to Chief Sebastian and recommending that SWAT be outfitted with AA-Suits. They're not going to like it, but they need to know that this Elliot Three dash Seven is more than worthy of their discomfort."

Williams raised his hand. "I'd like to join them. Temporarily, of course."

Frank regarded his partner for a long moment. He knew he was more than qualified for the position, considering his military background. *"What about your collarbone?"* he transmitted in a voice text.

"It's just fine, Frank. With the AA-Suit's strength-amps, I won't even notice," Marcus sent back.

Campanelli nodded. "Okay, Marcus. I'll have Frohm's squad take you on and we'll be the spear of the task force," he said, then addressed the rest of the room. "Any questions?"

No one said anything. They seemed anxious to move on.

"All right," Frank said and stood. "Lyman and Davies, I want you to spread this report to the rest of the homicide squad. I want everyone's input on this. I'll be meeting with Sebastian in a little while. Dr. Ruger, Agent Quinne, you'll be coming along with me. Marcus, go find Sergeant Frohm and relay my orders."

***

Frank walked in the door of his apartment that evening well after seven. Exhausted, he set his fedora on the kitchen counter, draped his overcoat on the back of a chair, and dropped his body upon it.

"Hi, hon," Tam greeted. "Wow. You're tired."

He could only nod.

"Let me warm up a plate for you."

"Thank you," he mumbled. "I need to shut the implant down. It needs a recharge."

"Okay," she replied. She had seen the feature on the news and assumed that he was still on loan to homicide. "Is this about the Nighthunter?"

"What?" Frank answered as his vision left him. In his darkness, his police instinct told him what had occurred. "Oh. Was the McCormick Place incident on the news?"

"Oh, yeah," she answered while placing a dish of food in front of him. She placed a fork in his hand and told him what was on the plate and where.

"Ah, thank you," he replied, and dug in. "So, Nighthunter, huh?"

"That's what the news people called him," she said from the chair next to him. "Is that not what you guys are calling him?"

"We don't give names to serial killers, Tam. That's media hype."

"Oh."

Frank ate his chicken stir-fry in silent contemplation as Tamara watched him. The exhaustion on his face was apparent and, with the news of the eleven bodies that this Nighthunter had slaughtered with no trouble, her fear for Frank's safety had known no higher peak.

"Man, this is just what I needed," he said as he felt around for his glass of water. He downed it in one try.

"Here, let me get you another," Billingsley said and took the empty glass to the counter. "So, I guess you'll be napping by the phone this evening," she said over her shoulder. It was put across as more of a question than a statement.

"Looks like it," he answered. "We have to find this guy and quick."

"Well, I hope you guys are calling out the National Guard or something." She set the fresh glass of water in front of him and retook her seat.

"The Guard's a possibility. It was brought up in our meeting with Sebastian," he said after another gulp of water. "Superintendent Dehner rejected the idea, but will keep it in mind."

"Well, that's just great," she said with disgust, and sat back hard.

"If it makes you feel any better, I've got three squads of SWAT outfit with full armor and gear on standby. Marcus is one of them."

"Really? He just got out of the hospital, Frank!" Her eyes searched the ceiling for an answer that was not, nor had ever been, there. It was a habit, nonetheless.

"I know," Frank replied and shrugged. "He assured me he was fine. With the added strength the armored gear can give him, he should be fine in hand to hand, if it comes to that."

"I'd just be happy if this asshole leaves the city," Tamara grumbled.

Campanelli had no reply to that. As much as Chicago would rejoice if that happened, Frank knew that he would just make life hell for the citizens of another town. He also believed it to be unlikely that Elliot would voluntarily leave a rich hunting ground.

He moved to the couch after he was finished eating and fell asleep within moments. Tam set the telephone within his reach and watched holovision from the recliner.

As she watched him sleep, she drifted as well.

***

That night and the next, Saturday, passed without incident. Despite this, the citizens of Chicago were terrorized by the repeated news items surrounding the mysterious killer they had dubbed the Nighthunter. As a result, the streets were nearly completely barren once the sun fell. Unable to sleep,

Frank cruised the streets early Sunday morning. Empty bars and clubs had closed due to the nearly complete absence of patrons. To Frank, the city at night had become even more daunting and unwelcoming than usual, as only the street lamps lit his way. The neon signs had gone dark, sucking the life from the city.

Convinced that there was nothing left to see but other police vehicles and stray, feral animals, he returned home, parked, and crawled back into bed.

The Nighthunter had either gone to ground or Tamara Billingsley had received her wish.

***

Monday, June 9th was a warm, sunny day, but for the Chicago Police Department, it was cloaked in gloom. It was time to lay one of their own to rest, a time all too frequently experienced. Detective Kirby McLain's casket was rolled into the hearse by several pall bearers. Frank and Marcus, along with Lyman, Davies and two other homicide detectives that had served under the man, all lent their hands.

As usual, Frank drove his cruiser in the multi-car procession to Rosehill with Marcus at his side. Both men wore their formal uniforms and caps.

"What does Dr. Ruger have to say about Elliot's disappearance?" Marcus asked. He could no longer take the silence. Frank's disdain for funerals always had a profound effect on the man.

"I talked to him this morning," he said through a cracking voice. He cleared his throat. "He can only speculate, but it's his opinion that Three-Seven is lying low to let the heat settle. After that, he may choose to move on or continue killing."

"I agree," Williams replied and nodded. "I was hoping he was badly injured and was healing up, but Lincoln's report on the garage scene killed that. Not a drop of Elliot's blood was found and the time between Kirby's murder and the attack on the Warlocks was determined to be a few hours."

"Yeah," Frank whispered.

This was Marcus's cue that the man no longer wanted to speak of it, at least for the time being.

Frank and Marcus met the hearse and took their places alongside the toffee colored casket and grasped the brass handles. Among the six men, they maneuvered it onto the stand at the graveside and lined up behind it.

The priest spoke his piece, as did the mayor and the superintendent. Soon after, it was time for the six of them to fold the flag as the bagpipers and drummers erupted into a rendering of "Going Home", a known preference of Kirby McLain's. The McLain family had long since departed from the face of the Earth in one way or another. It was Frank himself that presented the flag to Superintendent Dehner. They saluted one another and Campanelli returned to the line.

His eyes wandered about the crowd and, to his surprise, he found Tamara, dressed in a dark gray pantsuit. He wanted to ask her what she was doing there, as she never attended these funerals. She was crying quietly and dabbing her eyes with a handkerchief. The sight of her in such a state, together with the pipes and drums, brought tears to well in his eyes. Frank shut the lenses down, pitching him into darkness where he stood.

They remained off until the end of the ceremony. He found Tamara in the crowd.

"You did wonderfully, Frank," she said and hugged him tightly.

No words came to his mind, so he simply hugged her back.

***

After Kirby McLain was properly buried, Campanelli dropped Williams home, and drove to his own apartment in silence. He returned his dress uniform to the closet and dressed for a regular day at work in a black suit. Even though it was after noon, he was sure to at least be available in case a call came in from someone having spotted Elliot Three-Seven. Additionally, he may have Sentinel business to attend to, though he doubted it. His underlings were handling the department fine without him.

Frank stared at himself in the mirror for a time as he fumbled with the tie. He could not help but notice the lines near his eyes and forehead. His guard had been down and the worry was plain in his face. He decided he would have to be conscious about his expressions, at least in front of Tam.

He came out of the bathroom, fresh and ready. He was restless and did not know, for the moment, what to do with himself.

"You okay?" Billingsley asked. She had not yet changed out of her pantsuit.

"Yeah."

She nodded and they looked to one another for a long moment. "I'm heading out to see the Yardleys today."

"Who?"

"The couple I'm buying the restaurant from. We're signing the papers today."

Annoyed at himself, he slapped his palm onto the kitchen counter. "Sorry, I forgot."

Tamara smiled and walked up to him. She planted a kiss on his cheek and mouth. "It's more than okay, Frank."

He thought about it and recalled that the diner was only about a block south and one west of Kirby McLain's apartment. A vision of Elliot Three-Seven ripping into the small restaurant and killing the Yardleys and Tamara Billingsley both angered and frightened him.

"When are you going?" he asked.

"Right now."

"I better escort you. You'll still need to take your car. I could be called while you're in there."

Her face brightened. "Oooo...my own police escort? Wonderful."

Both of them went to their cars. Tam drove her old German roadster and Frank followed in his cruiser. Along the way and while he waited outside, he monitored the CPD computer's blotter. There was nothing unusual about the day. Traffic stops, burglaries, a mugging, and a stolen car were all quite routine. He smirked over the stolen car, wondering who would bother, considering the amount of junk just lying around. The perpetrator must have been in some need. He wondered if it could have been the FROG.

Campanelli checked on his partner's status and noted that he had reported in at SWAT HQ on Fillmore Street, several blocks west of his position.

Frank sat back in his seat and watched the restaurant, the pedestrians, and the traffic along Michigan Avenue. His thoughts wandered to the sad events of that morning. There was no way to halt it, despite what good was going on inside the restaurant that would soon belong to Tamara. He was happy for her, but the issue of the psychopathic FROG and the murder trail he was leaving behind weighed heavily.

He lazily watched a group of cars accelerate from the light at Cermak Road. Among them was a vehicle that was much louder than the others and it gathered his attention. Campanelli thought the driver's window down and watched as three cars and a motorcycle rolled by him. Upon the motorcycle, a dark-skinned male with a mass of greasy black hair eyed him back and gave him a crooked smile.

Frank blinked and quickly magnified his vision, focusing on the rider's face. The man's eyes were bright yellow, indicating the presence of bio-electronics. The mass of cars along with the motorcycle rolled on by. Campanelli looked up the model of motorbike and found that it was a rare, American-built cycle with an Italian engine called a Torpedo V-4. It had taken its name from an early twentieth-century machine, but resembled it not at all beyond having a four-cylinder engine. Its age was approximately seventy years old.

He watched the bike recede in his side view mirror. A couple of factors set off his detective's instincts. The rider was wearing a dirty black overcoat, and Dr. Ruger had stated that FROGs were capable of changing their skin pigmentation.

Frank doubted his luck, but started the cruiser's motor, slipped it into gear, and made a U-turn. He caught up to the small group of vehicles, so he could see the motorcyclist through the windows of the automobile ahead of him.

At the intersection of Michigan and Cullerton, the biker turned right. Cullerton was a two lane road, quite a bit narrower than Michigan and more residential. Frank turned the corner and followed, keeping roughly a dozen car lengths between himself and the loud machine. The rider seemed calm and was keeping his speed within the posted limits.

The traffic lights were with them, allowing Frank to stay back while he studied the back of the bike. The frame had been designed to be versatile, comfortable over long distances, but built with the legendarily powerful four-cylinder. It resembled café racers of the late twentieth century, only it possessed a larger frame. The black leather saddle bags seemed out of place, but they had been installed solidly. They did not shift when the bike hit bumps. The rear tire was wide and sparsely treaded, making it a high performance tire with a great amount of contact with the pavement.

Cullerton ended when it intersected with Calumet Avenue and featured a posted stop sign. The biker braked and began looking both ways. Campanelli stopped behind him, leaving more than a car length.

189 • Campanelli: Siege of the Nighthunter

The biker revved his motor loudly, sending out puffy white exhaust. He made eye contact with Frank in his left side mirror and turned back over his left shoulder.

In a pair of heartbeats, the rider's skin changed color to a light pink. He winked at Frank as he gunned the engine with the front brake still engaged. The rear wheel spun in place while the tire shrieked shrilly and created white smoke.

"Son of a bitch!" Frank shouted in his car. His hand flashed to his gun, but he had no chance to pull it as Elliot Three-Seven let go of the brake. In a shot, he turned it to the left and accelerated away.

Frank mashed the pedal on his cruiser. The twin turbochargers howled and made the four tires spin, matching the smoke the motorbike had left behind on the corner. He thought the command for his cruiser to go to Condition Three, pursuit mode.

"Dispatch! I have suspect, Elliot Three-Seven sighted!" he called out. "I am in pursuit! He's on a Torpedo V-4 model motorcycle!"

"*Five-one-six-two, roger,*" the dispatcher replied a scant second later.

She chatted on, alerting back up units, as Frank negotiated the gentle left curve in Calumet Avenue, where he knew from experience, the curvature increased as the road bent westward. He watched as Elliot leaned hard, nearly scraping his knee along the street. Campanelli found himself hoping for an oncoming truck, but he was left disappointed.

Once the street straightened out, Elliot opened up the throttle and put distance between himself and Frank's car. The street name changed to Eighteenth Avenue after this turn, the very street Frank and Tam lived on.

Campanelli floored the accelerator in an effort to catch up, and his cruiser responded, flying through the gears as it approached and passed one hundred KPH. The distance between himself and Elliot was held in check for a pair of heartbeats.

The motorcycle braked for traffic crossing its path at the intersection of Indiana Avenue. Both tires of the bike smoked and left black streaks along the pavement.

Frank hit the brakes hard as well, throwing his body forward into the restraints. His widened eyes watched as Elliot weaved around cars that had come to a panic stop upon his sudden appearance. These vehicles were without guidance computers and not under Campanelli's patrol car's influence, so the drivers had no warning.

Three-Seven accelerated hard once he was through and Frank did the same. Unexpectedly, the FROG hit the brakes again and guided the bike to the right side of the street, but the seasoned policeman was not fooled. He knew this was an attempt to make a left turn at high speed and as wide as possible, so he did the same.

Elliot pressed the motorcycle hard through the turn and bounded up a slight incline as it entered an alley behind a row of apartment buildings. He accelerated so hard, the rear tire slipped, making the FROG ease off the gas.

Frank confidently followed and pushed his car to catch up, which it was able to do in a hurry. The two vehicles raced southward down the alley only a few meters apart. Unlike the well-maintained roadway they had just left behind, the alley was rough and only patched with asphalt, which had been sloppily applied and left lumpy.

Elliot pushed his bike hard and weaved around the bumps as much as he could, but the bike still struck one, lifting it into the air for a scant second, filling Frank with hope that the FROG would fall. Compensating quickly by shifting his weight and briefly laying off the accelerator, he did not. The tires reacquired contact with the rough alleyway and continued on, only giving up another meter of distance to the pursuing police car.

Campanelli began to grin as he was close enough to his target that he could no longer see the bottom of the bike's rear tire. He also knew that the alley dumped out onto Cullerton again and terminated into an empty lot of decimated concrete and rubble that the motorcycle could not traverse.

Elliot shifted to the left side of the alley, apparently preparing for a right turn. Frank discovered quickly that this was only partly correct. He was forced to slam on his brakes and twitch the yoke to the left to avoid a parked pickup truck. Three-Seven made a high-speed right onto Cullerton, causing another motorist to swerve out of the way. The antique vehicle crashed into a pair of parked cars.

Campanelli made the turn after Elliot and continued the chase, calling in the mishap. He shot through the green light at Michigan Avenue, and Frank could see that they were both driving into traffic. As his cruiser's computer came within contact of most of the vehicles, they decelerated and moved out of the way. Only an old unmarked delivery truck remained in Frank's way as he gained on Elliot's bike.

The two of them came up on the truck as it was passing through the intersection with Wabash. Campanelli's police siren finally caught the attention of the truck driver, so he slowed and moved out of the way.

As they approached State Street, Frank was alerted to the presence of additional units moving to intercept. Reluctantly, he let off the gas and covered the brake pedal with his other foot.

Elliot, unaware of the upcoming hazard, was surprised to see a marked CPD cruiser enter the intersection from the north and come to a screeching halt directly in front of him. To Frank's amazement, the FROG put the bike in a skid, using the rear brake only. The rear wheel kicked out to the right, slowing the bike and allowing the rider to steer around the front end of the police car. Once straightened out, the powerful motorcycle put distance between himself and Frank once again.

Campanelli guided his car around the squad car and mashed the gas pedal.

Additional units were waiting ahead, where Cullerton met with Archer Avenue. The three squad cars lay in wait for him, sprawled across the odd intersection and blocking any northbound option.

Elliot shifted his weight hard to his left, again dropping the knee nearly to the pavement, continuing in a tight left turn and bleeding as little speed as possible until the motorcycle wound up on Clark Street, heading south.

Frank followed, but had to put his cruiser sideways to make the high-speed turn without striking civilian cars. He straightened out and kept Elliot in sight, chasing after him with two marked cruisers following behind them.

They were quickly approaching Cermak Road, another place that would make Elliot choose a direction, when Frank's car lost power. Everything on the dashboard went dark and the pedals and steering yoke all lost function. At well over eighty KPH, Campanelli's cruiser approached the T intersection.

For a moment, all Frank could hear was the Torpedo's four-cylinder, the sirens of the police cars behind him, the wind against his cruiser, and the whirring of rubber against pavement.

He gripped the useless yoke in one hand and yanked the parking brake lever with the other. His rear tires locked up, diminishing much of the car's speed as it entered the intersection. The dead car struck the curb on the far end and was launched up an embankment, where it met with a wooden fence and a pair of trees with a loud crunching, shrieking of metal, and the explosions from the airbags.

Campanelli was vaguely aware of this just before the world went white, then dark.

**

Frank's unconsciousness was neither complete nor long-lasting. He clearly remembered what had happened and his *CAPS-Link* device had not powered down, so he knew he had not been out long. He blinked, but could not clear his vision of the white. He lifted a hand to rub his eyes, but encountered something else on the way. *Ah, airbags.*

He took a deep breath and realized the he felt some pain in his back and limbs, but it was tolerable. He moved the center airbag from his face and looked through the windshield. He saw nothing but spider-webbed glass, trees, and blue sky.

A knock at the window startled him.

"Yes?" He could think of nothing else to say.

"You okay in dere?" someone asked from the other side of the door.

"Think so," he replied and tried the door. It opened. On the other side was a uniformed officer. "Where'd that biker go?" Frank unbuckled the belt and cautiously got out of the car.

"They're still chasin' 'im," the slightly overweight patrolman answered. "Looks like anudder squad crashed a little further on."

"Interesting," Campanelli commented as he stretched and checked himself for injury. Other than having the wind knocked out of him and his bell rung, he was sure there were no serious injuries. He gazed around and noted the gapers' block that his crash had caused.

Frank looked his car over. The front end had collapsed around the two trees it had collided with. The hot metal ticked and the destroyed radiator was letting its coolant free in white vapor. He tried, but could not connect to the vehicle's computer.

"Hey, Detective," the uniformed officer interrupted, "you sure you're okay?"

"Yes, but I'm out of contact," Campanelli explained. He looked over at the officer's vehicle and noted that it was a K-9 unit not involved with the pursuit. "Call a backup unit over here to come get me, please."

"Yer da boss," the officer, whose name was Willems, answered and moved quickly to his truck and jumped inside.

Frank reached inside the ruined car and retrieved his hat. He walked around the back of it and up along the other side to see if anything looked better over there. It did not. In fact, Campanelli decided that it looked far worse. The right front wheel was jammed upward into the depths of the fender, and that entire corner was bent upward.

"I got a wrecker and a squad on the way, sir," Willems called from the truck.

"Thank you," Frank replied and put his fedora on. The car wreck seemed to have temporarily shaken the urgency from him, but as he thought it over, his anticipation returned. Elliot Three-Seven was extremely dangerous and he had been so close to having him.

"So, what happened?" the officer asked from his side.

"Not sure," Frank shrugged. "Everything just went out. The engine, steering, dash, lights, everything just...out."

"Dat sounds just like what they're sayin' happened to da car that was just behind you, only a few blocks from here."

"Are the officers okay?"

"Oh, yeah," Willems confirmed. "Your wreck here seems worse."

Frank reached out with his implant and connected to the CPD server. He accessed the radio reports regarding the chase and found that Elliot had led the pursuing officers around McCormick Place and onto Lake Shore Drive. He was now headed northbound with a trail of three cruisers on his tail.

"He's not trying to escape," Frank whispered.

"What's dat, sir?"

"Elliot. Our serial killer. He's not attempting to leave the city, even with all of us on him," Campanelli said with conviction. "He's toying with us."

"Dat Nighthunter guy? Some toying," Willems said, and whistled.

Frank cycled to the end of the list of transmissions and listened to the most recent one. The unit indicated that Elliot had ridden into the abandoned and condemned Soldier Field.

Thinking fast, he added to the conversation via implant. *"All units, this is Campanelli, five-one-six-two. Do not pursue Elliot Three-Seven inside the stadium. To all units available, converge and surround all entrances and exits to Soldier Field. SWAT teams mobilize and meet me there ASAP."*

At that moment, a two-man squad arrived on the scene. Frank bolted for it, showed his badge to the passenger, and jumped in the back seat. "Soldier Field! Go!"

***

The last report given on the pursuit of Elliot Three-Seven described him leading several police cars on a chase around the old stadium and entering the facility from the south entrance. Campanelli was familiar with the layout of the place, as the abandoned sports arena had been a popular place for criminal activity ever since it was closed. Dozens of bodies had been dumped there over the years and it was often the center for gang-related activities, including wars, which took place on the now downtrodden dirt field.

"I want all surveillance drones to converge on Soldier Field and every helo we have on station. We have a chance to trap and capture Elliot Three-Seven," the Captain of Detectives sent to the CPD dispatcher, using the squad car's transceiver.

"*Roger, five-one-six-two,*" the dispatcher replied audibly.

It seemed to Campanelli that every police vehicle in the city was on its way to Soldier Field. The car he rode in eventually became surrounded by a sea of white and blue. His ears could barely register anything beyond the cacophony of sirens around him. Not a civilian vehicle remained on the streets.

"*Five-one-six-two, from fifty-two-oh-two,*" Marcus called over the radio.

Frank leaned as far forward as he could, restrained as he was by the critter-cage separated him from the front seats. "Go ahead, Williams."

"*Frank, the blotter says you wrecked, you okay?*"

He shook his head. It was not something he wanted announced over the radio. "I'm fine. Is your squad in place?"

"*Affirmative,*" Williams answered. "*We have three squads assembled at the south entrance, where the suspect was seen entering. Should we proceed?*"

"Negative. Wait for me."

"*Roger.*"

"I'm a few minutes out," Campanelli added. "Where are Quinne and Dr. Ruger?"

"*They are standing by,*" Williams answered.

The cruiser Frank was riding in bounced up a curb to approach the south entrance. Ahead, he could see the area, a wide concrete swath originally intended for pedestrians was now covered with squad cars and SWAT vans.

"I'm on scene, wait for me!" Frank shouted and opened the door before the driver came to a complete stop.

Campanelli ran for the entrance, weaving between vehicles and uniformed officers. Out of habit, he held up his badge, which minimized queries. He made his way to the center of the mass of humanity and began counting the armored personnel. He confirmed three squads and Frohm was the ranking officer over all three. He called the man's name and found him in the crowd.

"I've just sent a request for further SWAT units to assist in securing the facility. Your three squads will be going in with a small detachment of uniformed police and myself and we're gonna find this asshole!"

"Yes, *sir!*" Frohm agreed vehemently, though his voice was now a hollow representation of itself through the vent of the fully-encompassing helmet. Marcus Williams stood next to him, taller and more monstrous than ever in the AA-Suit due to the armor and articulating armatures.

"Detective! Detective Campanelli!" Dr. Mitchell Ruger called frantically as he bumped through the crowd of officers and SWAT.

"Dr. Ruger," Frank greeted.

"I need to go in with your group," Ruger demanded. "I can talk to Elliot."

Frank looked to Agent Quinne, who came up behind the old geneticist. The man shrugged.

"Look, Doctor. I don't think that's wise. Your presence may have the opposite effect, you know."

"I've thought of that, believe me. But I think that Elliot will talk to me," Mitchell insisted. "He had to know that I disagreed with the decision to eliminate the FROGs."

"Dr. Ruger…"

"Please, Detective!"

At that very moment, a surveillance drone transmitted the image of Elliot Three-Seven, riding the Torpedo across the uneven and muddy playing field. They had to move in and Frank knew it.

"Detective, Elliot hacked into your squad car's computer and caused your crash," Ruger explained quickly. "He did that to two others as well. He can hack into any implant he wishes. If he wanted to kill you, he would have hacked your implant directly."

"Look! I think this is a terrible idea, but we have to go!" Frank shouted. "Frohm! He's on the field! Let's go!"

Frohm replied in the affirmative and ordered his squads inside the facility. With a nod, Marcus Williams was off, sticking closely to Frohm's side.

"All right!" Campanelli called to the uniformed men around him. "You four on me! Quinne, protect Dr. Ruger!"

Quinne nodded and pulled his semi-auto from his shoulder holster. "Stick close to me, Professor."

The men, counting more than forty including the uniformed officers covering the rear, ran up the ramps and through the corridors that brought them to the first level of seating. Frohm split the SWAT squads, sending one east and one west. Spread as they were, they would emerge from the outer corridor and enter the seating area as one unit.

Once he got the confirmation that the other squads were in place, he ordered them forward. Each SWAT member stayed low and acquired the target through their rifle scopes once they had moved forward enough to see him on the field.

Frank ordered the uniformed officers, armed with semi-automatic rifles or shotguns in addition to their sidearms, to remain in the corridor to cover their rear. He then moved in with Frohm's squad and took a position near the sergeant. Quinne and Ruger came along, but stayed back and low.

Campanelli kicked concrete and glass debris out of his way and crouched next to Sergeant Frohm at the last row of lower deck seats. Marcus Williams remained at the ready on Frohm's right.

The roar of the motorcycle's four-cylinder resonated throughout the old crumbling structure. Elliot rode like a madman over the gutted football field, making fresh ruts in the mud with the powerful bike.

Frank was about to peek when his *CAPS-Link* received a ping. There were several hundred police officers surrounding the stadium, but he knew who it was.

"He knows we're here," he said to Frohm, who nodded.

As if to confirm that, Elliot slowed the motorbike and brought it to the center of the field. Once there, he gazed at the seating sections on the field's southern end and smiled. He held the bike in place and gunned the engine, flinging the rear end around and around as he cackled madly.

"Can someone *please* take him off that thing?" Frank asked of the SWAT commander.

"Sure," Frohm answered. "This may be our best opportunity to take him down."

"I can do it," Williams affirmed and focused his sights on the FROG.

"No! Wait!" Ruger called from behind them. "I haven't talked to him, yet...please!"

"Marcus." Frank leaned forward and looked to his partner. "Target the bike itself."

"Sure thing," Williams said with confidence.

Tired of spinning the Torpedo in circles, Three-Seven brought it to a stop and stared hard into the group of armed men. He could see them watching him from their rifle scopes. Elliot was about to shout up to them when a muzzle flash blossomed. The buzzing round came in quickly and struck the motorbike's engine block with a ringing report. The engine coughed and ran unevenly for a few seconds before a loud hammering came from deep within the contraption.

"No, no, no, noooo!"

With a final *thwack!* and a cough, the motor died. Black smoke exuded from the hole that was punched into its side and the exhaust pipes.

"Well, that's not *fucking cool!*" Elliot screeched. He reached back into a saddlebag, retrieved one of the Warlock submachine guns and appeared to take a casual, single shot in response to the received gunfire.

The domed top of Marcus's helmet was struck with the round. Had he not heeded Frohm's order to get down, the bullet would have entered through the helmet's visor.

"Shit!" Williams hollered. "That's *it!*" He shifted over to the next row of seats and raised his weapon to take out the FROG once and for all.

Other SWAT members opened fire on the FROG, forcing him to drop the hefty bike nearly on top of himself for cover.

"Cease fire!" Frohm called into the helmet radio.

"Hold it, Williams!" Campanelli shouted.

"Goddamn it!"

"Just stand down a minute!" the Captain of Detectives ordered his partner.

"Elliot!" Ruger called as he ran forward. "Elliot Three-Seven!"

Frank rolled his eyes, turned, and reached out with his left hand. His fingers grasped the elderly doctor by the belt and held him there.

The stadium fell nearly silent. Only a stiff breeze could be heard for several seconds.

"Dr. Ruger?" Elliot called from his place of hiding. He was virtually lying under the disabled motorcycle, despite the engine heat.

"Yes! It's me, Elliot!" He ceased any attempts to move further forward, but Frank held on to the belt.

"Can anyone get a clear shot of him?" Sergeant Frohm nearly whispered into the mic. No one answered, so the answer was negative.

"What the hell are *you* doing here?" Three-Seven shouted. He shifted under the Torpedo, trying to see if he could place the barrel of the gun through a bit of the machine's anatomy to return fire.

"I just wanted to talk to you," Mitchell Ruger replied. "I...want you to drop your weapons and come in. Surrender yourself, please. Whatever's wrong we can talk about it."

Agent Quinne come up alongside the doctor and remained in a low crouch behind the seats opposite the row Frank was hiding behind. Campanelli gave him a hard look for letting Ruger leave his side. Quinne shrugged in an apology.

"You've got to be yanking me, Doc!" Elliot yelled back angrily. "You bastards killed us! Almost all of us!" He magnified his vision upon the area where his ears had pinpointed Ruger's position.

"That wasn't my idea, Elliot! I swear to you, I never wanted that!" Mitchell bellowed sorrowfully.

Three-Seven found the voice and smiled. The geneticist was crouched behind the seats of the lower level like the rest of the policemen. To Elliot's delight, the blind detective was alongside him.

Placing the barrel of the submachine gun through the gap between the front forks and the frame of the ruined motorcycle, Elliot fired a single shot.

The lone report echoed throughout the quiet stadium. Dr. Ruger let out a short yelp of pain and crumpled to the concrete floor.

"Goddamn it!" Campanelli shouted, but was drowned out by sporadic return fire from the SWAT teams. He leaped to his feet and dragged the doctor back to the entrance.

Rounds struck the motorcycle, ringing off the thick metal frame and engine. Several led projectiles punched holes in the fuel tank. Gasoline rained down upon Elliot's face.

"Arrgh! Fuck!" he spat and shrunk into a ball. Straining to reach it, he fiddled through the saddlebag on that side of the slowly disintegrating machine and pulled the other weapons from within it, one by one.

Three-Seven waited for the firing to cease. He knew then that most of his attackers were reloading, so he made his move.

Sliding out from under the bike, he knocked the kickstand into place with the barrel of the submachine gun and jumped up into a crouch. His *FROG-ServLink* quickly assessed the threats and sent the location of each gunman in the stands, marking them with a red dot on his lenses. Each weapon in his hand was capable of firing automatically, but Elliot needed precision at this range, so he had left them set at single shot. He brought the guns close enough together that each of his eyes could make use of their sights and picked out one target after the other. He fired as he retreated.

One by one, SWAT members took a hit in their body armor or helmets and dropped, shouting in pain. Frohm and Williams returned fire, tracking the fast moving FROG. The reports from the falling SWAT members filled their helmet radios. They watched as their target skillfully evaded the rounds they fired. He hopped and ran, rolled along the dirt, jumped to his feet, and sprinted away with astounding agility and speed.

"How the hell?" Marcus mumbled as he took careful aim and fired. Round after round missed cleanly, though a couple appeared to come very close. He marveled at the FROG's uncanny ability to place such long range shots on target, even while evading fire.

Frohm emptied his magazine and began reloading just as Marcus did the same. Williams kept his eye on Elliot as he went about reloading his weapon. After a second, he was glad he did.

"Down!" Marcus shouted and spun about, throwing an arm across Sergeant Frohm's chest and bringing the both of them down to the concrete, hard.

Both of Three-Seven's shots at them missed.

Frank inspected Ruger's wound and determined that it was serious, but not life threatening. He told the geneticist to make his way back outside and alerted a uniformed officer that the doctor needed medical attention. The old man had taken a nine millimeter round in the shoulder and could walk.

Campanelli ran back to join the SWAT team, entering the seating area in time to duck the rounds meant for Williams and Frohm. He magnified his vision and caught a glimpse of the FROG as he disappeared into the shadow of a tunnel at the northwest corner of the field.

On impulse, Campanelli bolted down the steps between the weather-beaten and vandalized seats toward the field. He did not hear Marcus shouting after him. He vaulted over the wall at the bottom of the decline and landed hard onto the muddy field, letting out a cry of pain. His legs instantly ached from the impact, but he pushed them hard, reaching a near-sprint pace through the torn-up and rutted field. He did not take his eyes from the tunnel ahead.

Marcus ran after him and continued to reload his rifle on the way. "Frank!" he shouted again, but his older partner never faltered. Williams landed hard on the muddy field and ran after him.

Campanelli reached the far end of the field and put his back against the wall to the left of the tunnel opening. He hesitated for several seconds, catching his breath. He saw Williams had followed and was headed for the opposite side of the entrance.

"*Are you nuts?*" Marcus sent in an audible message. The sanitized digital voice of Williams only hinted at the ex-SEAL's angst, which was clearly stamped upon his face.

"*I think maybe, yes,*" Frank returned in kind. Quickly, he adjusted his vision for night and curled his head around the corner. He saw no one, just the tunnel which led to the innermost depths of the ancient stadium. On the ground lay the two submachine pistols. Apparently, they had been emptied.

Without wasting any more time, Campanelli came around the corner and stepped forward. Williams followed.

To their left, a pair of doors hung wide open. Whether or not this had just been done was doubtful, as Soldier Field had been at the mercy of gangs, criminals, and relatively harmless trespassers for decades.

As the Captain of Detectives approached the opening with his handgun raised, a radio message from Sergeant Frohm reached Williams's helmet radio. It would be a few seconds before it would reach Frank's *CAPS-Link.*

"He's flanked you! Above and left!"

"Look out, Frank!" Marcus shouted and brought his weapon up. He saw Elliot's face for the first time, taking it in during the second that passed before he could pull the trigger. Three-Seven appeared calm, even amused, as he smiled and looked down upon the two policemen. The bright yellow eyes locked on Marcus's face, though he did register the SEAL's intent to shoot him.

Frank anticipated what Elliot had done, assumed that he was about to fire on them, and raced around the corner through the open doors.

By the time Marcus had placed his finger on the trigger, Elliot had disappeared.

Gunfire erupted from the SWAT team, and rounds rained over the seating area above them. The assault was brief, as Three-Seven moved out of their sight as well.

With the assistance of the AA-Suit, Marcus launched himself upward and grasped the edge of the wall. The powerful actuators allowed him to pull himself up with one arm. Giving a glance about the area, he lifted his body over the top of the wall. He stayed low, covering the area around him with the rifle.

"Where'd he go?" Williams called into the microphone.

Campanelli ascended a staircase strewn with litter and refuse. He was careful, but quick. He reached the top and left the stairwell, finding himself inside the stadium. He increased the sensitivity to his ears and heard footfalls receding quickly at his left.

"*He went up the row right where you are, Marcus,*" Frohm answered. "*Then inside.*"

"Roger," Williams answered and ran past the stairs leading to the upper level, toward the first open doorway he saw. He saw Campanelli stride past. "Frank! Wait a minute!" he shouted.

He burst into the wide corridor and was relieved to find that his partner had waited. Williams gave him a nod as his eyes wandered over the place, even giving a glance up to the rafters. They could not afford to continue underestimating Elliot's abilities.

"*I heard footsteps this way,*" Frank sent to Marcus over the implant. He pointed to their left and stepped hurriedly in that direction.

Both men kept sharp, watching the long abandoned and emptied shops, vendor counters, and washrooms. The entire area reeked of mold, causing Campanelli's sinuses to itch and run.

Sunlight spilled into the area from the outer windows, setting the dusty air alight in long, foggy beams which spilled onto the gray floor. Frank thought the command to link with the CPD server. It took a moment to find a police vehicle within range to relay the signal, but in a moment, he was able to access the array of police drones that were patrolling the stadium.

Frank and Marcus traversed the interior of the stadium slowly, following its curving nature to the south.

Campanelli put his back to a dusty wall and paused for a moment. The moldy air was going to make him sneeze. He held up a finger to bring Marcus to a halt with him and shuffled through the images taken live from the camera drones.

Movement on one of them froze him in place. He studied it for a moment and sent the image link to his partner. The movement appeared to be on the upper levels, in the luxury suite sections of the structure. He ordered the drone operator to freeze in place and follow the movement.

"*Campanelli to Frohm,*" he composed, "*Elliot is in the luxury suite section. Watch this shot from the camera drone.*" He sent the message and turned to Marcus. "He's upstairs."

"Yeah," Marcus agreed in a whisper. The both of them walked past a bank of elevators, one of which had its doors forced open at some point. He looked about for directions to the stairwell that would lead them there and found one. "This way."

The two detectives rushed up the stairs, Marcus leading the way as he was far more prepared to do damage to the Marine FROG. Williams reached the lowest floor of the luxury boxes and halted before leaving the stairwell. In a moment, Frank joined him, and the two entered the sunlit corridor.

The wind had its way within the structure, as many windows had been broken out over the years. Still, a foul stench lay underneath the undulation of fresh air. Campanelli had known form the many reports of squatters on the premises, that many a crime had been committed in the old suites, and nearly as great a number of criminals had sought refuge here, not so much from police, but from rivals.

A squadron of gray pigeons took flight some distance ahead of them, having been disturbed by something. They burst from several of the suites and headed toward the stairwell from which the two men had entered.

Both men ducked as the flurry of winged vermin took a sharp turn as a unit and exited the premises through what had once been a window, now missing its pane of glass.

"Whew," said Frank as he cautiously rose to his full height. "So, that's what the smell is."

Marcus nodded and covered the area ahead of them with his semi-automatic rifle. He was fairly certain that neither he nor Frank had upset the birds.

Campanelli gestured for his partner to cover the door as he stepped forward and peered into the first suite. The floor was littered with pieces of broken furniture, empty bottles, cans, and unidentifiable bits of fabric, amongst other trash. The suites were separated by wood paneled walls and a clear partition at the front that would allow patrons to see down the row of suites, partially into the others. Frank slowly stepped inside, trying to keep the sounds of his footsteps quiet. It was difficult, due to the debris that littered the remnants of the carpeting.

The sun filtered into the room through splatters of unidentified fluids that had been deposited on the main window which overlooked the field. His shoes crunched underneath him.

Campanelli made his way to the front of the suite and looked through the filthy partition that had once been completely transparent. Sadly, the parade of vandals and criminals had done various deeds to just about every suite's partition, making it impossible to see very far.

Giving up that avenue, Frank headed back into the corridor and shrugged.

"We're going to have to check each one," he sent in an audible message. He turned and began to step to the next one.

"Frank," Marcus whispered.

Campanelli looked quizzically back at his armored partner.

Marcus tapped his helmet then made a swiping motion across his throat. It was at this time that the Captain of Detectives realized that his message had not been sent. His implant could no longer see Williams's, nor could it make contact with any other officers, for that matter.

"He's jamming us," Frank whispered harshly.

At that moment, a black blur crossed their field of vision and flew into an open elevator shaft. The object was large enough to be Elliot Three-Seven. Campanelli raced toward it, but was quickly overtaken by his faster partner.

Williams skidded to a stop and covered the open elevator with his rifle barrel. There was nothing but cables in the expanse, but they were swinging jerkily back and forth. Marcus stepped forward and glanced downward. He heard the noise of shoes and clothes sliding up a steel cable come from above him. Quickly, he exposed his head and looked up just as Three-Seven exited the shaft at the top floor.

"Damn that guy," Marcus hissed and headed for another stairwell.

"Can you transmit?" Frank asked as he followed.

"Frohm, come in," Williams attempted. In response, he heard only static and bits of words, unable even to identify the speaker. He turned to Frank and shook his head.

"Can his implant cook, too?" Campanelli muttered and cussed. Before he entered the stairwell, he called to his partner. "Marcus, hold on a sec."

Williams nodded and waited with his rifle covering the steps. It would not be beyond the realm of possibility that Elliot would try to double back, right at them.

Frank jogged down the corridor, looking into each suite until he found one that appeared similar to the one that the spy drone was hovering near. Near the center of the level he saw it and slid across the smooth concrete floor. He ran inside and waved to the small flying robot with both arms for about five seconds. He watched as the camera swung onto him and appeared to focus on his movement.

Campanelli made the same gesture that Williams just had to indicate jammed communications. Then, he pointed up and mouthed the words, "Top floor."

As the drone gained altitude, he turned and sprinted out of the suite, back up the corridor, and joined his partner in the stairwell.

"Let's go," Frank directed and explained what he had just done.

"That should do it," Williams concurred and led the way.

Marcus could see that this stairwell was different from the others. It brought the two detectives to the center of a large room, certainly, one of the more expensive suites in its day. The wind whistled as it passed over his helmet. It was obvious that many of the large window panes had been destroyed. The wind did little to cure the stench that met their noses. It smelled as if many dozens of vandals had used the once dignified location as a toilet. The fact that the entire stadium had served as a body dump for a myriad of criminals did nothing to help.

The sun shone throughout the wide open space, as the entire east wall was made up of curved panes of thick glass, many of which had been shattered. With his head the only thing above floor level, he turned in place as he scanned the area for Elliot.

There was nothing but broken furniture and garbage, just like everywhere else. Miscellaneous trash fluttered upon otherwise vacant countertops. Drawers hung open like lifeless tongues and many cabinet doors swung at the wind's mercy. They creaked and banged without rhythm.

Williams stepped onto the top floor and continued his sweeping of the area. He expected Three-Seven to pounce on them any second. Frank followed and stood nearby.

"Now what?" Marcus asked in a whisper. Annoyingly, his implant remained utterly useless for communication.

"We search," Campanelli answered plainly, though his heart pounded in his chest. He increased his serotonin levels to steady his hands. He found the suite's washroom and peeked inside. It reeked, but was empty. He pointed northward and Marcus moved that way with his assault weapon ready and level.

Around the corner they progressed and found nothing different in the next suite, though the big windows weren't busted out. The wind flew past them from other gaps in the structure, however, rising from a whistle to a howl.

Frank tried reaching the SWAT team again with his implant, but it was still blocked. The FROG had to be close by. Watching their backs, Campanelli progressed into the suite with his back to the wall and cleared that washroom as well.

A loud banging came from the suite they had just left and both men's heads swung toward it. Frank looked through the open doorway and realized what it was.

He turned to Marcus. "Cabinet...look out!" he exclaimed as he lifted his handgun to the fast moving target.

Williams was in the middle of spinning around to meet the threat when a foot met him. Elliot had administered a flying kick that found the ex-SEAL's dented helmet and sent him flying backward. He landed on his back and saw stars.

Frank was about to squeeze the trigger of his eleven-millimeter when the FROG dropped into a crouch and spun around with another outstretched foot. It struck Campanelli in his left calf and sent him to the floor as well.

Marcus could not focus his eyes for a moment, but he saw enough to understand that Elliot was rushing his way, bayonet in hand and lifted high. There was no time to aim the weapon. Instead, he chose to deflect the blade with it. As Three-Seven came down on him, he pushed with his right arm. The power of the AA-Suit came to his rescue, redirecting the triangular carbon fiber blade away from him. At the same time, the stock of the rifle struck Elliot in the cheek.

"Gawww!" Three-Seven shouted gutturally as he tumbled off of Williams.

Marcus rolled in the opposite direction and hopped up just as the FROG got to his feet. Before Williams could lift the barrel, he was on him again. The two entangled and spun. Even with the AA-Suit's powerful leg actuators, Marcus could not gain footing on his attacker. Every time he regained balance, the FROG shifted his weight in a different direction.

Campanelli regained his feet and aimed his weapon, but Marcus and Elliot moved through the room furiously, spinning one way, then another in an unpredictable pattern. Shockingly, Williams was slammed against the cabinetry, splintering a large door and sending it to the carpet in pieces.

"Aww!" Williams yelled. He kneed Elliot in the crotch and, though it did hurt him, it failed to crumple him to the floor. Instead, the FROG pulled his right arm back and prepared to plunge the blade into his opponent's chest armor.

Frank flew into action and ran around the back of Three-Seven and grabbed him by the forearm. He jammed the barrel of his pistol into the killer's ribs.

"Drop it!" Frank shouted.

Elliot looked back at Frank as he held Marcus's two powerfully augmented arms at bay. He smiled and thrust his right elbow backward, impacting Campanelli's cheek and driving him back to the wall of glass, which let out the sound of a gunshot when its inner pane cracked. Stunned, he watched his fedora fall from the top of his head. Outside and below them was the peaked roof of Soldier Field's Collonades. Once a beloved landmark, it was now a simple reminder of how serious their situation was.

"Nice to meet you in person, Detective Campanelli!" Elliot shouted over his shoulder. "Hope you enjoyed the ride over!" He crowed madly as he pulled and spun Marcus around to put him between himself and the dazed detective.

Seeing the opportunity, Williams thrust his right knee up again, striking the groin of Elliot Three-Seven for a second time. It was causing discomfort, but it seemed to only make the madman angry. His yellow eyes flared and he grinned evilly, showing his sharp, unnaturally perfect teeth.

"I think that will be enough," Elliot seethed. He braced against the wood paneled partition, brought his legs up and pressed the policeman his implant identified as a Navy SEAL. Intrigued, he read on as he worked to disentangle himself from the man. In a moment, he got his wish and struck out with a powerful sidekick.

The next thing Williams knew, he was flying across the suite. He impacted hard against the cabinetry and landed in the sink. The world went dark for several seconds.

"So, this is your partner, Detective Williams," Elliot said and grinned. He was breathing hard after tangling with the amplified muscular power of an already strong man, but he was recovering quickly.

Marcus's head had cleared enough to see that Elliot had paused in his gloating, so he raised his weapon and

213 • Campanelli: Siege of the Nighthunter

squeezed the trigger. Nothing happened. He stared at Three-Seven with his eyes wide.

Elliot laughed crazily and waved the rifle's magazine at the SEAL. "Feeling low, old man?"

Williams knew that a round was in the chamber. He noted that the safety had been engaged, but there was something odd about that, too, his mind registered, even as his fingers failed to budge it from its place.

Mad laughter filled the tattered suite. "I bent that up a bit. You might want to think of somethin' else!"

Elliot turned in time to see Campanelli raising his gun. In a flash, Three-Seven spun into a low crouch, closed distance with the detective and kicked up, striking the man's wrist and sending the pistol flying.

Infuriated, Frank reacted more quickly than the FROG would have dreamed, striking the killer's face with a left palm, followed by a solid punch from his right. Already near the floor, the FROG rolled away and retook a defensive stance. Campanelli was on him immediately. Wrapping the fingers of his left hand around Elliot's right wrist to keep the blade at bay, he struck out with his right fist yet again and connected. By the time he drew back it back for another strike, however, Frank was again thrown back against the glass wall by a straight kick.

Another loud crack reminded the Captain of Detectives that it was a way down to the Collonades.

Williams flew into the fight, swinging the disabled assault rifle. Elliot was fast enough to move his head out of the way, but not the rest of his body. He took the rifle butt in his left shoulder, but as he spun away with his right arm outstretched, the bayonet's blade sliced Williams's armor, creasing it at his lower right ribcage.

Marcus turned quickly to face Three-Seven once again, forced into ducking immediately away once more to keep from being skewered by the carbon fiber bayonet.

Elliot danced his way around Williams, kicked off the cabinetry and flew into Campanelli, who was bending to pick up his pistol. Frank was tackled into the opposite partition with a floor-jarring thud and slashed at with the bayonet as Three-Seven left them both behind.

"Frank!" Marcus shouted and scrambled to his fallen partner. He had seen the blade flick through the man's black overcoat, lifting it from his body as the blade passed through his side, near his hip.

To Campanelli, the voice sounded far away and muffled. His head, neck, and back throbbed harshly, and his left side burned.

"Frank!" Marcus repeated and placed a hand on the older detective's pale face. He looked into Campanelli's unfocused eyes and saw that the blow against the wall may have been the more devastating injury. "Okay, don't move, Frank. Hear me?"

"Get that son of a bitch!" Campanelli slurred.

"Yeah!" Marcus shouted and was on his feet, running after his suspect. He tried the helmet radio again and this time, there was chatter. In a moment, he realized why.

Elliot had been laying an ambush for Williams, when he himself was met with SWAT members entering from the staircase in the floor. He assaulted them immediately, disarming the first man he encountered and giving him a powerful sidekick.

The unfortunate police officer flew backward and through an already broken out window pane. Marcus broke into a run as his eyes followed the falling man until he could see him no more. His right hand fell to the holster on his hip and came away with his pistol. As he cycled the action, he watched Three-Seven rake the stairwell with rounds from the stolen officer's assault weapon, forcing the other men back down.

At the corner of the wooden partition, Marcus came around, found Elliot, and began firing. Three-Seven saw his movement and reacted in a blur, rolling along the floor as he returned fire. Williams was forced to drop to cover behind the partition, but not in time to dodge a round to his right forearm. It struck the thick aluminum alloy actuator and fragmented, sending a piece of shrapnel into Marcus's visor, where it lodged without harm.

Another SWAT member tossed a flash grenade out of the stairwell and onto the ruined carpet, landing not far from the FROG's feet. Seeing this, Williams steeled himself for the explosion.

In two seconds, the main room lit up with a loud report. The area filled with smoke and Marcus peered around the corner. Two SWAT members came up the steps, covering the area with their rifles.

As the wind carried the smoke from the room, Elliot Three-Seven was nowhere to be seen.

Williams stepped to the side of the SWAT member at the top of the stairs. It was Sergeant Frohm.

"Where the shit did that bastard go?" he grumbled over the static.

"Not sure..." Marcus began to reply. It was then his eyes found a possible escape route along with something moving at his extreme left. By the time he figured out that Three-Seven had escaped the central suite through a broken transparency which had once separated the suites at the field end, the FROG struck him with a sidekick.

Williams was thrust into Frohm and Frohm, in turn, tumbled into the next officer, sending the both of them down the steps.

Marcus was saved from following by Elliot, who pulled the big man toward him by the shoulder armor. With his other hand, he ripped the helmet off the ex-SEAL and struck him on the top of the head with it.

Sent to near unconsciousness, Williams reached out with his left arm and met Elliot's throat with his open palm. He squeezed. The AA-Suit was without actuators in the hands beyond the wrist, so it was up to the SEAL's powerful fingers.

In a flash, however, Three-Seven had Williams on the floor once again. Marcus saw the bayonet thrust coming and was forced to abandon the attempt at strangulation to keep from being pierced.

Three-Seven gave Williams a succession of left jabs to his head. Marcus tried desperately to block the assault, but was losing consciousness.

"I didn't want to kill you, brother," Elliot grunted out between strikes. "You've served your country with honor, but you pushed me."

Marcus tried to assault the creature with profanity, but he had no words as his head took another punch. He heard gunshots from directly above him and, to his horror, noted that it was his own weapon. Elliot was keeping the other SWAT members from coming up the stairs.

The point of the bayonet was now pressing into the AA-Suit's breast plate and Elliot drew his left hand high into the air to pistol whip Marcus into the final submission. Williams flashed out with his right arm, but its ruined actuator, struck by a bullet just moments earlier, could not help him.

"Elliot!" a voice screamed.

Through unfocused eyes, Marcus saw Elliot Three-Seven pivot his head to the sound. He followed the FROG's line of sight and found Frank Campanelli. The man was depending heavily on the wood partition to remain standing, and he did not look well, but he was there and so was his eleven-millimeter.

"This is what I get for being merciful!" Three-Seven howled at the man. Instead of backing off, he smiled and put more effort into his right arm. The point of the bayonet skewered the armor and it began to fail, bending inward from the pressure.

Frank squeezed the trigger three times in rapid succession. The three rounds drove into the FROG's torso, sending him sprawling to the floor. The carbon fiber bayonet fell into the stairwell and clattered at Frohm's feet.

Marcus took a few deep breaths as he watched Frank clumsily drop back onto the floor. With effort, Williams rolled and faced the downed killer, who was lying motionless.

Frohm came up to the top of the stairs with two other members of the SWAT team. Williams and he shared a look.

"Frohm here," he called into the helmet microphone. "We need three med units to the top floor, RFN!"

Marcus reached to his belt and pulled out his cuffs. "Somebody...get these on 'im," he called and tossed them to Frohm.

Another set landed on the floor near Elliot's feet. "Bind his damn legs, too!" Frank ordered.

Moments later, the area swarmed with more SWAT members, uniformed officers, and paramedics. Frank dropped off into unconsciousness and came back in time to see that Elliot had been bound by two pairs of handcuffs to both his wrists and his ankles. Williams was on his feet, looking tired and beat, but was otherwise all right. He could not hear his words over the out-of-tune symphony of voices in the room, but he was up and around.

Campanelli slipped off again. When he awoke the next time, Elliot was being taken down the stairs, as there was no power to Soldier Field to run the elevators. His aching mind wondered if they would work at all after all this time.

A young medic approached the Captain of Detectives and directed the two men carrying the stretcher to lay it down next to their patient. He produced a flashlight and inspected the detective's eyes.

Frank did not need to blink, as his *CAPS-Link* adjusted the light level for him.

"You've got quite the concussion, sir," the medic opined.

"No shit, Dr. Kildare," Campanelli snapped back. "You wanna take a look at this for me?" He pulled the ruined coat away from the bayonet wound.

"Oh!"

"Yeah," Frank grunted and lay his head down. He knew nothing more for some time.

***

Frank Campanelli awoke to darkness, which was not unusual. The air around him was cool and gave him chills. He felt that his arms were bare and that he was wearing very thin clothing.

He tried to speak, but coughed instead. His mouth was painfully dry. "Hello?" his roughened voice uttered. There was no answer.

Frank thought the command to activate his *CAPS-Link* and the world brightened to an empty hospital room. From the looks of things, it was identical to the room that Williams had stayed in. A sweater that he recognized as Tam's was hung over a chair. A Sherlock Holmes book sat on the table. He smiled, knowing that she was somewhere nearby, probably getting coffee or lunch, considering the time.

It was half past noon, Tuesday, June 10th. He remembered nothing since falling unconscious back at Soldier Field. Calculating it, he found he had been out for more than twenty-five hours.

Frank stretched his extremities, relieved to feel that he had all his toes, fingers, and other bits. He felt rested, but weak and achy everywhere, especially his head.

Relieved upon remembering that he had shot Elliot Three-Seven and that he was no longer a problem, Frank drifted in and out of sleep with a slight smile on his face.

A few minutes later, Tamara Billingsley returned to the room along with a nurse, both dressed in anti-bacterial suits.

"Frank!" Tam called and rushed to his side. She grabbed his hands and squeezed them.

"Hi," he said through a cracking voice.

"How do you feel?" she asked.

Frank shrugged and nodded. The nurse introduced herself and handed him a cup of water with a straw. He downed the clean, cool liquid until it was empty. Meanwhile, Tam chatted at a mile a minute. He wanted to hear nothing else in the world. He looked to her pretty face and smiled.

The nurse checked him over, covered him with another blanket, informed him that he had a severe concussion, some bruising along his upper back, and had been cut deeply just below the rib cage at his left side. This was all what he figured, but the fact that things seemed to have been put back into place pleased him.

"How's Marcus?" he asked when he found the space.

"He's fine," she said. "He's a floor up, watching your Nighthunter. Let me tell you, people were almost dancing in the streets when it hit..."

"*What?!*" Frank shrieked and pulled himself up on his elbows.

"Take it easy, Frank!" She was startled at his sudden harsh voice. She realized that he had not known the FROG still lived.

"How the hell...?"

"You shot him three times, but the doctors pulled him through," she explained as she watched Campanelli sit up in the bed and throw his legs over the side.

"For God's sake…*why?!*"

"Why what?"

"Why did they bother saving that…*monster?*" Frank was so angry the question came out in spurts.

Tamara stepped to him and took both of his forearms in her hands. "That's what a doctor is supposed to do, Frank. Heal people, no matter what."

"He's not *people*, Tam! He's a murdering monster!" he shouted as he tried to unhook his intravenous connection, but she held him hand tightly.

"Frank, no!" she called out loudly enough that her voice no longer sounded muffled in the suit's mask. "You're not well enough to go see him!"

Letting out a growl of frustration, he sat back down. His head had begun pounding and dizziness fell on him like a wet blanket.

"You don't understand," he tried again in a quiet, tired voice. "He can heal so fast, Tam. They built him so damn strong that Marcus, in a double 'A'-suit, had a hard time with him. He'll tear through this goddamned hospital like it was some old-fashioned meat market and bust outta here!"

"Nighthunter is out cold and Marcus is not alone, Frank. He has a couple of SWAT officers, a few uniforms, and Agent Quinne with him." Tamara spoke confidently as she tugged him back toward the bed.

"A lotta damned good an FBI guy'll do. Where the hell was he anyway?"

"I'm sure I don't know, dear."

The spinning room sent Campanelli back to his bed and on his back. "Hey. What happened to Dr. Ruger?"

"He's here on this floor, just a couple doors down."

"Good." Frank nodded and sighed, relieved that his prognosis of the man's condition had been correct. He had felt guilty when he sent the elderly man out to meet other officers and an ambulance, alone and bleeding.

"I'm sure Marcus wouldn't mind if you reached out and talked to him," Tam suggested.

Frank nodded and activated his *CAPS-Link*'s communications window. He found Williams and an entire squad of CPD available. Half of them were SWAT. FBI Agent Quinne was also in range. Suddenly, he felt guilty for wondering where the agent had been during the chase for Elliot.

"*What is Three-Seven's status?*" Campanelli sent in text after a brief exchange of greetings with his partner.

"*Still unconscious after surgery,*" Marcus replied. "*He's fastened to his bed frame with cuffs on each wrist and ankle, despite what the attending physician wanted.*"

"*So, what exactly are our orders? Why was he kept alive?*"

A few minutes went by before he received Williams's response. "*I just checked with Chief Treadwell. We're to turn him over to Dr. Ruger, Agent Quinne and a detachment of Marines on their way here.*"

Frank shook his head in frustration at first, but was relieved that a higher authority was to take charge. "*When are they getting here?*"

"*Friday.*"

"Shit," Campanelli spoke aloud as he turned his eyes to the ceiling.

"What?" Billingsley asked, concerned.

"We're to keep that monster in his bed until the Marines come get him…this Friday," he relayed to her.

"Shit," she agreed.

As the afternoon rolled on, Frank's headache continued, but lessened in intensity. Not one for a long bed rest, he insisted on getting up and going for a walk. His body was tight, achy, and uncomfortable.

Tamara and a nurse helped him to his feet. His back, bruised and inflamed from his impact with the shock from the car accident and the wooden partition at Soldier

Field, was alight with a fiery and deep throbbing pain. Once he stood straight, however, it abated slightly.

Frank announced his intention to visit Dr. Ruger's room, so the nurse brought him a full anti-bacterial suit like she wore. As Ruger's injury was also an open wound trying to heal, the chances of the older man contracting a staph infection or one of the many strains of influenza were great.

Once Campanelli was suited up, Tam and the nurse escorted him to the airlock door and let him in. As he was getting around well enough to not need a cane or a walker, the two ladies left him to visit Ruger alone.

"Hello, Detective Campanelli," Ruger greeted in a tired voice. His eyelids appeared heavy, staying closed for a couple of seconds at a time.

"Doctor," Frank returned. He saw that the man's heart rate, while a little low, was even and steady. His blood pressure appeared normal. "Good to see you made it."

Mitchell Ruger smiled. "Yes, thank you. He was an amazing shot, wasn't he?"

"You could say that," Campanelli said and smiled.

"Was anyone else hurt?"

"Yeah," Frank nodded and pulled the recliner closer. His head swam and he needed a seat. "He tossed a SWAT member out an open window and shot four others with that same accuracy."

"Oh, God."

"Yeah."

"How are you feeling, Detective?"

"Like an army of evil nanites is trying to escape the confines of my cranium with power tools," Frank said flatly. "But I can't complain. It could have been worse."

"I'm terribly sorry," Mitchell said and turned to look at the ceiling. His eyes closed and stayed there long enough that Frank thought the man had gone to sleep. "I wanted to...talk to him. Bring him in peacefully."

"He had other plans, Doctor," the detective replied and sat back to relieve the pain in his back.

"At least it's over," Ruger whispered and let out a heavy sigh.

"Well, if you can get him back to that classified location of yours." Frank added, "The laboratory or whatever."

"What?" Ruger opened his eyes and regarded Campanelli with a heavy frown.

"The transportation back to the base," the Captain of Detectives said a little louder for the older man, thinking he had merely misheard. "I hope the Marines are prepared with a good, strong cage."

"He's...*alive?*"

"Yes, Doctor," Frank affirmed and pointed a thickly gloved hand to the ceiling to the northwest. "He's upstairs. Unconscious after having my three bullets pulled out of him."

"Oh, my."

"Agent Quinne didn't tell you?"

"I haven't seen him."

"Dr. Ruger, my implant pinpointed his location as being in this room not fifteen minutes ago!" he exclaimed and leaned forward in the chair.

"I just awoke some minutes before you came in," he responded defensively.

"All right, all right." Frank held up his palms to calm himself and the old man. "No big deal, Doctor."

"There might very well be a big deal, Detective," Ruger explained with weakened urgency. "You say he's alive and upstairs. Is he bound? Cuffed? Chained? Anything?"

"Yes, of course." He told him as he checked for the location of Agent Quinne. His implant now indicated that the man was upstairs with the SWAT team and Marcus Williams.

"Is he any calmer? Or is he fighting his restraints?" the elderly geneticist begged to know.

"He's still unconscious."

Ruger appeared confused. "How long ago was the surgery?"

Frank shrugged. "Not sure. I'm sure it must have occurred immediately after arrival. That was probably late afternoon."

"How long was the surgery? Did he sit still for it?" Mitchell asked, speaking quickly.

"Dr. Ruger, you are starting to concern me. What do you mean? He's been unconscious the whole time. I'm sure he was given some anesthetic…"

"That won't have any effect, Detective!" exclaimed the unnerved old man.

"What the hell are you trying to tell me?"

"FROGs don't need to be put under for surgery, Campanelli," he explained as he forced himself to sit up. "They can turn off the pain receptors in their nervous system. Any drugs injected into the body are identified by the bio-nanite matrix. If they are of a toxic nature, including the drugs used for anesthetics, they are rerouted from the blood stream and sent to a waste channel."

Frank stood up. "Are you telling me that there's no sedating Elliot?"

"Exactly."

"Then why is he unconscious, Doctor?"

"I don't know. He can't be," Mitchell Ruger insisted. "If his injuries are enough to keep him unconscious this long, then perhaps they were fatal and the doctors only prolonged the inevitable."

Campanelli thought about this for a few moments. "Or…he's playing possum."

"Healing while he works out an escape plan," Ruger finished for him.

"Shit." Frank got to his feet and walked as quickly as he could manage to the door. "I'll let them know, Doc."

"Yes! Do that, please!"

Frank quickly unlocked the inner door and shut it behind him. As he tried to contact the nurse's station to be let out from the anti-bacterial chamber, he realized that no one was coming to his call.

"*Marcus. Answer me,*" he thought next and sent.

He watched his display as the message sat in the queue. He quickly came to the conclusion that he was being jammed. Frank looked through the glass portal of the outer door and saw a nurse sitting at the station to his extreme right. Frantically, he banged on the door, even though he knew that the fiberglass and steel construct was too thick for the sound to make it to her.

"Hey!!" Campanelli screamed loud and hard enough that his head became swimmy once more. Angered, he roughly removed the head gear of the anti-bacterial suit and tried again. "Let me out!! Heeyy!!"

Ruger saw the shadows dancing along the chamber's walls to Detective Campanelli's movements and deduced what was happening. The man was trapped in the chamber and kept from using his implant. Thinking quickly, he reached for the call button and pressed it several times.

"Come on," he hissed. "Come on!"

"*Yes, Dr. Ruger?*" the nurse at the station responded.

"Quick! Please help! Detective Campanelli is stuck in the chamber and needs out! Hurry!"

The nurse, a forty-something professional who kept herself in shape, said nothing further. She bolted from her seat and sprinted to Ruger's room. The fact that the Nighthunter was one floor up was enough to keep everyone on her staff on edge, so her reactions were on a hair-trigger as it was.

She pulled the handle of the outer door and let the red-faced policeman free. "Detective! Your suit!"

"Never mind that! Call CPD for me and get back up units here now!" he shouted at her and pushed his aching body into a fast jog. He remembered where the stairs were from his many recent visits and headed for them.

"Frank!" Tam shouted from a distance behind.

His sock-covered feet slid across the slick tile as he turned to look back. "Stay down here!"

"What's happening?!" she called back, frightened.

"Just stay down here!" he ordered her and took on the daunting task of vaulting up the stairs. Everything hurt as he went, but his worry propelled him. He was still unable to send anything from the *CAPS-Link* or even determine if any of the officers were still up there. He wished he had his gun.

Arriving near the top, he could hear loud male voices. They were shouting at each other. Frank reached the top of the staircase and yanked the door out of his way. There he found the SWAT team holding their weapons up, pointing into the open hospital room airlock. With the anti-bacterial suits on the bodies of every officer, the only way to determine SWAT from a patrolman was the assault weapons. Three of the SWAT members were inside the doorway, aiming their weaponry toward what certainly must have been Three-Seven's bed.

The rest of the group, another six men, remained outside and at the ready. Williams and Quinne were not among them.

"Let him go! Do it now!" one of the SWAT men on the inside shouted.

One of the officers approached Frank with his hand up. "Sir, you need to go back down the stairs!"

"I'm Detective Frank Campanelli, Sentinel Division," he replied sternly. "What's going on?"

227 • Campanelli: Siege of the Nighthunter

"Where's your badge?" the officer continued and blocked Frank's way.

"In my hospital room downstairs," Campanelli explained. "That is Elliot Three-Seven in there and I believe my partner, Marcus Williams and Agent Quinne are in there as well. Is that right?"

After a second, the officer nodded. There was no way to verify the man's claim, but no one other than another policeman would know who was in the room. "Okay. Yes, they're in there."

"Thank you," Frank said and moved past him and stood next to a SWAT member just outside the door. "Let me borrow your pistol."

"Get the hell back or I'm crushing this man's throat!" bellowed a voice from within the hospital room.

After Frank identified himself for a second time to the SWAT officer, the man reached into his anti-bacterial suit and retrieved his semi-automatic. He handed it to the detective. "There was a scuffle. Somehow, Elliot was able to grab a hold of Quinne."

"Thank you," he said and checked it for a round in the chamber before dropping it into the pocket of his own suit. Campanelli squeezed into the open space and got a look at what was happening inside the room.

Elliot was still cuffed to his bed, but his right arm had bent the safety bar enough so that he had been able to reach Jerry Quinne, who was missing the hood of his anti-bacterial suit. The FROG's long fingers had the FBI agent in a death grip. Quinne's face was blue and his eyes bulged.

Marcus Williams, also sans hood, had his pistol pointed to Three-Seven's head, but the wounded FROG simply stared hatefully back with a devilish smile on his pale white face. He was clearly not well, but still had considerable strength. Looking closer, Frank could see that not only had the bed's guard been bent, a few of the links in the cuff were stretched. The strands of the cuff cut into

Elliot's forearm deeply, causing the fresh wound to bleed, but it did not deter the killer in the least.

"There's no getting out of this, Elliot," Marcus warned him. "There's nowhere to go. Let him go, now!"

Three-Seven ignored Williams and caught Campanelli's eye. "Well! The blind cop! Welcome. Come on in. Make room for the detective or I'll squeeze my fingers together until they meet in the middle of this man's crushed esophagus."

"It's okay, guys," Frank spoke up. "He means me." He patted the three SWAT members on the shoulders to let them know where he was. "Everyone give this man some room."

"Frank, we got this," Williams said through gritted teeth.

"I know you do, Marcus," Campanelli said calmly. "I think we need to just have a talk with Elliot here and we need to clear the room."

Reluctantly, the three heavily armed SWAT officers slowly backed out of the room. They had no intention of going much beyond the line of sight. Frank nodded at them as they went.

"Why, thank you, Detective Campanelli," Elliot oozed. He let up on his grip and let Quinne suck in gales of air. Almost immediately, the man's color improved and life came back to his eyes. Instinctively, the agent reached up to try to free his throat. Three-Seven shook Quinne hard. "Don't touch me! Hands down!"

Jerry Quinne complied and dropped his arms.

"Just let him go, Elliot," Frank ordered. "There's no point to this."

"I disagree, Detective," the FROG responded almost kindly. "I want my freedom. I'll kill this man to get it."

"We can't let you go, Elliot," Frank explained. "You're responsible for killing a lot of people."

"Children, you mean," Three-Seven scoffed and studied Campanelli's face. "Barely conscious of their own existence. I reminded them of their fear!"

Frank and Marcus shared a glance. Even though their implants were prevented from communicating, their expressions made their thoughts clear to the other one. Elliot Three-Seven was quite insane.

Elliot laughed harshly and threw his head back. "You don't get it. I am preying on the weak, the stragglers. Look at your citizens, now! Afraid to leave their homes at night, they are embracing their survival instincts once again. Like our ancestors once did." As he spoke, Elliot increased the tension on the cuffs binding his left hand and began to tighten the muscles in his blanket-covered legs. He was determined to break free.

"A Marine detail is on its way here, Elliot," Frank revealed. "You won't be teaching anyone anything."

Elliot's demeanor changed from maniacal arrogance to subdued melancholy. His eyes lost focus as he recalled his home. "I will not go back there. Ever!" His left hand wrapped around the cuff's links and pulled as his legs worked on their restraints. The metal frame of the bed groaned with the strain.

"Shit," Marcus whispered. His fingers tightened on the pistol.

Frank slowly removed the pistol from the anti-bacterial suit's pocket.

"I'll kill this man, Detectives," Elliot reiterated and squeezed Quinne's throat once more. The man choked through groans of pain and turned a deep red.

Campanelli raised the pistol and took aim of Three-Seven's chest. "This won't work. We're not letting some caged animal loose and we're sure as shit not arresting you and putting you in jail. You do that and we're just going to shoot your worthless ass."

Williams glanced over his partner, checking for a sign of bluffing. There was none.

The bed creaked louder. The links in the cuffs around the FROG's wrists strained and opened with a cry. Jerry Quinne's face was now blue as Elliot and Frank stared at each other.

"You know, I hacked into your car and turned it off," Three-Seven explained with a tone of amusement. "I did it to two others, too. I can hack into that implant of yours and blind you, Campanelli."

"I don't care," Frank replied immediately. "You wouldn't be the first son of a bitch I killed while blind."

"Let him go, Elliot!" Williams shouted. Quinne looked horrific with his unseeing, bulging eyes.

"Williams, I like you," Three-Seven said as the chains of the cuffs binding his legs snapped. "As an ex-SEAL, I don't wish to kill you. You may go."

Marcus smirked and remained planted.

"Listen, buster..." Frank started.

"Ha! Buster?!" Elliot shouted gleefully. "Honestly! Who talks like that?"

"Let him go!" Campanelli all but screamed. He could see that Quinne had seconds.

The FROG smiled that horrific smile once again as his wrists came free. With shocking speed, his left hand flew to the agent's shoulder holster and pulled the handgun from it. At the very same instance, his right hand pulsed with tremendous strength, crushing Jerry Quinne's esophagus with a sickening crackling sound. He dropped the body to the floor as he brought the handgun to bear on Campanelli.

Both detectives opened fire, repeatedly tapping the triggers as fast as could be physically possible for man and machine.

Quinne's pistol dropped to the tile as Elliot Three-Seven's body withered from the gunfire and fell back to the bed. His chest, still healing from the previous day's surgery, had been opened afresh by sixteen nine-millimeter rounds.

Williams ceased fire before emptying his magazine into the FROG. He covered the bleeding body as Frank stepped forward. He had fired his borrowed weapon up to the last round.

"Frank," Marcus warned. He halted the swarm of intruding SWAT members and other officers with a giant hand.

Campanelli approached the heaving body of Elliot Three-Seven. He wheezed loudly through the inhale and coughed blood on the exhale. His yellow eyes followed Frank's approach. Slowly, he turned his head toward the detective.

"You...should finish..." Three-Seven began, but coughed, "...what you...st...start."

Frank Campanelli froze for a moment. He could see the man was dying. The mattress was quickly filling with dark blood.

"You know," Elliot spoke clearly in a moment of resolve, "you should really be sure that I'm dead this time, Campanelli!"

Frank stared into the face of the cannibalistic killer as the scales flourished with colors. With a roar, Elliot swatted his left arm out at him. Frank jumped back, took aim and fired his last round. It entered Three-Seven's forehead and sent blood and brains through the large hole it created at the rear. The wall behind the dead Marine became a mural of death in slow motion as the mess fell to the influence of gravity.

Campanelli stared for a time. Marcus stepped to his side and removed the empty pistol from his grip. "Are you hurt, Frank?"

"Huh? I don't think so. Why?" Campanelli heard his voice say.

"Jesus, he sliced right through that damned suit," one of the SWAT team said.

As if in a trance, Frank looked down and noted that the anti-bacterial suit was a tattered, shredded mess. Campanelli pulled the fabric away, frantically looking for evidence of a wound.

"We need a medic in here," Marcus called loudly. "You're sliced up pretty good, Frank."

Frank looked up at his immense partner and nodded. "Bastard...fought right to the end."

Marcus looked to the officers that had rushed to Agent Quinne. A shake of the head from one was enough to let him know that his friend and fellow SEAL was gone.

"Yeah," Williams answered in a whisper and guided his sole remaining friend to the lounger in the corner. "Just relax, Frank. I can't tell how deep you're cut."

Exhausted, Campanelli did not fight the blanket of unconsciousness that smothered him.

Epilogue

Captain of Detectives Frank Campanelli arrived home from Cook County Hospital six days later. He walked in without aid from cane or Tamara, though she remained close to his side. The ride home was made in silence, other than the rattling that the old German convertible made on its own along the way.

Frank hung up his newly replaced black overcoat, flipped his fedora up onto the shelf, and made his way to the living room, where he collapsed in his chair. The pain medication for his back pain was energy depleting, but effective.

"You hungry, Frank?" Tam asked from the kitchen.

"Starving."

"Let me make you a sandwich. That'll get you through until dinner."

"Thank you, my dear," he responded as he let his eyes go dark. He kept the *CAPS-Link* engaged for a time as he was expecting a communication. Williams had told him that CPD's Internal Affairs Division, at least one of the five remaining officers of the group, was investigating the shooting and had taken offense that Elliot Three-Seven, a United States Marine Corps FROG, had been executed in his bed.

It was a laughable case, and everyone knew it except for the IA officer in question. Pictures of the body of Agent Jerry Quinne, Frank's incurred lacerations, and his implant's visual recording of the incident had been forwarded as well as that of Detective Williams.

Until then, Frank had been suspended without pay.

In his self-imposed darkness, he sat in his chair, at the moment uncaring about a single thing beyond the woman in his apartment. He hoped that the suspension would be a while. A few weeks, maybe a month would be healing and good. The bayonet slash was the worst of it, and would take the longest to heal.

Hell, maybe Tam's right, he thought. *Maybe we should get the hell out of here. Move to...where? California? Canada?*

"Ha!" he barked suddenly. "Yeah, sure. Might as well try for the next ship to Alethea," he murmured.

"What's that, Frank?" Tamara called to him.

"Nothin', sweetheart," he returned and smiled, though he could not see if she was looking at him. "Nothin' at all. Everything's just fine."

About the Author:

Frederick H. Crook was born in Chicago in 1970 and now lives in Villa Park, Illinois with his wife, Rae and their three dachshunds. In 2010, Frederick's first novel, The Dregs of Exodus, was published. This was followed up with, The Pirates of Exodus in 2012. Throughout 2013, he continued writing and published four short stories for Kindle. In 2014, Solstice Publishing picked up his third novel, Campanelli: Sentinel. The novella, Minuteman Merlin was published in March, 2015. His fourth novel, Of Knight & Devil, launched in October, 2015.

Social Media Links:

Website: http://frederickcrook.wix.com/crooksbooks

Facebook:
https://www.facebook.com/TheDregsOfExodus/?ref=hl

Twitter: https://twitter.com/FrederickHCrook
@FrederickHCrook

33471305R00133

Made in the USA
Middletown, DE
14 July 2016